"Science Fiction, fantasy and historical stories by an established writer. Anderson is good at brisk, colorful adventure, sometimes with poignant touches."

—*Cleveland Plain Dealer*

"I recommend it to you." —Algis Budrys

HOMEWARD AND BEYOND

This is the best anthology of stories by Poul Anderson, winner of awards for best story of the year, including the famous "Goat Song," and his new story "The Peat Bog," printed here for the first time—a brilliant historical fantasy.

By the Same Author

STAR PRINCE CHARLIE
WITH GORDON DICKSON

HOMEWARD AND BEYOND

POUL ANDERSON

A BERKLEY MEDALLION BOOK
published by
BERKLEY PUBLISHING CORPORATION

To Linda
from her affectionate brother-in-law

Copyright © 1975, by Poul Anderson

Published by arrangement with Doubleday & Company, Inc.

Doubleday & Company, Inc.
Garden City, New York

SBN 425-0

*BERKLEY MEDALLION BOOKS are published by
Berkley Publishing Corporation
200 Madison Avenue
New York, N.Y. 10016*

BERKLEY MEDALLION BOOK ® TM 757,375

Printed in the United States of America

Berkley Medallion Edition, JULY, 1976

This is a book of science fiction stories, and my main hope is that you will enjoy them. But it is also, in a small way, an attempt—not to define science fiction, because that can't be done—but to explore some of the territory and even try to extend that a bit.

All fiction deals with imaginary people and events. This includes the *roman à clef* and the kind of history or biography whose author makes up occurrences and conversations he thinks might have taken place; but works of that kind do stick pretty close to reality, as nearly as we can know what reality is. A step further is the straight here-and-now story. The writer invents his characters and incidents, perhaps his entire setting, but these have actual exemplars.

The fantasy brings in whole classes of things that are, to the best of our knowledge, nonexistent: ghosties and ghoulies and long-legged beasties and things that go boomp in the night. Then can we not say that science fiction is the subdivision of fantasy whose classes of imaginary entity and event might possibly be, or become, real? For instance, spacecraft capable of going to the Moon did not exist, though they were a theoretical possibility, a generation ago; hence they were material for science fiction. Spacecraft capable of taking men to Mars are still in the theoretical stage; spacecraft capable of taking them to Alpha Centauri may or may not be possible someday to build; hence they remain material for science fiction. Do these criteria not mark off the different areas of literature?

No. To start with, they would—for example—make science fiction of the most meticulously realistic novel about a political campaign, though the author has set it in the near future merely because his purpose requires this. Then they would relegate—for example—any story about a spaceship which can travel faster than light to the realm of pure fantasy, because physicists have long insisted that that violates natural law. But does the idea of a ghostie or ghoulie necessarily contain any such violation and can we be absolutely certain that no such beings prowl around us?

And now some extremely distinguished physicists have started rethinking some of our most basic concepts. There may after all be ways to get around the light-speed limit. Hypothetical tachyons (which *may* just have been detected as I write these words) and hypothetical phenomena associated with black holes are simply the best known of several conceivabilities. In fact, there may be ways to travel in time! (I have the Tipler machine in mind, a suggestion respectable enough to be published in *Physical Review*.) Today we are making the same kind of quantum jump they made with Copernicus or Darwin. Suddenly we see much further and deeper than we had imagined we ever could, and what we see is mystery.

For such reasons, John Campbell argued that all fiction is science fiction, with "mainstream" nothing but a specialized subcategory. I wouldn't take so extravagant a position, but will point out that it is logically defensible. My own feeling is that literature is, or should be, a continuum, itself continuous with other arts and ultimately with the whole of life. Classifications have their uses, but we are mistaken if we regard them as anything more than conveniences.

To try to demonstrate that, I've set this collection in a certain order, and offer a brief commentary on each item. By no means does the book cover a complete range. Even among those who are labeled "science fiction writers," we find many whose admirable work is utterly different from anything I have ever done or would ever be able to do. But within the bounds of what a single man can master, it is possible to cross a sufficiently large number of borders to show how arbitrary and, in fact, unreal they all are.

Of course, that's incidental to the chief purpose, which is to entertain. You're welcome to skip the editorial matter and pay attention only to the stories. I hope you have fun.

CONTENTS

/242

HOMEWARD AND BEYOND

WINGS
OF
VICTORY

This is about as clearly identifiable science fiction as you're likely to find. The basic idea came from John Campbell, during the last conversation we ever had. I wondered aloud, "If reptiles are post-amphibian, and mammals are post-reptilian, what might a post-mammalian animal be like?" At once, almost casually, he tossed back a suggestion which I worked out in detail and used in several different narratives. Those who remember any of these know the answer to the problem that the characters confront here. But I trust they will nonetheless enjoy what is also an attempt to express the romantic spirit behind science and discovery.

OUR PART in the Grand Survey had taken us out beyond the great suns Alpha and Beta Crucis. From Earth we would have been in the constellation Lupus. But Earth was 278 light-years remote, Sol itself long dwindled to invisibility, and stars drew strange pictures across the dark.

After three years we were weary and had suffered losses. Oh, the wonder wasn't gone. How could it ever go—from world after world after world? But we had seen so many, and of those we had walked on, some were beautiful and some were terrible and most were both (even as Earth is) and none

1

were alike and all were mysterious. They blurred together in our minds.

It was still a heart-speeding thing to find another sentient race, actually more than to find another planet colonizable by man. Now Ali Hamid had perished of a poisonous bite a year back, and Manuel Gonsalves had not yet recovered from the skull fracture inflicted by the club of an excited being at our last stop. This made Vaughn Webner our chief xenologist, from whom was to issue trouble.

Not that he, or any of us, wanted it. You learn to gang warily, in a universe not especially designed for you, or you die; there is no third choice. We approached this latest star because every G-type dwarf beckoned us. But we did not establish orbit around its most terrestroid attendant until neutrino analysis had verified that nobody in the system had developed atomic energy. And we exhausted every potentiality of our instruments before we sent down our first robot probe.

The sun was a G9, golden in hue, luminosity half of Sol's. The world which interested us was close enough in to get about the same irradiation as Earth. It was smaller, surface gravity 0.75, with thinner and drier atmosphere. However, that air was perfectly breathable by humans, and bodies of water existed which could be called modest oceans. The globe was very lovely where it turned against star-crowded night, blue, tawny, rusty-brown, white-clouded. Two little moons skipped in escort.

Biological samples proved that its life was chemically similar to ours. None of the micro-organisms we cultured posed any threat that normal precautions and medications could not handle. Pictures taken at low altitude and on the ground showed woods, lakes, wide plains rolling toward mountains. We were afire to set foot there.

But the natives—

You must remember how new the hyperdrive is, and how immense the cosmos. The organizers of the Grand Survey were too wise to believe that the few neighbor systems we'd learned something about gave knowledge adequate for devising doctrine. Our service had one law, which was its proud motto: "We come as friends." Otherwise each crew was free to work out its own procedures. After five years the survivors would meet and compare experiences.

For us aboard the *Olga*, Captain Gray had decided that, whenever possible, sophonts should not be disturbed by preliminary sightings of our machines. We would try to set the probes in uninhabited regions. When we ourselves landed, we would come openly. After all, the shape of a body counts for much less than the shape of the mind within. Thus went our belief.

Naturally, we took in every datum we could from orbit and upper-atmospheric overflights. While not extremely informative under such conditions, our pictures did reveal a few small towns on two continents—clusters of buildings, at least, lacking defensive walls or regular streets—hard by primitive mines. They seemed insignificant against immense and almost unpopulated landscapes. We guessed we could identify a variety of cultures, from Stone Age through Iron. Yet invariably, aside from those petty communities, settlements consisted of one or a few houses standing alone. We found none less than ten kilometers apart; most were more isolated.

"Carnivores, I expect," Webner said. "The primitive economies are hunting-fishing-gathering, the advanced economies pastoral. Large areas which look cultivated are probably just to provide fodder; they don't have the layout of proper farms." He tugged his chin. "I confess to being puzzled as to how the civilized—well, let's say the 'Metallurgic' people, at this stage—how they manage it. You need trade, communication, quick exchange of ideas, for that level of technology. And if I read the pictures aright, roads are virtually nonexistent, a few dirt tracks between towns and mines, or to the occasional dock for barges or ships— Confound it, water transportation is insufficient."

"Pack animals, maybe?" I suggested.

"Too slow," he said. "You don't get progressive cultures when months must pass before the few individuals capable of originality can hear from each other. The chances are they never will."

For a moment the pedantry dropped from his manner. "Well," he said, "we'll see," which is the grandest sentence that any language can own.

We always made initial contact with three, the minium who could do the job, lest we lose them. This time they were Webner, xenologist; Aram Turekian, pilot; and Yukiko Sachansky, gunner. It was Gray's idea to give women that last assignment. He felt they were better than men at watching and waiting, less likely to open fire in doubtful situations.

The site chosen was in the metallurgic domain, though not a town. Why complicate matters unnecessarily? It was on a rugged upland, thick forest for many kilometers around. Northward the mountainside rose steeply until, above timberline, its crags were crowned by a glacier. Southward it toppled to a great plateau, open country where herds grazed on a reddish analogue of grass or shrubs. Maybe they were domesticated, maybe not. In either case, probably the dwellers did a lot of hunting.

"Would that account for their being so scattered?" Yukiko wondered. "A big range needed to support each individual?"

"Then they must have a strong territoriality," Webner said. "Stand sharp by the guns."

We were not forbidden to defend ourselves from attack, whether or not blunders of ours had provoked it. Nevertheless the girl winced. Turekian glanced over his shoulder and saw. That, and Webner's tone, made him flush. "Blow down, Vaughn," he growled.

Webner's long, gaunt frame stiffened in his seat. Light gleamed off the scalp under his thin hair as he thrust his head toward the pilot. "What did you say?"

"Stay in your own shop and run it, if you can."

"Mind your manners. This may be my first time in charge, but I *am*—"

"On the ground. We're aloft yet."

"Please." Yukiko reached from her turret and laid a hand on each man's shoulder. "Please don't quarrel . . . when we're about to meet a whole new history."

They couldn't refuse her wish. Tool-burdened coverall or no, she remained in her Eurasian petiteness the most desired woman aboard the *Olga*; and still the rest of the girls liked her. Gonsalves' word for her was *"simpático."*

The men only quieted on the surface. They were an ill-assorted pair, not enemies—you don't sign on a person who'll allow himself hatred—but unfriends. Webner was the academic type, professor of xenology at the University of Oceania. In youth he'd done excellent fieldwork, especially in the trade route cultures of Cynthia, and he'd been satisfactory under his superiors. At heart, though, he was a theorist, whom middle age had made dogmatic.

Turekian was the opposite: young, burly, black-bearded, boisterous and roisterous, born in a sealtent on Mars to a life of banging around the available universe. If half his brags were true, he was mankind's boldest adventurer, toughest fighter, and mightiest lover; but I'd found to my profit that he wasn't the poker player he claimed. Withal he was able, affable, helpful, popular—which may have kindled envy in poor self-chilled Webner.

"Okay, sure," Turekian laughed. "For you, Yu." He tossed a kiss in her direction.

Webner unbent less easily. "What did you mean by running my own shop if I can?" he demanded.

"Nothing, nothing," the girl almost begged.

"Ah, a bit more than nothing," Turekian said. "A tiny bit. I just wish you were less convinced your science has the last word on all the possibilities. Things I've seen—"

"I've heard your song before," Webner scoffed. "In a

jungle on some exotic world you met animals with wheels."

"Never said that. Hm-m-m . . . make a good yarn, wouldn't it?"

"No. Because it's an absurdity. Simply ask yourself how nourishment would pass from the axle bone to the cells of the disk. In like manner—"

"Yeh, yeh. Quiet, now, please. I've got to conn us down."

The target waxed fast in the bow screen. A booming of air came faint through the hull plates and vibration shivered flesh. Turekian hated dawdling. Besides, a slow descent might give the autochthons time to become hysterical, with perhaps tragic consequences.

Peering, the humans saw a house on the rim of a canyon at whose bottom a river rushed gray-green. The structure was stone, massive and tile-roofed. Three more buildings joined to define a flagged courtyard. Those were of timber, long and low, topped by blossoming sod. A corral outside the quadrangle held four-footed beasts, and nearby stood a row of what Turekian, pointing, called overgrown birdhouses. A meadow surrounded the ensemble. Elsewhere the woods crowded close.

There was abundant bird or, rather, ornithoid life, flocks strewn across the sky. A pair of especially large creatures hovered above the steading. They veered as the boat descended.

Abruptly, wings exploded from the house. Out of its windows flyers came, a score or better, all sizes from tiny ones which clung to adult backs, up to those which dwarfed the huge extinct condors of Earth. In a gleam of bronze feathers, a storm of wingbeats which pounded through the hull, they rose, and fled, and were lost among the treetops.

The humans landed in a place gone empty.

Hands near sidearms, Webner and Turekian trod forth, looked about, let the planet enter them.

You always undergo that shock of first encounter. Not only

does space separate the newfound world from yours; time does, five billion years at least. Often you need minutes before you can truly see the shapes around, they are that alien. Before, the eye has registered them but not the brain.

This was more like home. Yet the strangenesses were uncountable.

Weight: three fourths of what the ship maintained. An ease, a bounciness in the stride . . . and a subtle kinesthetic adjustment required, sensory more than muscular.

Air: like Earth's at about two kilometers' altitude. (Gravity gradient being less, the density drop-off above sea level went slower.) Crystalline vision, cool flow and murmur of breezes, soughing in the branches and river clangorous down in the canyon. Every odor different, no hint of sun-baked resin or duff, instead a medley of smokinesses and pungencies.

Light: warm gold, making colors richer and shadows deeper than you were really evolved for; a midmorning sun which displayed almost half again the apparent diameter of Earth's, in a sky which was deep blue and had only thin streaks of cloud.

Life: wild flocks, wheeling and crying high overhead; lowings and cacklings from the corral; rufous carpet underfoot, springy, suggestive more of moss than grass though not very much of either, starred with exquisite flowers; trees whose leaves were green (from silvery to murky), whose bark (if it was bark) might be black or gray or brown or white, whose forms were little more odd to you than were pine or gingko if you came from oak and beech country, but which were no trees of anywhere on Earth. A swarm of midgelike entomoids went by, and a big copper-winged "moth" leisurely feeding on them.

Scenery: superb. Above the forest, peaks shouldered into heaven, the glacier shimmered blue. To the right, canyon walls plunged roseate, ocher-banded, and cragged. But your attention was directed ahead.

The house was of astonishing size. "A flinking castle,"

Turekian exclaimed. An approximate twenty-meter cube, it rose sheer to the peaked roof, built from well-dressed blocks of granite. Windows indicated six stories. They were large openings, equipped with wooden shutters and wrought-iron balconies. The sole door, on ground level, was ponderous. Horns, skulls, and sculptured weapons of the chase—knife, spear, shortsword, blowgun, bow and arrow—ornamented the façade.

The attendant buildings were doubtless barns or sheds. Trophies hung on them too. The beasts in the corral looked, and probably weren't, mammalian. Two species were vaguely reminiscent of horses and oxen, a third of sheep. They were not many, could not be the whole support of the dwellers here. The "dovecotes" held ornithoids as big as turkeys, which were not penned but were prevented from leaving the area by three hawklike guardians. "Watchdogs," Turekian said of those. "No, watchfalcons," They swooped about, perturbed at the invasion.

Yukiko's voice came wistful from a receiver behind his ear: "Can I join you?"

"Stand by the guns," Webner answered. "We have yet to meet the owners of this place."

"Huh?" Turekian said. "Why, they're gone. Skedaddled when they saw us coming."

"Timid?" Yukiko asked. "That doesn't fit with their being eager hunters."

"On the contrary, I imagine they're pretty scrappy," Turekian said. "They jumped to the conclusion we must be hostile, because they wouldn't enter somebody else's land uninvited unless they felt that way. Our powers being unknown, and they having wives and kiddies to worry about, they prudently took off. I expect the fighting males—or whatever they've got—will be back soon."

"What are you talking about?" Webner inquired.

"Why, . . . the locals." Turekian blinked at him. "You saw them."

"Those giant ornithoids? Nonsense."

"How? They came right out of the house there!"

"Domestic animals." Webner's hatchet features drew tight. "I don't deny we confront a puzzle here."

"We always do," Yukiko put in softly.

Webner nodded. "True. However, facts and logic solve puzzles. Let's not complicate our task with pseudo-problems. Whatever they are, the flyers we saw leave cannot be the sophonts. On a planet as Earthlike as this, aviform intelligence is impossible."

He straightened. "I suspect the inhabitants have barricaded themselves," he finished. "We'll go closer and make pacific gestures."

"Which could be misunderstood," Turekian said dubiously. "An arrow or javelin can kill you just as dead as a blaster."

"Cover us, Yukiko," Webner ordered. "Follow me, Aram. If you have the nerve."

He stalked forward, under the eyes of the girl. Turekian cursed and joined him in haste.

They were near the door when a shadow fell over them. They whirled and stared upward. Yukiko's indrawn breath hissed from their receivers.

Aloft hovered one of the great ornithoids. Sunlight struck through its outermost pinions, turning them golden. Otherwise it showed stormcloud-dark. Down the wind stooped a second.

The sight was terrifying. Only later did the humans realize it was magnificent. Those wings spanned six meters. A muzzle full of sharp white fangs gaped before them. Two legs the length and well-nigh the thickness of a man's arms reached crooked talons between them. At their angles grew claws. In thrust after thrust, they hurled the creature at torpedo speed. Air whistled and thundered.

Their guns leaped into the men's hands. "Don't shoot!" Yukiko's cry came as if from very far away.

The splendid monster was almost upon them. Fire speared

from Webner's weapon. At the same instant, the animal braked—a turning of quills, a crack and gust in their faces— and rushed back upward, two meters short of impact.

Turekian's gaze stamped a picture on his brain which he would study over and over and over. The unknown was feathered, surely warm-blooded, but no bird. A keelbone like a ship's prow jutted beneath a strong neck. The head was blunt-nosed, lacked external ears; fantastically, Turekian saw that the predator mouth had lips. Tongue and palate were purple. Two big golden eyes stabbed at him, burned at him. A crest of black-tipped white plumage rose stiffly above, a control surface and protection for the backward-bulging skull. The fan-shaped tail bore the same colors. The body was mahogany, the naked legs and claws yellow.

Webner's shot hid amidst the left-side quills. Smoke streamed after the flameburst. The creature uttered a high-pitched yell, lurched, and threshed in retreat. The damage wasn't permanent, had likely caused no pain, but now that wing was only half useful.

Turekian thus had time to see three slits in parallel on the body. He had time to think there must be three more on the other side. They weirdly resembled gills. As the wings lifted, he saw them drawn wide, a triple yawn; as the downstroke began, he glimpsed them being forced shut.

Then he had cast himself against Webner. "Drop that, you clot-brain!" he yelled. He seized the xenologist's gun wrist. They wrestled. He forced the fingers apart. Meanwhile the wounded ornithoid struggled back to its companion. They flapped off.

"What're you doing?" Webner grabbed at Turekian.

The pilot pushed him away, brutally hard. He fell, Turekian snatched forth his magnifier.

Treetops cut off his view. He let the instrument drop. "Too late," he groaned. "Thanks to you."

Webner climbed erect, pale and shaken by rage. "Have you gone heisenberg?" he gasped. "I'm your commander!"

"You're maybe fit to command plastic ducks in a bath-tub," Turekian said. "Firing on a native!"

Webner was too taken aback to reply.

"And you capped it by spoiling my chance for a good look at Number Two. I think I spotted a harness on him, holding what might be a weapon, but I'm not sure." Turekian spat.

"Aram, Vaughn," Yukiko pleaded from the boat.

An instant longer, the men bristled and glared. Then Webner drew breath, shrugged, and said in a crackly voice: "I suppose it's incumbent on me to put things on a reasonable basis, if you're incapable of that." He paused. "Behave yourself and I'll excuse your conduct as being due to excitement. Else I'll have to recommend you be relieved from further initial-contact duty."

"*I* be relieved—?" Turekian barely checked his fist, and kept it balled. His breath rasped.

"Hadn't you better check the house?" Yukiko asked.

The knowledge that something, anything, might lurk behind yonder walls restored them to a measure of coolness.

Save for livestock, the steading was deserted.

Rather than offend the dwellers by blasting down their barred door, the searchers went through a window on grav units. They found just one or two rooms on each story. Evidently the people valued ample floor space and high ceilings above privacy. Connection up and down was by circular staircases whose short steps seemed at variance with this. Decoration was austere and nonrepresentational. Furniture consisted mainly of benches and tables. Nothing like a bed or an *o-futon* was found. Did the indigenes sleep, if they did, sitting or standing? Quite possibly. Many species can lock the joints of their limbs at will.

Stored food bore out the idea of carnivorousness. Tools, weapons, utensils, fabrics were abundant, well made, neatly put away. They confirmed an Iron Age technology, more or less equivalent to that of Earth's Classical civilization.

Exceptions occurred: for example, a few books, seemingly printed from hand-set type. How avidly those pages were ransacked! But the only illustrations were diagrams suitable to a geometry text in one case and a stonemason's manual in another. Did this culture taboo pictures of its members, or had the boat merely chanced on a home which possessed none?

The layout and contents of the house, and of the sheds when these were examined, gave scant clues. Nobody had expected better. Imagine yourself a nonhuman xenologist, visiting Earth before man went into space. What could you deduce from the residences and a few household items belonging to, say, a European, an Eskimo, a Congo pygmy, and a Japanese peasant? You might have wondered if the owners were of the same genus.

In time you could learn more. Turekian doubted that time would be given. He set Webner in a cold fury by his nagging to finish the survey and get back to the boat. At length the chief gave in. "Not that I don't plan a detailed study, mind you," he said. Scornfully: "Still, I suppose we can hold a conference, and I'll try to calm your fears."

After you had been out, the air in the craft smelled dead and the view in the screens looked dull. Turekian took a pipe from his pocket. "No," Webner told him.

"What?" The pilot was bemused.

"I won't have that foul thing in this crowded cabin."

"I don't mind," Yukiko said.

"I do," Webner replied, "and while we're down, I'm your captain."

Turekian reddened and obeyed. Discipline in space is steel hard, a matter of survival. A good leader gives it a soft sheath. Yukiko's eyes reproached Webner; her fingers dropped to rest on the pilot's arm. The xenologist saw. His mouth twitched sideways before he pinched it together.

"We're in trouble," Turekian said. "The sooner we haul

mass out of here, the happier our insurance carriers will be.''

"Nonsense," Webner snapped. "If anything, our problem is that we've terrified the dwellers. They may take days to send even a scout.''

"They've already sent two. You had to shoot at them.''

"I shot at a dangerous animal. Didn't you see those talons, those fangs? And a buffet from a wing that big—ignoring the claws on it—could break your neck.''

Webner's gaze sought Yukiko's. He mainly addressed her: "Granted, they must be domesticated. I suspect they're used in the hunt, flown at game like hawks though working in packs like hounds. Conceivably the pair we encountered were, ah, sicced onto us from afar. But that they themselves are sophonts—out of the question.''

Her murmur was uneven. "How can you be sure?''

Webner leaned back, bridged his fingers, and grew calmer while he lectured: "You realize the basic principle. All organisms make biological sense in their particular environments, or they become extinct. Reasoners are no exception—and are, furthermore, descended from nonreasoners which adapted to environments that had never been artificially modified.

"On nonterrestroid worlds, they can be quite *outré* by our standards, since they developed under unearthly conditions. On an essentially terrestroid planet, evolution basically parallels our own because it must. True, you get considerable variation. Like, say, hexapodal vertebrates liberating the forelimbs to grow hands and becoming centauroids, as on Woden. That's because the ancestral chordates were hexapods. On this world, you can see for yourself the higher animals are four-limbed.

"A brain capable of designing artifacts such as we observe here is useless without some equivalent of hands. Nature would never produce it. Therefore the inhabitants are bound to be bipeds, however different from us in detail. A foot which must double as a hand, and vice versa, would be too grossly inefficient in either function. Natural selection would weed out any mutants of that tendency, fast, long before intelligence could evolve.

"What do those ornithoids have in the way of hands?" He smiled his tight little smile.

"The claws on their wings?" Yukiko asked shyly.

" 'Fraid not," Turekian said. "I got a fair look. They can grasp, sort of, but aren't built for manipulation."

"You saw how the fledgling uses them to cling to the parent," Webner stated. "Perhaps it climbs trees also. Earth has a bird with similar structures, the hoatzin. It loses them in adulthood. Here they may become extra weapons for the mature animal."

"The feet." Turekian scowled. "Two opposable digits flanking three straight ones. Could serve as hands."

"Then how does the creature get about on the ground?" Webner retorted. "Can't forge a tool in midair, you know, let alone dig ore and erect stone houses."

He wagged a finger. "Another, more fundamental point," he went on. "Flyers are too limited in mass. True, the gravity's weaker than on Earth, but air pressure's lower. Thus admissible wing loadings are about the same. The biggest birds that ever lumbered into Terrestrial skies weighed some fifteen kilos. Nothing larger could get aloft. Metabolism simply can't supply the power required. We established aboard ship, from specimens, that local biochemistry is close kin to our type. Hence it is not possible for those ornithoids to outweigh a maximal vulture. They're big, yes, and formidable. Nevertheless, that size has to be mostly feathers, hollow bones—spidery, kitelike skeletons anchoring thin flesh.

"Aram, you hefted several items today, such as a stone pot. Or consider one of the buckets, presumably used to bring water up from the river. What would you say the greatest weight is?"

Turekian scratched in his beard. "Maybe twenty kilos," he answered reluctantly.

"There! No flyer could lift that. It was always superstition about eagles stealing lambs or babies. They weren't able to. The ornithoids are similarly handicapped. Who'd make utensils he can't carry?''

"M-m-m," Turekian growled rather than hummed. Webner pressed the attack:

"The mass of any flyer on a terrestroid planet is insufficient to include a big enough brain for true intelligence. The purely animal functions require virtually all those cells. Birds have at least lightened their burden, permitting a little more brain, by changing jaws to beaks. So have those ornithoids you called 'watchfalcons.' The big fellows have not.''

He hesitated. "In fact," he said slowly, "I doubt if they can even be considered bright animals. They're likely stupid . . . and vicious. If we're set on again, we need have no compunctions about destroying them.''

"Were you going to?" Yukiko whispered. "Couldn't he, she, it, simply have been coming down for a quick, close look at you—unarmed as a peace gesture?''

"If intelligent, yes," Webner said. "If not, as I've proven to be the case, positively no. I saved us some nasty wounds. Perhaps I saved a life.''

"The dwellers might object if we shoot at their property," Turekian said.

"They need only call off their, ah, dogs. In fact, the attack on us may not have been commanded, may have been brute reaction after panic broke the order of the pack." Webner rose. "Are you satisfied? We'll make thorough studies till nightfall, then leave gifts, withdraw, hope for a better reception when we see the indigenes have returned." A television pickup was customary among diplomatic presents of that Turekian shook his head. "Your logic's all right, I suppose. But it don't smell right somehow.''

Webner started for the airlock.

"Me too?" Yukiko requested. "Please?''

"No," Turekian said. "I'd hate for you to be harmed.''

"We're in no danger," she argued. "Our sidearms can handle any flyers that may arrive feeling mean. If we plant sensors around, no walking native can come within bowshot before we know. I feel caged.'' She aimed her smile at Webner.

The xenologist thawed. ''Why not?'' he said. ''I can use a levelheaded assistant.'' To Turekian: ''Man the boat guns yourself if you wish.''

''Like blazes,'' the pilot grumbled, and followed them.

He had to admit the leader knew his business. The former cursory search became a shrewd, efficient examination of object after object, measuring, photographing, commenting continuously into a minirecorder. Yukiko helped. On Survey, everybody must have some knowledge of everybody else's specialty. But Webner needed just one extra person.

''What can I do?'' Turekian asked.

''Move an occasional heavy load,'' the other man said. ''Keep watch on the forest. Stay out of my way.''

Yukiko was too fascinated by the work to chide him. Turekian rumbled in his throat, stuffed his pipe, and slouched around the grounds alone, blowing furious clouds.

At the corral he gripped a rail and glowered. ''You want feeding,'' he decided, went into a barn—unlike the house, its door was not secured—and found a haymow and pitchforks which, despite every strangeness of detail, reminded him of a backwoods colony on Hermes that he'd visited once, temporarily primitive because shipping space was taken by items more urgent than modern agromachines. The farmer had had a daughter. . . . He consoled himself with memories while he took out a mess of cinnamon-scented red herbage.

''You!''

Webner leaned from an upstairs window. ''What're you about?'' he called.

''Those critters are hungry,'' Turekian replied. ''Listen to 'em.''

''How do you know what their requirements are? Or the owners'? We're not here to play God, for your information.

We're here to learn and, maybe, help. Take that stuff back where you got it.''

Turekian swallowed rage—that Yukiko should have heard his humiliation—and complied. Webner was his captain till he regained the blessed sky.

Sky . . . birds . . . He observed the "cotes." The pseudo-hawks fluttered about, indignant but too small to tackle him. Were the giant ornithoids kept partly as protection against large ground predators? Turekian studied the flock. Its members dozed, waddled, scratched the dirt, fat and placid, obviously long bred to tameness. Both types lacked the gill-like slits he had noticed. . . .

A shadow. Turekian glanced aloft, snatched for his magnifier. Half a dozen giants were back. The noon sun flamed on their feathers. They were too high for him to see details.

He flipped the controls on his grav unit and made for the house. Webner and Yukiko were on the fifth floor. Turekian arced through a window. He had no eye, now, for the Spartan grace of the room. "They've arrived," he panted. "We better get in the boat quick."

Webner stepped onto the balcony. "No need," he said. "I hardly think they'll attack. If they do, we're safer here than crossing the yard."

"Might be smart to close the shutters," the girl said.

"And the door to this chamber," Webner agreed. "That'll stop them. They'll soon lose patience and wander off—if they attempt anything. Or if they do besiege us, we can shoot our way through them, or at worst relay a call for help via the boat, once *Olga*'s again over our horizon."

He had re-entered. Turekian took his place on the balcony and squinted upward. More winged shapes had joined the first several; and more came into view each second. They dipped, soared, circled through the wind, which made surf noises in the forest.

Unease crawled along the pilot's spine. "I don't like this half a bit," he said. "They don't act like plain beasts."

"Conceivably the dwellers plan to use them in an assault," Webner said. "If so, we may have to teach the dwellers about the cost of unreasoning hostility." His tone was less cool than the words, and sweat beaded his countenance.

Sparks in the magnifier field hurt Turekian's eyes. "I swear they're carrying metal," he said. "Listen, if they are intelligent—and out to get us, after you nearly killed one of 'em—the house is no place for us. Let's scramble. We may not have many more minutes."

"Yes, I believe we'd better, Vaughn," Yukiko urged. "We can't risk . . . being forced to burn down conscious beings . . . on their own land."

Maybe his irritation with the pilot spoke for Webner: "How often must I explain there is no such risk, yet? Instead, here's a chance to learn. What happens next could give us invaluable clues to understanding the whole ethos. We stay." To Turekian: "Forget about that alleged metal. Could be protective collars, I suppose. But take the supercharger off your imagination."

The other man froze where he stood.

"Aram." Yukiko seized his arm. He stared beyond her. "What's wrong?"

He shook himself. "Supercharger," he mumbled. "By God, yes."

Abruptly, in a bellow: "We're leaving! This second! They *are* the dwellers, and they've gathered the whole countryside against us!"

"Hold your tongue," Webner said, "or I'll charge insubordination."

Laughter rattled in Turekian's breast. "Uh-uh. Mutiny."

He crouched and lunged. His fist rocketed before him. Yukiko's cry joined the thick smack as knuckles hit—not the chin, which is too hazardous, the solar plexus. Air whoofed from Webner. His eyes glazed. He folded over, partly conscious but unable to stand while his diaphragm spasmed. Turekian gathered him in his arms. "To the boat!" the pilot shouted. "Hurry, girl!"

His grav unit wouldn't carry two, simply gentled his fall when he leaped from the balcony. He dared not stop to adjust the controls on Webner's. Bearing his chief, he pounded across the flagstones. Yukiko came above. "Go ahead!" Turekian bawled. "Get into shelter, for God's sake!"

"Not till you can," she answered. "I'll cover you." He was helpless to prevent her.

The scores above had formed themselves into a vast revolving wheel. It tilted. The first flyers peeled off and roared downward. The rest came after.

Arrows whistled ahead of them. A trumpet sounded. Turekian dodged, zigzag over the meadow. Yukiko's gun clapped. She shot to miss, but belike the flashes put those archers —and, now, spearthrowers—off their aim. Shafts sang wickedly around. One edge grazed Webner's neck. He screamed.

Yukiko darted to open the boat's airlock. While she did, Turekian dropped Webner and straddled him, blaster drawn. The leading flyer hurtled close. Talons of the right foot, which was not a foot at all but a hand, gripped a sword curved like a scimitar. For an instant, Turekian looked squarely into the golden eyes, knew a brave male defending his home, and also shot to miss.

In a brawl of air, the native sheered off. The valve swung wide. Yukiko flitted through. Turekian dragged Webner, then stood in the lock chamber till the entry was shut.

Missiles clanged on the hull. None would pierce. Turekian let himself join Webner for a moment of shuddering in each other's embrace, before he went forward to Yukiko and the raising of his vessel.

When you know what to expect, a little, you can lay plans. We next sought the folk of Ythri, as the planet is called by its most advanced culture, a thousand kilometers from the triumph which surely prevailed in the mountains. Approached with patience, caution, and symbolisms appropriate to their psyches, they welcomed us rapturously. Before we left, they'd thought of sufficient inducements to trade that I'm sure they'll have spacecraft of their own in a few generations.

Still, they are as fundamentally territorial as man is fundamentally sexual, and we'd better bear that in mind.

The reason lies in their evolution. It does for every drive in every animal everywhere. The Ythrian is carnivorous, aside from various sweet fruits. Carnivores require larger regions per individual than herbivores or omnivores do, in spite of the fact that meat has more calories per kilo than most vegetable matter. Consider how each antelope needs a certain amount of space, and how many antelope are needed to maintain a pride of lions. Xenologists have written thousands of papers on the correlations between diet and genotypical personality in sophonts.

I have my doubts about the value of those papers. At least, they missed the possibility of a race like the Ythrians, whose extreme territoriality and individualism—with the consequences to governments, mores, arts, faiths, and souls— come from the extreme appetite of the body.

They mass as high as thirty kilos; yet they can lift an equal weight into the air or, unhampered, fly like demons. Hence they maintain civilization without the need to crowd together in cities. Their townspeople are mostly wing-clipped criminals and slaves. Today their wiser heads hope robots will end the need for that.

Hands? The original talons, modified for manipulating. Feet? Those claws on the wings, a juvenile feature which persisted and developed, just as man's large head and sparse hair derive from the juvenile or fetal ape. The forepart of the wing skeleton consists of humerus, radius, and ulna, much as in true birds. These lock together in flight. Aground, when the wing is folded downward, they produce a "knee" joint. Bones grow from their base to make the claw-foot. Three fused digits, immensely lengthened, sweep backward to be the alatan which braces the rest of that tremendous wing and can, when desired, give additional support on the surface. To rise, the Ythrians usually do a handstand during the initial upstroke. It takes less than a second.

Oh, yes, they are slow and awkward afoot. They manage, though. Big and beweaponed, instantly ready to mount the wind, they need fear no beast of prey.

You ask where the power comes from to swing this hugeness through the sky. The oxidation of food, what else? Hence the demand of each household for a great hunting or ranching demesne. The limiting factor is the oxygen supply. A molecule in the blood can carry more than hemoglobin does, but the gas must be furnished. Turekian first realized how that happens. The Ythrian has lungs, a passive system resembling ours. In addition he has his supercharger, evolved from the gills of an amphibianlike ancestor. Worked in bellows fashion by the flight muscles, connecting directly with the bloodstream, those air-intake organs let him burn his fuel as fast as necessary.

I wonder how it feels to be so alive.

I remember how Yukiko Sachansky stood in the curve of Aram Turekian's arm, under a dawn heaven, and watched the farewell dance the Ythrians gave for us, and cried through tears: "To fly like that! To fly like that!"

THE
LONG
REMEMBERING

Among the greatest rewards of being a science fiction writer, especially one who does a lot of the "hard science" kind, are the rather frequent contacts made with readers. They have an extraordinarily strong tendency to be likable and lively, maintain a wide range of interests, and, in their own work, do some of the most fascinating things around. Understandably, a good many of them are scientists. These will cheerfully accept a fantastic premise for the sake of a story, but want to have the verifiable details in it correct—and quite rightly. Every workman slips every now and then, but that's no excuse for being slipshod.

Such a reader is my old friend François Bordes, a pioneer in modern methods of studying prehistory, now professor of the subject at the University of Bordeaux. (When he can find time, he writes mighty good science fiction himself under a pen name. Somebody ought to consider English-language publication of those novels and short stories.) He liked this tale well enough to translate it for the French magazine *Fiction*. Being an honest scholar, he arranged for the editorial introduction to state where I had made errors. I have corrected these in the present version (Bordes is not responsible for any that remain), but can't resist sharing the gossip with you.

One observation was to the effect that the bow and arrow had not been invented in Aurignacian times, as I had assumed. In another passage, I had mentioned a "longtooth." He pointed out that while *Machairodus*, the saber-toothed tiger, was still alive in America, it was then extinct in Europe. To me he remarked, "It seems that long-toothed carnivores always survive later in America."

Ah, well, we still love each other's countries very much, and I look forward to the next glass we can hoist together.

CLAIRE TOOK my arm. "Must you go right away?" she asked.

"I'd better," I said. "Don't worry, sweetheart. I'll bring back a nice fat check and tomorrow night we'll celebrate." I stroked her cheek. "You haven't gotten much celebration lately, have you?"

"It doesn't matter," she said. "It's enough just having you around the place." After a moment when we could not have spoken: "Okay. Run along."

She stood in the door and smiled at me all my way down the stairs. During my bus ride, I decided for the thousandth time that I was a lucky fellow in spite of everything.

Rennie's house was big and old, the neighborhood somewhat better than ours. When I rang the bell, he admitted me himself, a tall gray man with tired eyes. "Ah, Mr. Armand," he said gently. "You are punctual. Come in."

He led me down the hall to a cluttered living room where books hid the walls. "Sit down," he invited. "Do you care for a drink?" We were alone, I realized.

"Thank you. A little wine, if you please." I looked out the windows to the undistinguished sunlight. A car went past, the newest and most blatant model. My leather armchair was solid, comfortable; when I moved, its horsehair stuffing rustled. I needed such assurances of everyday reality around me.

Rennie brought in a decanter and poured for us both. The Burgundy was pretty good. He sat down opposite me and crossed interminable legs.

23

"You can still back out," he said. "I won't think the worse of you." His half-smile faded. "My subjects don't sign those elaborate legal waivers for nothing. And you're married, aren't you?"

I nodded. That was no reason for retreat. Rather, it was my reason for being here. Claire worked, but we had a baby on the way, and as for me, graduate assistants in the chemistry department are not exactly overpaid. Rennie's spectacular experiments in psychophysics had won him a large grant, and he offered good money to volunteers. In a few hours with him, I could earn what would make all the difference to us.

Still—"I've never heard of any danger," I said. "You don't send people physically into the past."

"No." He looked beyond me. His words came stiff: "But this is such a new thing . . . full of wild variables. . . . I can't predict how far back you'll go, or what will happen then. Suppose your ancestor has—or had—a bad shock while you're there. What would the effect be on you?"

"Why, uh, has anybody had experiences like that?"

"Yes. No permanent psychological damage resulted, but some did return terrified and needed days to calm down. Others reported no events that were unpleasant *per se*, but nevertheless were deeply, unaccountably depressed for a while afterward. Everyone has, at best, felt disoriented at first. You mustn't expect to accomplish much in the next few days, Mr. Armand."

"I've been warned, sir, and made arrangements." I buried my gaze in the wineglass.

"You should be back to normal within a week. I want you to understand, though, I can promise nothing."

"I do."

"Very well, then." Rennie smiled and leaned back. "Let's get acquainted. I know little about you except that your psychoprofile indicates you'll be an excellent subject. Is your ancestry French?"

I nodded. "From the Dordogne. My parents were over here when I was born because my father worked for the diplomatic corps. I like France, but decided I'd rather be an American.''

"Well, you won't necessarily find yourself back there," said Rennie. "The races of Europe are so scrambled. I'm going to try to send you across a longer timespan than the few generations I've managed hitherto." He sipped. "How well do you know the theory of temporal psycho-displacement?"

"Just what I've read in the popular science magazines and such," I admitted. "Let's see. . . . My world line through the space-time continuum goes back further than my birth. At the point where I was begotten, it connects to those of my parents, and so on for grandparents, as far as the first living cell on Earth, possibly. The mind, the consciousness, whatever you want to call it, seems to be a function of the world line itself, as well as of the individual body. At least, you've found that under the proper conditions the mind can move back to a different part of the line—or scan back; the theorists are still arguing which, and the theologians are claiming that what's involved is actually the soul.''

Rennie chuckled. "Not bad. What's your personal opinion?"

"I don't feel qualified to have any," I said. "What's yours, sir? You insist in public you're suspending judgment till more data come in, but surely the pioneer—''

My voice trailed off in embarrassment. He must have sensed how I admired him, for he said quietly: "Please. I've done nothing more than systematize the work of predecessors, from as long ago as Dunne and Rhine if not further. I owe a tremendous debt to Mitchell and his colleagues; in fact, what I've done amounts largely to fusing their discoveries in noetics with some new concepts of physics and cosmology, and using modern laboratory equipment to check out the hypotheses that followed.''

"I've wondered—why can't you send me into the future?" I asked.

"I don't know," he replied. "I just can't—so far, anyway. None of the various explanations satisfy me."

He became the parched professor, maybe as a shield: "In spite of the countless news stories you must have seen, Mr. Armand, let me summarize for you the subjective experience you will undergo. Your body will lie unconscious for several hours. Your mind will be in the brain, or scanning the brain, of some ancestor, for the same period of time. But you will not be aware of that, of any separate identity. On arousal—return—you will remember what went on, as if that other person had been you. Nothing more, nothing less."

It was Faustian enough for me. My heart thuttered. "Can we get started soon, please?" I begged.

His laboratory had once been an upstairs bedroom. I loosened my clothes, took off my shoes, stretched on a couch. A pill I took was merely a tranquilizer, the biofeedback exercise merely to establish the desired brain rhythms. Then the laser-drive induction field took over and I fell into night.

I was Argnach-eskaladuan-torkluk, which means He Who Casts the Rope Against the Horse; but my true name I hold secret from warlocks and the wind ghosts, and will not reveal. When my first thin beard sprouted, I got my open name because I lurked near a water hole till a herd of horses came by, then threw a line around one neck, thus holding the beast till I could cut its throat and drag it home. That was on my Journey, which boys make alone. Afterward we are taken off to a certain place in the dark, and the wind ghosts dance in aurochs' hides before us, reindeer-antlered, and the first joint of the left middle finger is cut off and given them to eat. More I may not say. When it is over, we are men and can take wives.

This had happened—I do not know how long ago. The Men do not count time. But I was still in the pride of my youth. Tonight it was a cold pride, for I went by myself with small hope of coming back.

Snow gusted across my path as I walked down the hillside. Trees, dwarfish and scattered, talked in a huge noisy wind. Afar sounded a lion's roar. Maybe that was the same lion which had eaten Andutannalok-gargut when last the fall season had kindled rain-wet leaves. I shuddered and fingered the Mother charm in my pouch, for I had no wish to meet a beast with Andutannalok's ghost looking out of its eyes.

The storm was waning. I saw low clouds break overhead and stars tremble between sere branches. Still the dry snow hissed by my ankles and crusted in the fur of my clothing. Still there was little save darkness to see; I made my way as hunters do, my whole skin feeling what lay around.

This was in spite of heavy coat, trousers, and boots, whose leathers should be proof against spearthrust. But the goblins had more strength in their arms than a Man does. Any of them could hurl a stone that would smash my skull like a ripe fruit. And then my body would be left for wolves to devour, and where should my poor gaunt ghost find a home? The wind would harry it through the forests and up over the northern tundra.

I bore weapons: three flint knives at my belt, several spears in a bundle across my shoulder, a throwing-stick in my hand. The foremost spear was tipped with wolf bone to bite the deeper, and Ingmarak the Ghost Man had chanted over it. The rest had keen, fresh-chipped stone points. And my free fingers caressed the great comforting breasts of the Mother. Yet my single companion was the wind.

Trees thickened when I came down into the valley, mostly scrub oak and willow. At last I had woods around me and must part underbrush with arms and shins to pass through. Ahead, the river's brawling began to fill the gloom. Our cave seemed very far behind, unclimbably far in the cliffs.

Nobody there had forbidden me to go after Evavy-unaroa, my white witch girl. How could they? But all had spoken against it and none would come along. Ingmarak shook his bald head and blinked dim rheumy eyes at me. "This is not well, Argnach," he said. "No good can be found in Goblin Land. Take a new wife."

"I only want Evavy-unaroa," I told him.

The elders mumbled. Children stared frightened from

shadowed corners. What thing possessed me? I did not know myself.

I had gotten her only last summer, when my eyes grew suddenly hungry for her and she smiled back on me. No man had had her before, and her father drove an easy bargain. For everyone else was the least bit afraid of her—that dearest, merriest of creatures ever to walk the earth—and still did not ask to borrow her. This suited me, whether or not it lowered my standing a bit. We could afford that, since I was among the best hunters and people liked us both. It was only that other men didn't want to take a needless risk.

Soapstone lamps guttered and flared. Wind flapped the skins hung on poles before the hollow in the cliff where we sat. The fires gave such warmth that folk wore little clothing or none. Near the cave mouth was a good store of meat, gloriously ripening. We should have been cheerful. But when I told them I would go into Goblin Land and fetch Evavy back, fear had walked in and squatted among us.

"They have already eaten her," said Vuotak-nanavo, the one-eyed man who braided his beard and could smell game half a day's walk into the breeze. "Her and the unborn child, they are eaten, and lest their ghosts do not stay in the goblin bellies but come back here, we would do well to lay another hand ax under the hearth she used."

"Perhaps they have not been eaten," I replied. "It is my weird to go."

When I had said this, there was no turning back, and silence dropped from the night. Finally Ingmarak, the Ghost Man, rose. "Tomorrow we will make spells," he said.

We did a great deal on that day and in the twilight. All saw me take a lamp, the twig brushes, and the little pots of paint, deep into the cave. I drew myself overcoming the goblins, and colored my face. What else went on may not be spoken of.

Well, Ingmarak did relate to me at tedious length what I had always known about the goblins. Old stories told how they once held the entire land, till the Men came from the direction of winter sunrise and slowly crowded them out. Now the two kinds seldom glimpsed each other and hardly ever fought. We were afraid to attack them—what unknown powers were theirs?—and ourselves had nothing worth their robbery; they flaked tools somewhat differently from us, but no worse, and seemed to have less need of clothes. The river divided our countries, and few ever crossed it from either side.

But Evavy had gone there to fetch stones from its bed. They were strong stones in that water, for it flowed from the far north, where Father Mammoth walked the tundra and shook his tusks beneath the heights of the Ice. She wanted lucky pebbles to make a necklace for her child when it was born. She went alone because of having secret words to say, carried a spear and a torch against beasts and was not afraid.

When she made no return, I tracked her and in the trampled snow saw what had happened. A goblin party had stolen her. If she still lived, she was on their side of the water.

Now, on my quest, I reached the shore. The stream was broad, a snake of blackness between white banks and icy trees, in spots dully a-shimmer as if scales caught light. This bottom of the valley was sheltered from the wind, which was falling anyhow; but cold breathed from the currents, and I saw ice floes whirl past.

During the day, with proper apologies, I had chopped down a small tree. An ax is not a good weapon, I think, but does make a useful tool. Most branches I had lopped, leaving some which ought to keep me from upsetting and drowning, and one I had made into a rough paddle.

I took off my boots and hung them around my neck. The snow bit my feet like teeth. The clouds were black, sundering mountains above me. Northward the air stood clear and the dead hunters danced in the sky, their many-colored mantles waving and their long spears shaken at the stars. For them, I drew a knife and cut off a lock of hair, stood by the river and said into the dying wind:

"I am Argnach-eskaladuan-torkluk, a man of the Men,
who here gives you a piece of his life. For this gift, of course,
I ask no return. But know, Star Hunters, I am bound into
Goblin Land to fetch back my wife, Evavy-unaroa the white
witch girl, and our child that she bears. For any aid I may
receive, I offer a fat part of every kill I make for the rest of my
days on earth."

The brightnesses flapped huge. The chill gnawed in toward
my foot-bones. My voice had come out very small and
lonely. So with a grunt, as a man grunts when he spears a boar
that may die or may live to slash him apart, I launched my
log.

At once the river had me. I sped downstream while I drove
my paddle into foam and craziness. The waters roared. I was
numbed in the feet, numbed in the head. What happened to
me seemed to be happening to a stranger far off while I, the I
of my secret name, stood on a high mountain thinking strong
thoughts. I thought it was really needless to freeze my feet
this way, when by fire and scraping a trunk could be hollowed
out for men to sit dry inside and fish or chase marsh fowl.

Then my deadened toes bumped on stones, the log grated
in shallows. I sprang off and hauled it ashore after me. For a
while I sat rubbing life back into my feet with a fox skin.
When that was done, I put on my boots again and started into
Goblin Land, marking well the path I took.

We knew where the goblins denned, closer to the river than
us on our side. I went at an easy pace, snuffing the almost
quiet air for smoke to guide me. I was somewhat afraid, but
not much, because my weird was on me and nothing could
change whatever was going to happen. Besides, the whole
world had felt not quite real to me since the evening I saw
goblin tracks across Evavy's bootprints. It had been as if I
were already half a ghost.

I do not understand why I should have lost all wariness
toward her, I alone among the Men. They agreed she was tall
and well-shaped, brave of heart, skilled of hand, and free
with her laughter. But she had blue eyes and yellow hair like a

goblin. Folk did say, to be sure, that of old, matings had taken place between the two breeds, so that now and again the light-hued strain appeared in us; but no one alive could remember another such child. Thus a Power clearly dwelt in Evavy-unaroa, and while she gave no reason to suppose it was harmful, still, nobody was quite sure what might come of coupling with her, and shied off from taking the chance.

I, Argnach, had not. My spirit saw that her Power was the Mother's and could only be good. Now I knew that it was, as well, the same which makes a bull elk stand and die for his mates.

The racket of a herd, alarmed by something and crashing off through young trees, put that thought in me. A dim wintry light had begun to steal between the boughs. I spied signs of plentiful game, more than we had on our side of the river. Much more!

And we were breeding more mouths than men who hunted, boys who fished, women and girls who gathered could readily feed.

I came out on an open slope, grassy in summer, which climbed northward to bulk wan across the last stars. A low breeze brought me smoke. My flesh prickled. I was near the goblin haunt.

If they were indeed such warlocks as the stories told of, they would soon smite me. I would fall dead, or turn into a worm and be crushed underfoot, or run screaming and foaming into the woods as sone have done who were never seen again.

But Evavy was yonder, if she lived.

Therefore I made myself into smoke, drifting amidst shadows, curling behind boulders, winding from bush to thicket to tussock, throwing-stick in my left hand and foremost spear in my right. The eastern sky had blanched when I saw the goblin cave.

It was bigger and wider-mouthed than ours. They did not make a shelter outside and mostly use that, like us. Instead, they stayed inside and kept a fire always at the entrance.

Ingmarak had told me that in his childhood the Men had done the same, but this was no longer needful; the beasts had learned not to approach us. Hereabouts were more beasts than in our country, and they must be bolder. I had supposed the abundance came from goblin spells, raising game out of dawn mists. But as I stood and peered through the branches of a low-sweeping juniper, a very great thought came to me.

"If they have the Power," I whispered to myself, "then they should not be afraid of lion or bear. They should not need a fire in front of their home. But they do. Then perhaps, O Star Hunters, this is because they do not have the Power. Perhaps they are not even such good hunters as the Men, and that is the reason there are many animals in their land."

I shuddered with the thought, strength lifted in me, I had no more fear at all.

Most softly, then, I stole over the last stretch to the goblin lair.

An old one was tending the fire. This was the first time I had seen any at close range. The sight was less dreadful than I had awaited. He was much shorter than me, thickly shaped, but would have been as erect had age not stooped and gnarled him. His hair, once tawny, hung grizzled and unkempt past his shoulders, which were still broad, the arms on them still brawny. His head was the strangest part, long, flattened on top, low of brow, eyes nearly lost under great ridges, no chin behind the thin beard.

He stamped his feet, beat hands together, puffed frost out of a craglike nose. Well must he be cold, for his dress was no more than a few hides clumsily lashed to each other and to him, while his feet were bare. He stayed alert, though. When I broke from cover and sped across the last few man-lengths, he yelled and snatched for a club.

My spear butt seemed of itself to find the angle of the throwing-stick. The cast whirred. The wolf bone struck. The goblin lurched, clutched at the shaft in his belly, fell onto the snow where his blood shouted louder than his pain. I sprang past him to the cave mouth, drew a second spear from my harness, and roared for Evavy.

A goblin came out with a spear of his own. Its point was merely fire-hardened. Outreaching him, I stabbed mine in. A third male lifted a hand ax; they don't make the hafted kind. Before I could unlimber a fresh weapon, but also before he could smite, I seized a brand from the fire and thrust. The flame drew a wail from him. He fell backward to escape more.

It boiled with naked bodies in there. I dimly glimpsed the squat, ugly women scramble rearward, to guard their cubs and clash teeth at me. The goblin men bumbled in half-darkness, crying out, and the knowledge thrilled in me that they were afraid.

"Evavy!" I called. "Evavy, Argnach is come for you!"

Through one lost heartbeat, I knew fear again, that her ghost would answer from a goblin mouth. Then she had pushed her way to the front. I looked into eyes like summer's heaven, and tears stung my own.

"This way!" I loosed a spear blind into the murk. A goblin yelped. "Run!" I said needlessly.

Our flight must have heartened them. They pounded after us, howling and grunting. Evavy's feet paced mine, her hair streamed near my face. They had not taken her clothes, but even through the heavy furs I could see the grace of her, even then I savored it.

Down the slope we dashed, into the forest. Soon a deer trail helped us draw farther ahead of pursuit. They could not run as fast as Men. Once, when we crossed a glade, a stone whooped past me with more speed than I could have given it. But no spears came close.

Breath was harsh and hot in our throats by the time we reached the riverside where my log waited. "Get that launched!" I ordered. We could not hope to swim this icy torrent. While she strained at the weight, I leaned my remaining spears against a bole—none too early.

The goblins burst out of crackly, glittery brush. I wounded two of them. A third got in arm's length, caught the shaft I had, and wrenched it from me. I drew a knife and slashed him. Someone else stabbed at me, but my leather coat turned the wooden point. Evavy took a spear and jabbed back, hurting the naked creature. The goblins roiled in withdrawal from us. Our log was almost afloat. We waded, gave a last push, straddled it, and were in the river's arms.

I looked behind. The goblins hopped about, yelled, shook fists. Whatever fallen tree they had come raiding on was nowhere near, and the current had borne us out of casting range—swiftly bore us around a bend and out of sight. I laughed aloud and dug my paddle deep.

Evavy wept. "But you are free!" I said.

"That is why I weep," she answered. The Earth Powers are strong and strange in womankind.

"Did they hurt you?" I asked.

"No," she said. "One of them . . . I had seen before, watching me from his side. He and a few caught me by surprise and brought me across to their cave. They would not let me go. But they did no harm, did not even mount me; they gave me their best food and crooned gentle, unknown words. Yet I could not go back to you—" She wept afresh.

I thought that her fair coloring must indeed have made her a lovely sight to the goblins, as she was to me, while her height and features lent wonder, yes, mystery. They must have reckoned it well worth the risk to have her for—what? Their Mother?

I stopped my toil to stroke her hair. "There has been a weird in this," I said. "We were afraid of the goblins because they look so strange we thought they must command a Power."

The river hallooed in the first long light of the sun. My paddle wrestled the water again. "But that is not true," I said. "They are poor and awkward folk, slow on their feet and slow in their souls. Our fathers who hunt in the sky on winter nights drove the goblins off—not with spears or axes, I believe, but because they could think more widely and run more swiftly. Thus they could kill more game and raise more children. The goblins must leave or starve.

"Now we are outgrowing our grounds. When summer comes, I will gather the Men and cross the river. We will take those lands too for our own."

We struck the shallows on the home side and waded ashore. Evavy clung to me, her teeth clapping in her head. I wanted to make haste, back to the fires before the cave and the victory song I would sing for the Men. But a sound drew my gaze back across the water.

The goblins had reappeared there. They stood clustered, staring and staring. One of them reached out his arms. He was a goodly ways from me, but I have sharp eyes and saw his tears.

Because he also cares for Evavy, I will try to spare his life when we cross the river.

I came awake. A fluorescent lamp shone pale, for night lay beyond the drawn curtains.

Rennie guided me back to the living room and offered his wine. I had spoken no word.

"Well?" he said at last. "Where . . . when did you go?"

"A hell of a long way," I answered from the dream which still had me.

"Yes?" His look smoldered.

"I don't know the date. Let the archaeologists figure it out." In a few sentences I told him what had happened.

"My God," he whispered. "The Old Stone Age. Twenty thousand years ago, maybe, when half the northern hemisphere lay under the glacier." He reached out to grip my arm. "You have seen the first true human beings, the Crô-Magnon people, and the last Neanderthal ape-men."

"No, wrong," I muttered. "The difference wasn't that big between them. I feel sorry for the Neanderthals. They tried hard. . . . Look, I'm dazed. Can I go home and sleep it off?"

"Certainly. Typical reaction. You'll come back tomorrow, won't you? I want to record a full statement from you. Everything you can remember—everything! Good Lord, I never imagined you'd go so far."

He escorted me to the door. "Can you make your way all right?" he asked.

"Yes. I'm okay. Okay enough, anyhow." We shook hands.

"Good night." His tall form stood black in the yellow-lit doorway.

The bus I wanted stopped at the corner within minutes. When I had boarded, it rumbled and whined so that for a moment fear tensed my guts. What monster was this, what alien stenches? Then I remembered I'd inhabited the skin of another man, who was twenty thousand years in his grave.

That did not at once make the world come real. I walked through a winter wood where elk bugled, while ghosts crowded around me and twittered in my ear.

Climbing the stairs in my apartment building restored a measure of solidity. I swung aside an unlocked door and entered our general-purpose room. Claire put down a cigarette, rose from her chair, and came to me. "How are you, darling?" Her tone trembled. "How'd everything go?"

"Not too bad. Fantastic, in fact." I braced myself. "Except I'm bushed. Before I tell you, how about some coffee?"

"Of course, of course. But where did you *go*, darling?" She dragged me by the hand toward the kitchenette.

I considered her, clean, kindly, a trifle plump, rouged, creamed, girdled, with glasses and carefully waved hair and tobacco stale upon her breath. A face rose before me that was brown from sun and wind, weather-bleached yellow mane, eyes like summer's heaven. I remembered freckles dusted across a nose lifted sooty from the cookfire, and low laughter and work-hardened small hands reaching for me. And I knew what my punishment was for what I had done, and knew it would never end.

PEEK!
I
SEE
YOU!

The late John Campbell, editor of the magazine *Astounding* (until he changed its name to *Analog*), is rightly credited with being very nearly the single-handed founder of modern science fiction, through his policies and his encouragement of bright new writers as well as bright older ones. But he has seldom gotten praise for another set of major contributions. He was an absolute fountainhead of ideas, which he gave away freely to each and every person who might conceivably like to incorporate them in stories. If this then came about, he was delighted. But he never, never mentioned his own part in it. I know from the authors, not him, that some of the most important, even epoch-making tales he published were based on concepts he supplied. From this, plus personal experience, I can guess how many more.

The following yarn is scarcely of prime significance, but it does illustrate how Campbell operated and how—sometimes—the writer's own machinery does. For years I had had lying in my files a notion which had occurred to me, that visitors from advanced extraterrestrial civilizations might not necessary be interested in contacting Washington or Moscow. I couldn't quite see a story in that alone. Then a letter from Campbell threw off, independently and along with a lot of other fireworks, the suggestion that if such visitors didn't want to be bothered by Washington or Moscow, they wouldn't sneak into our atmosphere, they'd arrive with maximum display of a certain kind. Suddenly the two thoughts clicked together; I saw what to do, and had a lot of fun doing it.

Thank you, John.

THE FATHER of Sean F. X. Lindquist was an amiable, easygoing Seattle Swede. His mother was, as might be guessed, an O'Kelly with a will of her own. Their genes combined to produce a son who was good-natured, a bit raffish, intelligent, disinclined to toil—but, on occasion, stubborn as Lucifer. And thereby hangs a tale.

Being expelled from college, for reasons having less to do with his grades than the president's daughter, he impulsively joined the Army. True to its promise of showing him the glamorous parts of the world, it shipped him to Thailand, where he served his hitch clerking on what had to be the world's hottest, dustiest, most isolated and dismal station as part of a miniscule military advisory mission which the general truce throughout Asia had made altogether superfluous. Nonethless, he was enchanted with Bangkok, where he spent his leaves, and pulled wires to be demobbed in that city. In due course, with a certain feeling of mutual relief, the Army gave him his honorable discharge.

The enchantment wore off—she married someone else—and he made a leisurely way home around the world. Whenever his funds ran out, he did odd jobs. Some were very odd indeed. He was twenty-six before he reached the States again, and long out of touch. So he might have caught up on newspapers and technical journals; but he went instead to Las Vegas and updated himself in other fields. A true cliché calls luck a lady, apt to smile most upon men who do not pursue her. Lindquist departed with several thousand dollars in his pocket.

Tourism was booming in the Southwest. Lindquist remembered boyhood camping trips in the area. It occurred to him that he could make a pleasant living, and have his winters free, by starting an air ferry service. Though industry had spoiled much of the Four Corners country, a great deal of solitude and splendor remained in those uplands. But the effort and expense of packing into roadless mountains discouraged most potential visitors. Now if they and their gear could be flown in, and out again at an agreed-on time—if the pilot was available by radio meanwhile, to handle emergencies like lost can openers—

He took lessons and got his license. Then he bought himself a used VTOL aircraft and went to scout the territory.

Thus it was that he saw the spaceship.

He was droning leisurely along at about 3500 meters. The peaks were not extremely far below him. Their landscape was awesome: vast, steep, cragged, a ruddiness slashed by mineral ochers and blues, a starkness little relieved by scattered mesquite, greasewood, and sagebrush. Here and there, a streamlet turned the bottom of a canyon green. But mostly this was desert land, people-empty land, hawk, buzzard, jackrabbit, and coyote land. The sun was westering in a deep, almost purple sky. Updrafts boomed briefly and trickily, shaking the plane in its course.

Lindquist's lean, sandy-haired, shabby-clad form sat relaxed. He puffed a corncob pipe and hummed a bawdy song. But alertness was in him. Before he tried carrying passengers, he must get familiar with this kind of flying. And he needed a place to roost for the night, preferably containing water and firewood. His eyes roved.

The vision slanted down before him. It moved at incredible speed, banked at impossible angles. Yet its passage was so silent that his own motor, his very pulse hammered at him. The shape, as nearly as he could tell, was roughly like a disk thickened in the middle. But the lambent, shifting colors that played across it, enveloped it in aurora, made such things hard to gauge.

It swung around, slid near, and his magnetic compass went crazy. For a moment he stared at what seemed to be a row of ports, glowing as if furnaces burned behind them. Far in the back of his mind, a reckoner clicked: *Diameter something like thirty meters.* Otherwise he felt sandbagged.

The thing spun off. He grew aware that the pipe had dropped from his jaws. No matter. His hands were a-dance across the radar controls. He locked on. Reflection, yes! His compass steadied again. The vision dwindled . . . a mile away, two miles, three, shrinking to a rainbow dot, like the diffraction dots you see when you look sunward through your lashes . . . vanishing to nothing against mountain flanks and canyon shadows.

But it was real. Not just his rocking mind said so. His instruments did.

Other memories from boyhood and youth boiled up. "Judas priest," he whispered. "That's a sho-nuff flying saucer."

He opened the throttle. His plane leaped forward, roaring and shivering with power. He hadn't a chance of overhauling in a flat-out chase. But the thing did seem to be on a long downward track. Could he but stay within range, would it but land—

"Well, what then, laddy?" he challenged himself.

He didn't know. But he relived vividly the arguments that had once fascinated him. The radicals had insisted that flying saucers were ships from outer space, operated by benevolent though green little men. The conservatives denied that anyone had ever seen anything. In this hour he, S. F. X. Lindquist, had been handed a chance to investigate personally. He had nothing to lose, and perhaps—if he could solve the mystery—a great deal to gain. Like fame and money.

Though no intellectual, he followed the news around him. Had he not spent the past several years in out-of-the-way places, he would have known that pursuit was a waste of time, that the riddle had in fact already been answered. But no one had mentioned this to him. Quite simply and naïvely, he lined out after the vision.

In the different cultures of the galaxy, Dorek's Law is known by many different names. Some call it Shepalour's Rule, some the Basic Law of Thermodynamics, some the Principle of Most Effort, and so on for millions of languages. But the formulation is invariant, because we all inhabit the same universe.

"Everything that can go wrong, will."

On their present voyage, the partners in the hypership had seen it in full glorious operation. There is no need to detail their woes with rickety hull, asthmatic engines, and senile computer. Nor need one describe what cargoes they carried, with what infinite trouble, from planet to planet. A tramp has to take anything she can get, and this is apt to be stuff too weird for the sleek cargo liners.

But they did think their fortunes had turned when they reached Zandar. A message from the brokers lay waiting for them. After discharging their load of sandorads—and, hopefully, getting most of the mercaptan odor out of the vessel— they were to pick up some machine tools for New Ystankikkinikkitantuvo. Plain machine tools, harmless crated metal! Of course, the destination was far out on the Rim. So much the better, though. It would be a peaceful haul, with lovely pay accumulating; and then, having been gone as long as they'd signed for, they would head home, loaded or not; and the fleshpots of the Core had better be filled in advance for them.

But a summons came from the port co-ordinator.

Pazilliwheep Finnison went alone to the office. The co-ordinator was not of any species he recognized, possessing three eyes and a good many tentacles. They studied each other for a few seconds.

The spacefarer was from Ensikt. He was a diopt himself, though the eyes were quite large and dark, contrasting with blue stripes upon glabrous orange skin. (The air being thicker, wetter, and hotter than he was used to, he went nude except for a musette bag.) His body was slender, centauroid, with a gracefully waving tail. He breathed through rows of gill-like organs on either side of his long neck, which alternated with aural tympani. Albeit he thus had no nose, he did sport a muscular trunk above his mouth. It split into two arms that ended in boneless four-fingered hands. This was entirely practical on Ensikt, where gravity is comparatively weak and animals comparatively small. Pazilliwheep stood one meter high at the rump.

"Ah . . . Navigator-Pilot Finnison, H/S *Grumdel Castle* . . . yes, yes. Welcome," said the co-ordinator in Interlingo-5 with a flatulent accent. He punched a button on his data screen and regarded what appeared. "Yes. Correct what I was informed. You are clearing for . . . yes, that part of the Rim . . . with a stopover at—what is the name of the planet?"

Pazilliwheep automatically jerked his tail, then said in haste: "My gesture indicated indifference."

"Were you afraid it might be objectionable in my culture? No, we have no tails. Now about this . . . yes . . . confounded planet. Never heard of it till the other day. Cataloged as— But what's the name?"

"Tierra, Earth, Mir, Jorden, die Erde, et cetera, et cetera." Pazilliwheep's vocal apparatus formed the sounds rather well, except for a lack of nasal quality. "Hundreds of autochthonous words. Most of them translate as 'Dirt.' "

"So. Yes. I see." The co-ordinator had kept one eye on the unrolling data. "Primitive world. What do you call it?"

"Restocking Station 143."

The co— ordinator waved a tentacle in the air. "I indicate assent and understanding. Well, Navigator-Pilot, this is quite fortunate. Yes, fortunate. You came at, shall we say, the strategic moment. You are therefore able to be of material assistance to the Galactic Federation. Intergovernmental

Department of Planetary Development, Bureau of Supervisions, to be exact.''

Oh, oh! thought Pazilliwheep, and braced himself for bad news. But it was worse than he feared:

"Yes, you can, and therefore you . . . are herewith instructed to . . . furnish transportation and every necessary assistance . . . to the Sector Inspector.''

''No!'' Pazilliwheep cried. His four hoofs clattered on the floor when he sprang backward. ''Not the Sector Inspector!''

''Yes. The Sector Inspector. New one, you know. Anxious to make a good showing in . . . this latest assignment. Came here to check local records. Found no official investigation of that particular planet had been made for a long time. Yes, much overdue. Entire intelligent species being neglected. Perhaps, even, slyly exploited by the less scrupulous. Eh?''

''Exploited, my lowest left operculum!'' Pazilliwheep protested. ''What the entropy would there *be* to exploit? Besides, their principal culture belongs to the Federation. They have any complaints, they can go through regular channels, can't they? And say, why doesn't the Inspector go in his own ship?''

Remorselessly, the co-ordinator answered: ''Economy drive at GHQ. Inspectors for outlying regions do not, shall we say, rate their own vessels any longer. They use available transportation. Yes, I know, that delays them in their work, but they're always behindhand anyway. Too many planets. And a sector like this—not even important enough for records on it to clutter central data banks on any Core world—do you see?''

''But . . . listen, the *Grumdel*'s an old wreck. We've got the stingiest owners in the galaxy. My engineer's trying to repair a fusion tube right now. The interior maintenance units keep breaking down too. Our top hyperspeed is a hypercrawl. Anything would be better!''

''No doubt. No doubt. But nothing else available. Not

soon. Every other vessel due here within the next several weeks is a liner or else on time charter. Or, of course, not crewed by oxygen breathers. You may be old, Navigator-Pilot Finnison; you may be rusty; you may be underpowered, vermin-infested, and all but certifiably unspaceworthy; but you are the best I can do for the Sector Inspector. And, yes, my own career—promotion off this dreary mudball—his reports to GHQ—you understand. Yes. You are hereby commandeered.'' And the co-ordinator handed over the official orders with a flourish.

Thus Hypership *Grumdel Castle* departed Zandar with a third being aboard.

The Inspector was a good fellow at heart: young, inclined to take himself and his work overly seriously, but well intentioned. He apologized for the trouble he was causing, and reminded his hosts that their owners would be compensated according to law. His hosts showed no great enthusiasm at this. He explained that a major reason for his having picked their ship was that she was already scheduled to lay over on 143—''And might I inquire, out of a wish to become more intimately acquainted with my companions as well as for the technical information itself, not to mention simple curiosity, what activities you have planned on this planet?''

He used Interlingo-12 rather than any language of his own world, Ittatik. Unfortunately, Pazilliwheep did not speak Interlingo-12. Engineer-Supercargo Urgo the Red did, more or less, and translated into his version of Interlingo-7:

''He says what're we gonna do there?''

''Well, no reason not to tell him the truth,'' Pazilliwheep replied. ''Unless you've got some or other little racket you haven't told me about.''

''When we touch maybe once in three years? Don't make me laugh. It hurts.''

In point of fact, Pazilliwheep had a racket of his own. It was a mild one, and might even be legal, for all he knew. He swapped small quantities of ondon oil, which had turned out to have powerful aphrodisiac effects on the natives of 143, for kitchenware. The latter was unusual and artistic enough to command good prices on several more advanced worlds. This was one reason he did his restocking on 143 whenever possible.

"Let's answer his question by reciting common, elementary knowledge," he suggested to Urgo. "Might put him to sleep, at least."

"Is any knowledge common?" wondered the engineer-supercargo. "Like, it's a big galaxy. *I* never heard o' whatzisname's muckin' civilization till now. And still he says it fills a whole muckin' star cluster! Maybe he don't know how we operate in this spiral arm."

"Oh, I suppose the basic procedures are similar everywhere. If nothing else, in the course of ten thousand years or however long it's been around, wouldn't the Federation have had some leveling influence on the member species?" Pazilliwheep tail-shrugged. "We haven't anything better to do. Suppose you translate as I talk." He filled his lungs and began:

"It's a long way between stars in this thin outer part of the galaxy. And it's even longer between up-to-date systems that are normal ports of call. So ships are apt to need fresh supplies en route. Maybe the deuterium runs low, or the protein, or—lots of things. Or else, because no ship has perfect biochemical balance, it's necessary to stop on a homelike world and flush out accumulated by-products with fresh air. Planets suitable for the various types of space-going life forms are listed in the *Pilot's Data Bank and Ephemerides* for each region."

"He says we gotta tank up," Urgo told the Inspector.

Klat't'klak of Ittatik nodded, signifying assent in the same way as most 143an cultures. The head he used for this purpose also resembled the 143an, and those of both his shipmates, in that it had two eyes and a mouth. However, mouth and nostrils were set in a beak that brought the narrow skull to a point. A fleshy aileron grew from the top, counterpart to the rudderlike fluke at the end of a thin tail. The body in between had, like Pazilliwheep's, evolved from a hexapod. But on Ittatik the rear limbs had become legs terminating in claws to grasp branches; the middle limbs had become skinny arms with six-digited hands; the forelimbs were now leathery wings. A keelbone jutted from the deep-chested torso. When he stood erect, Klak't'klak's nude gray-skinned frame was of slightly less stature than Pazilliwheep's; but his wingspan was easily four meters. Nonetheless, he could not fly here. The ship's gee-field was set lower than his home gravity, but the air was so much thinner that he couldn't stay healthy without artificial help. This took the form of a pomander which he kept lifting to his face. The oxygen-generating biochemicals within smelled like rich swamp ooze.

"The requirement is understood," he said, "And obviously biological maintenance problems alone suffice to compel your descent into the planetary atmosphere. The point, however, which it was desired to make, is that a primary reason for the selection of this vessel as my transport was that you were, indeed, planning to restock on the world in question. Furthermore, your cargo is not perishable nor urgently required by the consignee. Thus the sum total of inconvenience and delay is minimized. Admittedly, I may be the cause of your remaining for more than the few 37.538-hour periods you presumably reckoned with. But if all appears to be in order, if there is no clear need at this point in time for further investigation of the possibility that ameliorative action may be required somewhere upon the globe, then we should be able to proceed within two or three months. I will not insist upon being returned to Zandar, but will rather continue with you to the Rim, where I shall debark in order to instigate a study of conditions prevailing upon that frontier."

"Oh," said Urgo. To Pazilliwheep: "He says we'll be stuck there for at least two or three months."

"Oh!" said the navigator-pilot, rather more pungently. "Will you ask his unblessed bureaucratship why the inferno he wants to excrete away so loving much time on one unseemly little ball of fertilizer?''—likewise rather more pungently.

"No fair," grumbled Urgo. "I can't talk to him like that."

Klat't'klak explained. He wasn't really much interested in 143. His primary mission was to make sure that things were going well on the civilized plants of the Rim, and recommend remedies to the Federation authorities for whatever he found amiss. Still, 143 was overdue for inspection—seeing that it housed one nation that belonged to the great confraternity.

Such membership confers certain privileges. They are not many, because a galactic-scale league is necessarily a loose one, little more than a set of agencies serving the common interests of wildly diverse cultures. But a member is entitled to some things: for example, technical assistance if it wishes to modernize in any way.

"No," said Pazilliwheep, "our friends on 143 aren't what you would call the go-getter type. They're content to sell us their services, use of landing space, a few kinds of goods. Mainly they take biologicals in exchange—you know, longevity pills and, uh, other medicines. Ask them yourself if you doubt my word."

"I do not, of course," Klat't'klak answered through Urgo. "But I gather the planet holds numerous cultures. Perhaps they are being treated unfairly. Might they not, for example, be worthy of Federation membership too?"

"Chaos, no!" Pazilliwheep paused. "Well, I suppose they're no worse than some I could name. But no better, either. We do make spot checks, we traders, in the hope of finding new potential markets. But the majority of 143ans haven't shown any improvement in the more than two centuries that the blob's been visited. They've got a drab, fragmented, quarrelsome, early-mechanical kind of civilization. Last time I was there, we noticed traces of manned landings on the single moon. That indicates the stage they're at. If they learned the Federation exists—"

"They would have to be admitted to membership if they asked."

"Exactly! And can you imagine the results? Those dismal characters would yell for so much technical assistance that their whole planet would be one gigantic college for the next fifty years. Sector taxes would go up ten percent, I'll bet, to finance it. We'd have to stop using our base, probably, because of their confounded nationalistic regulations about passports and I don't know what other nonsense. And there isn't as handy a planet for us within a hundred light-years." Pazilliwheep gestured violently. "And all this sacrifice on our part for what? To add one more lousy space-traveling species—competing right in our trade lanes to the Rim!"

"You are satisfied with the status quo, then?"

"Right. The 143ans who do know about us and do have membership are friendly, dignified, unaggressive, mind-their-own-business people who'll work for us when we need help at an honest wage for honest labor, and who produce salable handicrafts. Do you wonder that we hide our existence from everyone else?"

"No. Frankly, I cannot help suspecting you underpay your native help; that is what "honest wage for honest labor" usually means. But I am more concerned with ascertaining whether the planet has other civilizations that would, on balance, prove an asset to the Federation. Rather than read the sporadic reports of untrained and biased observers, I want to investigate and decide for myself."

Even through Urgo's translation, Pazilliwheep noted how Klak't'klak had dropped his elegant periods for shorter sentences in a sharper tone. The navigator-pilot sighed and resigned his soul. All right, he'd be hung up for a while on 143, chauffering the Sector Inspector around, assisting with instruments, catching natives for interviews. (This was done in such wise that, after they were released, no one believed their story. Experience had shown that the best ploy on 143 was the Benign Observers of Elder Race.) He and Urgo would be at once busy and bored.

Yet . . . eventually they'd start drawing overtime pay. And the mission on 143 wouldn't likely be prolonged. If nothing else, *Grumdel Castle* was uncomfortable. Her cramped cabins, vibrating decks, rusty metal, chipped plastic, wheezy ventilators, and uninspired galley saw to that. In addition, she carried so few books and tapes suitable for Klak't'klak that he would have them memorized in weeks. Pazilliwheep and Urgo always laid in recreational materials before a voyage. But what use to an Ittatikan were Ensiktan murder mysteries and Bontuan pornography?

And so *Grumdel Castle* creaked and groaned the long dark way to the Solar System. She took up orbit around the third planet while Pazilliwheep checked for indications of excessive radioactivity, smog, and other hazards of an early-mechanical culture. Meanwhile, Urgo the Red went outside to install camouflage tubes on the hull.

His shipmates saw his fur as bright blue; but then, they didn't use a visual spectrum identical with the Bontuan. The engineer-supercargo was a tailless biped, three meters tall and broad to match. His head was round, short-muzzled, big-eyed, fuzzy, and rather endearing. His hands were five-fingered, his feet four-toed. In spite of his hirsute skin, he affected white coveralls, sandals, and an ornate tool belt.

He clumped in again and shed his spacesuit. "Guess they'll hang together awhile," he reported, "but if the owners don't spring for a new set when we get home, I'm gonna look for another berth. How's the planet doin'?"

"About as before. I note more air traffic each time, though, damn it," Pazilliwheep said. "Also, today, what appears to be a manned orbital satellite. We'll have to wait here till the stupid thing's on the opposite side of the globe."

Klak't'klak inquired why they lingered. Urgo explained. *Grumdel Castle* used a camouflage standard on worlds of this atmospheric type, where it was desired to fly unbeknownst. The natives could not detect an operating hyperdrive; if they had that capability, they'd soon be making their own star ships! And antiradiation screens served to control air molecules as well as atomic particles, making even the fastest travel soundless. But you were still stuck with the fact that your ship was a solid, visible, radar-reflecting object.

So you wrapped her in the gaudiest ionized gas-discharge effect you could generate. You added powerful magnetic and electrostatic fields, and varied them randomly. You sailed in, alerting every eye and every instrument for a hundred miles around—

Just like a natural traveling plasmoid.

But since those erratic masses of molecules and electrons occur in atmosphere, and the ship was in space, she must first sneak down.

Presently she did. Near her destination, she spied a native aircraft. At Klak't'klak's request, she veered close so he could get a good look. Then she headed off for the home of that 143an people who, during the past two hundred years, had been members in good standing of the Galactic Federation.

On the assumption that the flying saucer would continue in a straight line, Sean Lindquist zigzagged along the same general path. After half an hour he was rewarded. He crossed above an immense red ridge. Its farther slope tumbled into a canyon whose bottom was the most vivid green he'd spied in a long while. Squarish adobe buildings were stacked against one rock wall, overlooking a stream lined with trees. But what made his pulses jump afresh was the object that lay before the houses. The dazzling, confusing play of colors was gone; the shape had definite outlines and a dark gray hue; but it was surely the thing that had buzzed him. And by all the saints and any heathen gods who cared to join in—it *was* a vessel!

He tilted his airplane's wings, crammed on power, and whipped back the way he had come. A thermal nearly tossed him from control. But he must get out of sight before he was observed and—

And what? Some kind of ray gun shot him down? He ran his tongue across lips gone sandpapery. The ship had to be from outer space: real outer space, the unimaginable abysses

that held the stars. He'd followed the progress of flybys and
landings within the Solar System. Hence he knew that, while
the saucerians might be little and emerald-colored, they were
not from any neighborhood planet. He also knew enough
aerodynamics to be sure no Terrestrial organization was
experimenting with stuff that advanced. Even if he had been
ignorant of the engineering requirements, he was learned in
the ways of public relations offices. . . . "Stop maundering,
will you?" he croaked.

What to do?

He kept the plane wobbling back and forth on the far side of
the mountain while, feverishly, he studied his charts and tried
to discover where he was. Uh, yes . . . "Wuwucimti," plus
the symbol for Pop. 0-1000 . . . evidently a pueblo, and
lonely as hell, to judge from the fact that nothing led away
from it except a dim mule trail. . . . Numbly, like parts of a
machine rather than a body, his fingers activated the radio. If
he could raise, oh, Gallup or Durango or wherever . . . make
his location known, so it wouldn't do the aliens any good to
destroy him. . . . A distant seething filled his earphones.
Whether atmospherics or They were responsible, he couldn't
get through.

He got his pipe off the floor, reloaded and relit it, and
fumed himself into a measure of calm. A long gulp from a
bottle that lived in his sleeping bag was equally helpful.
Consider, Lindquist, he thought. *You've stumbled on a
secret to shake the world. But this is hardly our first visit from
yonder. Leaving aside the mistakes, the hoaxes, and the
claims of the nut cults, there always was a certain amount of
saucer observation that couldn't be explained away. At least,
it was easier to believe in spaceships than in some of those
concatenations of coincidences that the orthodox scientists
postulated! And now you've got proof that the ship hy-
pothesis is right. Only, who's going to take your unsupported
word? Supposing you could go fetch witnesses, the thing's
bound to be gone when you return. You'd get classed with
Adamski and his breed.*

For which same reason, you'll keep your mouth shut.

Hey! he reflected in rising eagerness. *How many people have actually met saucerians, and been disbelieved afterward? And, on that account, how many more have met them and—not wanting to be laughed at—simply kept mum?*

After all . . . what little consistent evidence there is—indicates the saucerians aren't evil. They're shy, or snobbish, or something, but I can't remember anyone ever claiming that they do any deliberate harm. So maybe, this time, I can—

Allowing himself no second thoughts, Lindquist brought the plane about. He roared back over the mountain, chose his position, tilted wings, and commenced vertical descent.

Updrafts were tricky; and this was a somewhat battered, cranky craft he had. For a while he was too occupied with controls, instruments, hiss and shudder around him, to heed much else. He did see how the saucer squatted imperturbable in the bright late sunlight. Tawny mud-brick walls, red canyon sides, deep blue sky, green meadows and cornfields, green cottonwoods and willows along the quicksilver stream, dusty sage and juniper farther back—and in the middle, a spaceship from the stars!

His landing gear touched. He cut the power. Silence hit him like a thunderclap. He unharnessed, opened the door, and sprang shakily forth. The air was thin, dry, pungent with resinous odors. Except for a breeze, tinkle of water, bleating from a pasture shared by sheep and goats, the silence continued.

It was not broken by the approaching locals. They were ordinary Pueblo types, a few hundred medium-sized dark-complexioned folk of every apparent age. Men and women both wore their hair in braids. Clothing varied, from more or less traditional breechcloths, gowns, and blankets, to levis and sport shirts. Lindquist's sharpened perceptions noted that the people were better clad, seemed more healthy and prosperous, than the average Southwest Indian. And they were strangely uncordial. Not that they threatened him. But they drew up in a kind of phalanx, and stared, and said never a word. Even the littlest children sucked their thumbs in a marked manner.

Lindquist gulped. "Uh . . . hello," he said. His voice sounded very small to him. "I'm afraid I, uh, don't speak your language." They might know Spanish. *"Buenas días, mis amigos."* Trouble was, that damn near exhausted his Spanish.

A grizzled, weather-beaten man called softly, "sik-yabotoma." Lindquist said, "I beg your pardon?" but decided it was the name of a young man who stepped to the elder. They put heads together and conferred in mutters.

Lindquist gulped again, nodded, pasted on a smile, and started toward the flying saucer. At once he grew so conscious of it—so astonished, for instance, at the pitted, corroded metal of what had once been a smooth unitized shape—that the Indians faded from his mind. Colliding with them was a shock. Several had moved to intercept him.

They were embarrassed. The pueblo dwellers are among the politest beings on Earth. They smiled, in a forced way, bobbed their heads, and waved their hands. They pushed gently on Lindquist's arms, as if to urge him toward their houses.

Anger flared. "No, thanks!" he snapped, and planted his heels.

The young man rescued the situation. He was among those who wore modern clothes, including the gaudiest sombrero Lindquist had ever met. He sauntered forth, tapped the newcomer on the back, and said, "Excuse me, buddy. That's not the way."

"What?" Lindquist whirled to confront him.

"Welcome to Wuwucimti Pueblo," the Indian said. "I'm Sikyabotoma. But in the Army I used the name Joe Andrews. Picked that because it's handy being near the head of the alphabet. So if you want, call me Joe. Come on inside and have a drink."

"I—I thought—you—"

"You needn't be surprised. Sure, the Hopi don't approve of liquor as a rule. But they need somebody like me, who's equipped to handle white men. Like, I interpret when we take the mules to town and stock up on things. And I did do a military hitch. So I've gotten a few outsider habits. It's good bourbon."

"But—I mean—" Lindquist twisted his neck to goggle at what now lay behind his back. "I never imagined—"

"Yes, it is unusual," Sikyabotoma agreed cordially. He linked arms with Lindquist, who must needs come along as he ambled in the direction of the village. "We're the most isolated pueblo in the country. Not awful old. A bunch of Shoshonean-speaking Hopi moved here to get away from the Spaniards after the revolt of 1680 was put down. So we have a tradition of minding our own affairs, and we discourage visitors. Nothing rude, you understand. We just don't do anything interesting when the anthropologists come. And we got rid of the missionaries by telling the last padre who showed that we'd already been converted to hard-shell Baptists."

The other Indians trailed after at some distance. They kept their silence. "Please don't think we're hostile," Sikyabotoma urged. "We're only satisfied. We combine the old and the new as suits us best; and we do quite well for ourselves, on the whole; and everybody among us knows it. Regular contact with the outside world would upset our applecart. So we act pretty unanimously to defend our privacy. Unanimity comes natural in the Hopi culture anyhow. If you're in trouble, we'll help you, Mr., uh—"

"Lindquist," said Lindquist feebly.

"We'll do what we can for you. But if you dropped in out of curiosity, well, I hate to sound inhospitable, but the fact is you'd find Wuwucimti a mighty dull place. Lively young fellow like you, huh? I'd suggest you proceed right away. And, uh, I'd take it as a favor if you don't mention this stop you made. We're not after tourist business and that's that. You savvy?"

"Dull?" Lindquist tore loose. He spun, flung out both arms toward the great spaceship, and shouted, "You call that dull?" so echoes rang.

"Well, not to me, of course," Sikyabotoma said. "I get my kicks. And the average pueblo dweller is staid by nature."

"Flying saucers and—and—"

Sikyabotoma regarded Lindquist narrowly. "Do you feel okay?" he asked.

"Sure I feel okay! What about that flying saucer over there?"

Sikyabotoma squinted. "What flying saucer?"

"What do you mean? I, I, I chased it . . . to here . . . and there it sits!"

"Awa-Tsireh," called Sikyabotoma, "do you see a flying saucer?"

A middle-aged Indian looked solemnly back and shook his head. "No," he grunted. "No see fly sawsuh."

"I'll ask the others in Hopi if you want-" Sikyabotoma offered. "But you know, Mr. Lindquist, when people aren't used to this thin air and sun-glare, they can mistake mirage effects for some of the damnedest things. I'd be careful about that if I were you. Flitting around in an airplane, a guy has to be mighty sure what's real and what's an optical illusion. Doesn't he?"

Lindquist stared for an entire minute into the broad bland face. The others moved closer, and had also begun to smile and murmur soothing words. Briefly, in his tottering mind, he wondered if he was not indeed the crazy one.

No! He sprang back and launched himself. His legs flew. Dust spurted, the footfalls slammed through his shins, and he made an end run around the tribe. Meanwhile he bawled:

"Do radars have illusions? Do compasses? By heaven . . . let me . . . at my instruments . . . and I'll show you!"

He reached the ship. Its curve swelled immense above him, casting a knife-edged shadow. He snatched a rock and pounded the metal. It boomed. A lizard ran away. The sandstone crumbled under repeated impacts. "Is that optical?" he screamed.

The Hopi had been running toward him. But once more they halted at a distance. Sikyabotoma came nearer. The young Indian stopped, regarded Lindquist, and sighed.

"Okay," he said. "I didn't really expect it'd work. Have your way, Charlie."

He semaphored with his arms.

Lindquist stepped back from the ship, panting, sweating, trembling. The canyon brooded in a quiet immense and eternal; only the wind had voice. Then came a rusty creak.

Someone had been watching from inside, through some kind of television. And in some fashion, a part of the hull detached itself on three sides and unrolled, to make a gangway to the ground. Three creatures came forth. Lindquist saw them and strangled on an oath that was half a prayer.

Sikyabotoma took a philosophical attitude. "You ought to see what membership in the Galactic Federation has done to our kachina dolls," he remarked. "The real ones, that we don't show the anthropologists."

"This is most annoying," Klak't'klak said. He flapped his wings. They made a parchment rustle where he squatted in the sunshine, under the spaceship, confronting the bug-eyed 143an.

"Sure is," Urgo the Red agreed. "We gotta get rid of this bum. And then we gotta stay away from here for several days—prob'ly go into orbit—in case he does somehow talk somebody into comin' back with him. Right when I was hopin' to get that Number Three regulator tuned!"

"I was thinking more personally," the Inspector admitted. "I am not prepared to conduct interviews. That is, my translating computer has not yet assimilated the records of this planet's dominant languages which the autochthons brought me from their—ah—what did they call it?—their kiva. And I hate working through interpreters."

"So don't."

"No, as long as we have captured this being, I feel my duty is to examine him for whatever information he can give. And, too, I should endeavor to allay his fears. To this poor unsophisticated semisavage, we must resemble veritable demons. Consider how he staggered to his aircraft for that bottle of tranquilizing medication he now clutches so tightly."

Urgo waved a massive blue hand. Pazilliwheep trotted over, using his nose-tendrils in turn to summon one of the Indians. "I don't speak this barbarian's jabber," the navigator-pilot explained, "but Sikyabotoma does." Urgo passed on the datum.

The galactics, including the Pueblo man, formed a semicircle confronting Lindquist. The rest of the village watched aloofly. Klak't'klak lifted a gaunt arm. "Greeting to you, O native," he said in Interlingo-12. "Rest assured that you are in the grasping organs of civilized and benevolent entities who intend you no harm; who may, indeed, prove to be the promoters of a benign revolution upon your planet. Whether this eventuality materializes or not is dependent upon my official judgment as to whether a general announcement of the existence of a galaxy-wide Federation of technologically and sociologically advanced races will serve the larger good, including your own good. Hence the outcome is to a small extent dependent upon what you yourself, individually, today, choose to give me in the way of information. May I therefore initially request—request, mind you; we shall not compel you—request and advise that you relate to me in circumstantial detail what I wish to be apprised of, beginning with the events which led to your untoward arrival."

"He wants to know how the bum got here," Urgo said in Interlingo-7.

"The honorable envoy of the Federation's guiding council asks what gods led hither the stranger's path," Pazilliwheep said in Hopi.

"The pterodactyl character is a kind of inspector," Sikyabotoma said in English. "He won't hurt you, but he would like to know a few things, like how come you stopped by."

Lindquist took another pull on his bottle. "I . . . I saw the flying saucer . . . and followed it," he whispered.

"Yeah, sure. Look, pal, I don't believe you can tell him a thing that I can't. But let's go through with the game and make him happy, okay? The other two are plain merchant sailors. Old buddies of mine; I even made a voyage with 'em once, to help establish an outplanet market for our local handicrafts. But Beak-and-Wings, he's come to find out whether the galactics ought to let the rest of Earth know about them; whether they should invite every country to join their Federation. In other words, he's one of those do-gooder types."

"You—don't think—we should join?" Lindquist got forth.

"Frankly, no." Sikyabotoma shrugged. "Not that this pueblo is selfish, or holds a deep grudge against the white man, or anything. However, you can't expect we'll fall over ourselves to do the white man a favor, can you? Especially when that'd end our own comfortable monopoly on trade and services with the galaxy. We're not ostentatious about it, and of course we're pretty small potatoes in the Federation . . . but you'd be surprised at some of the stuff we keep in our adobes."

Lindquist braced himself. "*I* look at the matter differently," he said. "Can I trust you to give him my side of the story?"

"Sure. I may be prejudiced, but I'm honest. Besides, he figures to study the whole planet. Don't loft your hopes, though. One dollar gets you ten that he turns thumbs down."

"How can he?" Lindquist cried.

Sikyabotoma looked closer. "I'll be damned, you're right. He has thumbs on both sides of his palms. . . . Oh. You mean how can he refuse the USA, and the USSR, and France, and

Britain, and China, and—Well, it's easy. They haven't anything unique to offer. Not in a galaxy loaded with civilizations. All that Wuwucimti has, really, is a convenient location, and people who don't swarm over every ship that lands, stealing things and asking stupid questions. You start letting in the riffraff, and first you've got to disestablish institutions like war, and then you've got to give them technical assistance, and then—anyhow, it's a mess. That's why secrecy is preserved, you know. If you guys ever found out the truth, collectively, you'd have to be invited to join. Otherwise, the do-gooders say, your precious little egos would be so bruised that what culture you have would fall to pieces.'' The Hopi checked himself. ''Sorry. I didn't mean to sound smug. Or malicious. It's just the way the ball bounces.''

''How about my ego?'' Lindquist demanded, close to tears.

Sikyabotoma patted his shoulder. ''Nothing personal, Charlie,'' he said. ''Individual humans who got interviewed in the past don't seem to've suffered harm. Look at it this way: You won't be any worse off than you were. Huh?''

''I'll tell the world!'' Lindquist said furiously. ''I'll call in the FBI, the news reporters, the—''

''For both our sakes,'' The Indian answered, ''I wish you wouldn't. You'd only make a fool of yourself. At most, you'd bring in somebody else, and the village 'ud have to go through the same old cover-up schtick as before. You wouldn't do that to us, would you, now? A nice guy like you?''

''No, I'll keep watch—'' Lindquist snapped his mouth shut.

''Till another ship arrives, eh?'' Sikyabotoma chuckled. ''You'd wait a mighty long time, podner.''

''Not many come?''

''M-m-m, well, it varies. With thousands of shipping outfits plying these lanes, we can expect several craft per year to stop by, though we never know in advance. However, what we do know is if anybody's within thirty-forty kilome-

ters. A little gadget that detects thoughts. So you can't
monitor us unbeknownst. We can warn off ships; they do
radio us from orbit before landing. Chances are they'd come
down anyway, but maintain camouflage. All you'd observe
or photograph would be a colored blur like ordinary ball
lightning. If worst comes to worst, a bunch of us can deal
with a spy. Nothing violent, understand. We'll kind of escort
him away, no more. If we have to break his camera, we'll pay
him full value. You see, we're Federation members; we live
by Federation rules.''

The Inspector spoke words which went along the chain of
interpreters. Sikyabotoma nodded and sat down on his
haunches. "You might as well relax," he said. "Over here,
in the shade. You're about to be interviewed."

Time passed. Shadows lengthened. The Pueblo women
cooked dinner. They brought some to Lindquist. It was Hopi
food, based on cornmeal tortillas, but the filling was like
nothing on Earth. Quite literally so. Sikyabotoma explained
that a lot of interstellar trade was in spices.

When the sun went below the mountains, stars leaped
arrogantly forth. Coyotes yipped across a gigantic silence.
Lindquist stared heavenward and shivered in the sudden cold.

Sikyabotoma rose, yawning. "That's that," he said.
"They'll fly you out now, to make sure you don't hang
around. Any special place you'd like to go?"

"Colorado Springs?" Lindquist faltered.

"I wouldn't. NORAD headquarters, remember. They spot
your plane on their radars without any flight plan filed, they
might get a little unpleasant."

"That's my problem." Lindquist could scarcely keep his
tone level. He had not dared hope his precarious scheme
would work to this extent.

"Okay, then. Hm, I think I'll ride along. You might enjoy
being shown around a genuine hypership. Something to tell
your grandchildren, if you don't mind 'em thinking you're an
awful liar."

The three aliens embarked. Lindquist and Sikyabotoma followed, after the village elders had bidden the former good-bye with every ritual courtesy. A largery opening gaped elsewhere in the hull; the aircraft rose on some silent, invisible beam of force; it was stowed aboard. The great ship closed herself. Soundlessly, but swathed again in rainbow haze, she lifted and swung north.

Inside, she was less impressive. In fact, she was grimy, battered, noisy, and ill-smelling. Sikyabotoma shrugged when Lindquist dared remark on it. "What do you expect in an old tramp with cheapskate owners? Red plush toilet seats? C'mon, we better stash you in your plane. Be over Pike's Peak soon."

When Lindquist was harnessed, the Hopi stuck a hand through the open cabin door of the aircraft. His brown face was bent in a wry smile. "Shake," he offered. "I hope there aren't any hard feelings. You're a right guy. I could damn near wish Birdbrain does certify this whole planet for membership. But I know he won't. So long, Charlie, and good luck to you."

He closed the door. For a minute Lindquist sat alone, in the thrumming, coldly lit cavern of the hold. The hull opened. Stars glittered in the aperture, brilliant against crystalline black. Air puffed outward, popping his eardrums, and chill flowed inward. He started his engine. But it was the impalpable force beam that carried him forth and released him.

Town lights glittered far beneath. The spaceship hovered close, like a swirling, shifting, many-hued light-fog. She departed, gathering speed until no human-built rocket could have paced her. Night swallowed the vision.

Lindquist shuddered. His radio receiver squawked with challenge. An interceptor jet winged toward him. "Sure," he said. "I'll come down. Anyplace you want." Excitement torrented through him. "And then . . . take me to your leader!"

In the morning they turned him over to Lieutenant Harold

Quimby. Maybe that press officer could get rid of him.

Sunlight slanted through a window, beyond which stretched the neat buildings and walked the neat personnel of a United States Air Force base. Light glowed on immaculate office furniture, on Quimby's polished insignia and practiced toothpaste smile. Lindquist grew doubly aware of how unshaven, sweaty, and haggard he was. His eyes burned; the lids felt like sandpaper.

"Cigarette?" Quimby invited. "Coffee?"

"No," Lindquist grated. "Some common sense. That's all I ask. The common sense and common decency of listening to me."

"Why, surely our people—"

"Yeah, they grilled me. For most of the night. Oh, polite enough. But they kept after me and after me."

"Well, you must realize, Mr. Lindquist, when you suddenly appear over a sensitive area like this, you must expect that men charged with the national defense will ask for details."

"Damn it, I *gave* them details! Every last stinking detail I could dredge up. Look, the fact that I did appear, without your fool radars registering me till I was there . . . doesn't that mean anything?"

"It means that the plasmoid blanketed your approach. Not unknown. An unusually fine plasmoid, wasn't it?" Quimby leaned forward with a sympathetic air. "I can easily understand why you would follow such a beautiful and fascinating object. And, ah, how the interplay of colors . . . hypnotic, even epileptogenic effects . . . mistaking a vivid dream for reality—no, wait!" He lifted his hand. "The Air Force is not calling you a lunatic, Mr. Lindquist. What happened to you could happen to anyone. I talked with Major Williams of our psychiatric division before my appointment with you today. He assured me that illusion and confusion are the normal result of lengthy exposure to certain optical phenomena. We lodged you overnight precisely in order that our intelligence officers could make a few phone calls, checking on your background and recent activities. I assure you, Mr. Lindquist, we are careful here. We have established that you are sane and well intentioned. We appreciate the patriotism that led you to seek us out, even in your, ah, slightly delirious condition. You are free to go home, Mr. Lindquist, with the warmest thanks of the United States Air Force.''

Quimby paused for breath. "But you saw the spaceship yourselves!" Lindquist groaned. "You radared the thing. You recorded electric and magnetic effects. Your technical man admitted as much to me. How can you call it an illusion?"

"We don't, sir, we don't," Quimby beamed. ''It was absolutely real. The Air Force is not dogmatic. The Air Force has been interested in this subject for many years. When the first so-called flying saucer reports were made in the later 1940s, the Air Force mounted its own investigation. Here.'' He handed Lindquist a glossy-paper pamphlet off a stack on his desk. "A brief summary of Project Blue Book. Certain people continued unsatisfied. They charged—quite wrongly, I assure you—they charged distortion and suppression of evidence. Accordingly, to clear its good name, in the late 1960s the Air Force supported a new, independent investigation under the leadership of the late distinguished Dr. Condon. An unclassified project, mind you.'' He gave Lindquist another pamphlet. "Here is a history of that effort.'' And another. "Here is information on the final effort, which produced a theory to account for the facts. This is a summary of the technical findings. Here is a somewhat more popular account, and here is a reprint of what proved to be the key physical data, and here is a—''

Lindquist slumped. "I know,'' he said. "They told me last night what they believe. Ball lightning.''

"Well, no, not exactly that,'' Lindquist said. "The subject is pretty complicated. Yes, sir, pretty complicated, if I do say so myself. Flying saucer reports had many different sources. Early during the furore, it was shown that most were caused by sightings of weather balloons, or mirages, or reflections, or Venus, or any of several other things. There did remain a certain small percentage which could not be accounted for in that way. But at last it was shown that nature can generate plasmoids in the atmosphere. You know, traveling masses of ionized gas, held together for a few minutes or hours by a kind of self-generated magnetic bottle. Ball lightning is one kind of plasmoid. There are others. Including the kind that shines, produces erratic magnetic and electric fields, reflects radar, shuttles about at incredible speed but with never a sound, and is roughly disk-shaped. In short, the classical flying saucer apparition. This was *proven*, Mr. Lindquist. It was observed, analyzed, and reproduced in the laboratory. By now, any good electrophysicist who wanted to take the trouble could fake his own flying saucer. Here is an account by the Nobel Prize winner Dr.—''

''Never mind,'' Lindquist mumbled. ''I don't doubt there are natural neon signs zipping around. So the saucerians don't need anything for camouflage except a false one.''

''Well, Mr. Lindquist,'' Quimby replied, the least bit severely, ''don't you believe it's high time you looked at the matter like the reasonable man you are? You had a, ah, an involuntary psychedelic experience. You would not have had it if you had known the truth. Then you would have realized there was no point in chasing that plasmoid. Nobody does anymore, you know. Because of your, ah, long foreign residence, you weren't kept up to date. But the truth is that the flying saucer hysteria vanished years ago. Once the clear light of science was thrown on this murky subject, the American people realized that everything had been due to an easily explainable natural phenomenon. They turned their attention to better topics. You won't find anyone any longer who claims that flying saucers are, ah, spaceships crewed by little green men.''

''Would you believe a surly blue giant?''

''No, Mr. Lindquist, I would not. Nor, ah, pterodactyls and centaurs with arms on their noses. Least of all that a bunch of poverty-stricken, mostly illiterate Pueblo Indians are— Well, you have a very imaginative subconscious mind, sir, but I'm afraid no one cares to listen. So you had better settle for everyday reality.''

Lindquist raised eyes in which hope still struggled with exhaustion. "No one?" he asked. "Absolutely no one in the world?"

"Oh, I suppose a few cranks are left, like in California," Quimby laughed. "People to whom the outer-space— visitors idea became a sort of religion that they still can't bear to give up." His tone sharpened. "It would not be advisable to prey on their gullibility. Not that you would, Mr. Lindquist. But some confidence man who, ah, tried to squeeze a dollar from those poor deluded souls—yes, I think the authorities might deal rather harshly with him."

Lindquist rose. "I know when I'm licked," he said bitterly. "I won't take any more of your time."

"Well, thank you, that's appreciated." Quimby stood too, with almost indecent haste. "We are rather busy at the moment, preparing press kits about General Robinson's promotion to four-star rank."

Lindquist ignored the proffered hand and shambled toward the door. "Too busy to bring Earth into the Galactic Federation!" he spat.

"That's not the job of the Air Force," Quimby reminded him. "Foreign relations belong to the State Department."

The bar which Lindquist found was noisy with college students. He didn't mind that. For the most part he sat hunched over his beer. When his awareness did, occasionally, return from interstellar immensities—to order more beer—he got a little encouragement from the sight of coeds passing by. A universe which had produced girls couldn't be all bad.

Contrariwise, it must be a hell of a good universe. Rich, wonderful, various, exciting, mind-expanding, soul-up-lifting: if only you could get out into the damned thing.

"Rats!" Lindquist muttered around his pipestem. "Got to be *some* way to make a buck with what I know."

He wasn't entirely cynical. The galactics were, he thought. They denied to the human race every marvel, opportunity, insight, help, comfort that a millennia-old science must have to give. Not that they were monsters. With—how many suns in the galaxy? a hundred billion?—they rated intelligent species at a dime a dozen, and probably this was inevitable. Indeed, it was astonishing how altruistic they were. They could have conquered Earth in an afternoon. But instead, they slunk about in disguise for fear of what the knowledge of their presence might do to men . . . if, following the revelation, they did not promptly act to lift man to their own level.

Sure, you can't blame them. Why should they solve our problems for us? Especially when it'd be a lot of trouble and expense to them. What did we ever do for the galactics?

Lindquist fumed smoke into the racketing, beer-laden air. *That's not the point,* he thought grimly. *The point as far as I'm concerned is that I and my whole ever-lovin' species will keep on being poor, ignorant, war-plagued, tyrannized, restricted, short-lived, and I don't know what else—unless the Federation can be forced to take us in.*

Which it can be, if we the people of the United States learn for sure that the Federation exists.

How? The galactics, including those damn Injuns, understand how to keep us blindfolded. They didn't even bother to silence me. Who'd listen?

Maybe, momentarily, the chance had existed. In 1950, or whenever the flying saucer craze started, human civilization had advanced to the point where it could imagine extraterrestrial visitors; and it had not yet gotten the idea of plasmoids, or rather, it was denying that any such thing could be. So the standard spaceship disguise had been ineffective for a decade or two. Unfortunately, though, no one had happened to catch a sitting spaceship during those years. At least, not enough people had happened to do so, and their unsupported word was insufficient. Now research had established that flying saucers could be plasmoids. Therefore, humankind concluded, they were plasmoids. As the galactics had foreseen. The bastards.

Today no one would believe the crazy truth. Except maybe some pathetic remnants of the discredited saucer cults. They might. But what could they do, except invite the narrator into their mutual admiration society?

What . . . could . . . they . . . do?

Sean Lindquist leaped to his feet. His table went over, scattering beer and broken glass. His pipe fell to the floor. "Eureka!" he bellowed.

The bartender approached. "You had enough, buster," he said ominously. "Start taking off your clothes and I call a cop."

The Reverend Jacob Muir, pastor of the First United Church of the Cosmic Brotherhood, was a surprise. Though Lindquist had done considerable research beforehand, he had expected someone more, well, far out. Reverend Muir was soft-spoken, self-contained, and conventionally dressed: for Los Angeles, at least. He lived with his wife in an apartment near the shop that earned him his daily bread. The place could have belonged to any middle-class, middle-aged couple. Only the books were unusual. They formed probably as complete a library of sauceriana as existed anywhere on Earth.

"Please sit down, Mr. Lindquist," he invited. "Would you care for some coffee?—Joan, brew us a pot, will you dear?—Smoke if you wish. It's bad for the health, but until the Elder Brethren see fit to raise us to the next rung of evolution's ladder, we can't much help our frailties. Pardon me. I didn't intend to preach at you. You came to tell me something, not vice versa."

Lindquist wondered what his best gambit was. From what he could learn of the C. B. Church, its few score active

members, and its influence on several hundred saucerists of
other kinds, he didn't believe that he could be entirely truthful. Muir's credo held that the extraterrestrials were the
benevolent, well-nigh omnipotent agents of a civilization
which was the chosen instrument of God. That wouldn't fit
well with a rusty old tramp ship, pinchpenny owners, and so
forth. Would it?

"I've had an Experience," he said.

"Really?" Muir's tone did not alter. "Do you know, I
never have been vouchsafed one. Few who were are left
alive; and the last confirmed report of a talk with Them was
fifteen years ago." His gaze was quite steady. Traffic noises
came through the window, to underscore his voice with
muted thunder. "Hoaxes are not unheard-of."

Lindquist achieved a smile. "You're skeptical, Reverend?"

"Well, let us say I'm open-minded. I've often stated, in
sermons and articles, that I think the Elders have abandoned
us for a while because we grew too skeptical. They will come
back when faith has come back. But—forgive me—there
have been deliberate frauds, and there have been far more
honest mistakes. For your sake as well as ours, we must sift
your story carefully—whatever you tell."

"You're very tactful, sir." Lindquist's lanky frame
relaxed in the armchair. As he felt his way into the situation,
he gained confidence. "And I might as well confess at the
outset, I want money. Furthermore, I haven't a scrap of
physical evidence. Only the recent sighting over Colorado
Springs, which thousands of people saw." He drew a breath.
"However. if I can get financing, your auditors will keep
track of every nickel. What we need is to build and transport a
certain device which the Elders have described to me. For
this, we'll have to buy materials and hire expensive technicians. We'll have to do a little R & D, perhaps, because the
Elders didn't give me any blueprint, only a general verbal
account. We'll have to do this on the QT until we're ready to

roll, or you can imagine what a field day the news media will have.''

Muir opened his mouth. Lindquist hurried on:

"In earnest of my sincerity, as well as to help, I can mortgage what little I own and toss several thousand dollars into the kitty. If you can double that, I believe we'll have the necessary. I checked on your people before I phoned you. They're not rich by a long shot. But between your congregation and, uh, its sympathizers—if you launch an appeal yourself—a few dollars contributed per person—the thing can be swung financially without hurting any individual except me if it fails.''

He paused. "I do not guarantee success,'' he finished.

Muir sat quiet for a long time. His eyes never left his visitor. Finally he whispered, "You're not a con artist. You may be a crank, but you're honest. Go on, in God's name.''

Lindquist saw tears. However noble his purpose, he felt a touch guilty as he gave his doctored account. The benevolent Elders had returned. They found Earth in dire straits. Disaster was imminent. Yet they could not destroy the human spirit by acting as dictators. They could only work through such persons as had faith in them.

Nor could they linger here. Other planets also needed their attention. But if enough humans had faith—if the veritable mustard seed existed upon Earth—then they could manifest themselves at last, and lead mankind to salvation. To this end, let the faithful build a communication device such as they demonstrated and explained to Sean F. X. Lindquist. In time, they would receive its message and they would come.

Did no such call reach them, they would sadly know that man was beyond redemption.

Passing through the ship's observation veranda—an elegant phrase for a crummy little cabin outfitted with an exterior visiscreen and a few seats adjustable to most species—Urgo the Red saw Klak't'klak. The Sector Inspec-

tor stood hunched before the view that slid beneath. The
scene was of high desert, raw mineral hues under a blazing
sun. His winged shape was etched in black by contrast. And
yet he looked so frail, bowed, utterly tired and discouraged,
that Urgo's equivalent of a heart went out to him. The
engineer-supercargo had grumbled at length during the past
tedious weeks. Nevertheless, against his will, he had come to
like the official passenger. It hurt him, now, to see the little
Ittatikan stand thus alone. He went and joined him.

"You're really quittin', huh?" he asked inanely.

Klak't'klak uttered a mournful whistle. "Yes. Not that the
natives have no potential. They seem about average, insofar
as any such concept is meaningful. But I could not justify a
recommendation that missions be sent to elevate them."

"Troublemakers. Yeh, I could'a told you that right off,"
Urgo rumbled.

"No. Not really." Klak't'klak spread his wings and
folded them again. "They would not be a detriment to the
Federation. But neither would they be an outstanding asset,
as far as I can judge on the basis of my examinations. They
would, in short, be . . . merely one more member species.
Therefore, as long as they remain in happy ignorance of us, I
cannot honestly say that the Federation taxpayer should be
burdened with the cost of incorporating them. Let them
invent the hyperdrive for themselves, in a thousand or two
years."

Urgo belched, which out of him corresponded to a sigh of
relief. "That's the spirit, Inspector! I knew you'd decide
right. But how come are you lookin' down in the chops you
haven't got?"

"I don't rightly know," Klak't'klak said. "Depression, I
suppose. So much time, effort, expense, inconveniencing
you and Navigator-Pilot Finnison—you've been extraordinarily kind, you two, and I won't forget it when I write my
official report—but for nothing."

Urgo waved his mighty arms. "Ah, don't worry. The job
was a drag, sure, but it's over with now. We'll stop off at the

pueblo to snatch a rest and some trade goods. Then ho for the Rim!''

At that moment, the buzzer sounded. Pazilliwheep's voice followed. *"Attenta!"* He had amused himself by acquiring a few 143an phrases as *Grumdel Castle* prowled around the globe. *"Pericolo!* All hands to stations!''

"What the blazes?" Urgo was already loping for the engine room. Klak't'klak flapped and hopped toward his quarters, where he would at least be out of the way. You don't argue when someone calls emergency on a hypership. The deck gonged to the engineer-supercargo's footfalls. "What's'a matter?" he roared.

"I don't know," Pazilliwheep said tautly over the intercom. "Electromagnetic field . . . variable . . . registered a few seconds ago. Might be a natural plasmoid, but we'd better have a look.''

Urgo felt relieved. The news could have been something nasty, like the bottom dropping out of this hull. "Where are we, anyhow?" he asked.

"About a hundred kilometers west of Wuwucimti. Which is to say, the emanations could be from a galactic ship in distress—a little ways beyond mind detector range from the pueblo.'' Pazilliwheep swung his craft through a ninety-degree turn. The acceleration compensators were so badly out of phase that Urgo slipped on the deck and hit his nose.

Nevertheless, the engineer-supercargo confined his remarks to a muttered *"Snagabagabartbats!"* That was cruel country below, especially for beings who had not evolved on this planet. A vessel grounded helpless in those arid mountains and canyons might soon be crewless. And that—aside from every moral consideration—invited the disaster of discovery by non-Hopi autochthons. It was well that *Grumdel Castle* had happened by in time.

Once in the engine room, Urgo activated his own visiscreen. He saw a wild landscape, heat shimmers and dust devils . . . and, yes, a saucer shape on a small mesa. Its outlines were blurred by a weak camouflage field, and neither he nor Pazilliwheep could identify the make of ship. But with millions of different makes—

"Why aren't they transmitting?" Pazilliwheep wondered.

"Transmitter busted, I guess," Urgo said. "They could'a lain here for, cometfire, days or weeks, you know. Aimin' to land at Wuwucimti but not makin' it. Expectin' somebody else'd come by eventually, and keepin' their field goin' so's they'd be detectable at a distance."

"But not daring to strike out on foot for the pueblo," Pazilliwheep added. "Right you are. Let's get down."

Grumdel Castle descended to the mesa and cut her own camouflage and her engines. The galactics emerged into brilliant, silent, sagebrush-pungent air. Hulking Urgo, graceful Pazilliwheep, broad-winged Klak't'klak moved across the sand toward the beached hypership.

Only, now that they were close, it looked less and less like a hypership. It looked more and more like—

"Surprise, surprise!" caroled a native voice. Sean F. X. Lindquist's lean form sprang from the false hull. He ran to meet them, arms spread in welcome, face wide open in a silly grin. "Am I glad to see you! Two weeks waiting! And you turn out to be the very same guys who— Come on and have a cold beer!"

Klak't'klak had brought his translator machine, which was keyed to several federation as well as 143an languages. But it was his pomander behind which he retreated. His eyes rolled. He gasped. Urgo bawled, "Oh, no!" and Pazilliwheep looked ill.

Other humans emerged. So did a television camera on a dolly. "We alerted the news services," Lindquist said happily. "Of course they thought this was a lunatic-fringe project, but they did agree to stand by, in case we came up with anything good for laughs. Smile, you're on candid camera! Now we better break the news gently to my assistants, that you aren't quite the godlike beings most of them think you are." He stopped, blushed through his stubble, and beckoned to a companion. "Pardon me. I was so excited I forgot.

Here's Professor Rostovtsev from Colorado U. He speaks Hopi.''

Klak't'klak had already adjusted his machine to English. He turned it off for a minute, while he expressed himself in his own tongue. Then he closed the circuit again.

"Never mind," he said resignedly. "Welcome to the Galactic Federation."

MURPHY'S
HALL

So far the book has been straightforward, mostly optimistic science fiction storytelling. Now it's time to move on. There are other themes, other treatments and emphases, possible even within the strictest definition of the field.

My wife Karen gave me so much help in thinking this one out that I in turn gave her half the by-line on the original publication, and want the same understood here.

THIS IS A LIE, but I wish so much it were not.

Pain struck through like lightning. For an instant that went on and on, there was nothing but the fire which hollowed him out and the body's animal terror. Then as he whirled downward he knew:

> Oh, no! Must I   Only a month,
> leave them already?   a month.
> *Weltall, verweile doch, du bist so schön.*

The monstrous thunders and whistles became a tone, like a bell struck once which would not stop singing. It filled the jagged darkness, it drowned all else, until it began to die out,

74

or to vanish into the endless, century after century, and meanwhile the night deepened and softened, until he had peace.

But he opened himself again and was in a place long and high. With his not-eyes he saw that five hundred and forty doors gave onto black immensities wherein dwelt clouds of light. Some of the clouds were bringing suns to birth. Others, greater and more distant, were made of suns already created, and turned in majestic Catherine's wheels. The nearest stars cast out streamers of flame, lances of radiance; and they were diamond, amethyst, emerald, topaz, ruby; and around them swung glints which he knew with his not-brain were planets. His not-ears heard the thin violence of cosmic-ray sleet, the rumble of solar storms, the slow patient multiplex pulses of gravitational tides. His not-flesh shared the warmth, the blood-beat, the megayears of marvelous life on unaccountable worlds.

Seven stood waiting. He rose. "But you—" he stammered without a voice.

"Welcome," Ed greeted him. "Don't be surprised. You were always one of us."

They talked quietly, until at last Gus reminded them that even here they were not masters of time. Eternity, yes, but not time. "Best we move on," he suggested.

"Uh-huh," Roger said. "Especially after Murphy took this much trouble on our account."

"He does not appear to be a bad fellow," Vladimir said.

"I am not certain," Robert answered. "Nor am I certain that we ever will find out. But come, friends. The hour is near."

Eight, they departed the hall and hastened down the star paths. Often the newcomer was tempted to look more closely at something he glimpsed. But he recalled that, while the universe was inexhaustible of wonders, it would have only the single moment to which he was being guided.

They stood after a while on a great ashen plain. The outlook was as eerily beautiful as he had hoped—no, more, when Earth, a blue serenity swirled white with weather, shone overhead: Earth, whence had come the shape that now climbed down a ladder of fire.

Yuri took Konstantin by the hand in the Russian way. "Thank you," he said through tears.

But Konstantin bowed in turn, very deeply, to Willy.

And they stood in the long Lunar shadows, under the high Lunar heaven, and saw the awkward thing come to rest and heard: "Houston, Tranquility Base here. The Eagle has landed."

Stars are small and dim on Earth. Oh, I guess they're pretty bright still on a winter mountaintop. I remember when I was little, we'd saved till we had the admission fees and went to Grand Canyon Reserve and camped out. Never saw that many stars. And it was like you could see up and up between them—like, you know, you could *feel* how they weren't the same distance off, and the spaces between were more huge than you could imagine. Earth and its people were just lost, just a speck of nothing among those cold sharp stars. Dad said they weren't too different from what you saw in space, except for being a lot fewer. The air was chilly too, and had a kind of pureness, and a sweet smell from the pines around. Way off I heard a coyote yip. The sound had plenty of room to travel in.

But I'm back where people live. The smog's not bad on this rooftop lookout, though I wish I didn't have to breathe what's gone through a couple million pairs of lungs before it reaches me. Thick and greasy. The city noise isn't too bad either, the usual growling and screeching, a jet-blast or a burst of gunfire. And since the power shortage brought on the brownout, you can generally see stars after dark, sort of.

My main wish is that we lived in the southern hemisphere, where you can see Alpha Centauri.

Dad, what are you doing tonight in Murphy's Hall?

A joke. I know. Murphy's Law: "Anything that can go wrong, will." Only I think it's a true joke. I mean, I've read every book and watched every tape I could lay hands on, the history, how the discoverers went out, farther and farther, lifetime after lifetime. I used to tell myself stories about the parts that nobody lived to put into a book.

The crater wall had fangs. They stood sharp and grayish white in the cruel sunlight, against the shadow which brimmed the bowl. And they grew and grew. Tumbling while it fell, the spacecraft had none of the restfulness of zero weight. Forces caught nauseatingly at gullet and gut. An unidentified loose object clattered behind the pilot chairs. The ventilators had stopped their whickering and the two men breathed stench. No matter. This wasn't an Apollo 13 mishap. They wouldn't have time to smother in their own exhalations.

Jack Bredon croaked into the transmitter: "Hello, Mission Control . . . Lunar Relay Satellite . . . anybody. Do you read us? Is the radio out too? Or just our receiver? God damn it, can't we even say good-bye to our wives?"

"Tell 'em quick," Sam Washburn ordered. "Maybe they'll hear."

Jack dabbed futilely at the sweat that broke from his face and danced in glittering droplets before him. "Listen," he said. "This is Moseley Expedition One. Our motors stopped functioning simultaneously, about two minutes after we commenced deceleration. The trouble must be in the fuel feed integrator. I suspect a magnetic surge, possibly due to a short circuit in the power supply. The meters registered a surge before we lost thrust. Get that system redesigned! Tell our wives and kids we love them."

He stopped. The teeth of the crater filled the entire forward window. Sam's teeth filled his countenace, a stretched-out grin. "How do you like that?" he said. "And me the first black astronaut."

They struck.

When they opened themselves again, in the hall, and knew where they were, he said, "Wonder if he'll let us go out exploring."

Murphy's Hall? Is that the real name?

Dad used to shout, "Murphy take it!" when he blew his temper. The rest is in a few of the old tapes, fiction plays about spacemen, back when people liked to watch that kind of story. They'd say when a man had died, "He's drinking in Murphy's Hall." Or he's dancing or sleeping or frying or freezing or whatever it was. But did they really say "Hall"? The tapes are old. Nobody's been interested to copy them off on fresh plastic, not for a hundred years, I guess, maybe two hundred. The holographs are blurred and streaky, the wounds are mushed and full of random buzzes. Murphy's Law has sure been working on those tapes.

I wish I'd asked Dad what the astronauts said and believed, way back when they were conquering the planets. Or pretended to believe, I should say. Of course they never thought there was a Murphy who kept a place where the spacefolk went that he'd called to him. But they might have kidded around about it. Only was the idea, for sure, about a hall? Or was that only the way I heard? I wish I'd asked Dad. But he wasn't home often, these last years, what with helping build and test his ship. And when he did come, I could see how he mainly wanted to be with Mother. And when he and I were together, well, that was always too exciting for me to remember those yarns I'd tell myself before I slept, after he was gone again.

Murphy's Haul?

By the time Moshe Silverman had finished writing his report, the temperature in the dome was about seventy, and rising fast enough that it should reach a hundred inside another Earth day. Of course, water wouldn't then boil at once; extra energy is needed for vaporization. But the staff would no longer be able to cool some down to drinking temperature by the crude evaporation apparatus they had rigged. They'd dehydrate fast. Moshe sat naked in a running river of sweat.

At least he had electric light. The fuel cells, insufficient to operate the air conditioning system, would at least keep Sofia from dying in the dark.

His head ached and his ears buzzed. Occasional dizziness seized him. He gagged on the warm fluid he must continually drink. *And no more salt,* he thought. *Maybe that will kill us before the heat does, the simmering, still, stifling heat.* His bones felt heavy, though Venus has in fact a somewhat lesser pull than Earth; his muscles sagged and he smelled the reek of his own disintegration.

Forcing himself to concentrate, he checked what he had written, a dry factual account of the breakdown of the reactor. The next expedition would read what this thick, poisonous inferno of an atmosphere did to graphite in combination with free neutrons; and the engineers could work out proper precautions.

In sudden fury, Moshe seized his brush and scrawled at the bottom of the metal sheet: "Don't give up! Don't let this hellhole whip you! We have too much to learn here."

A touch on his shoulder brought him jerkily around and onto his feet. Sofia Chiappellone had entered the office. Even now, with physical desire roasted out of him and she wetly agleam, puffy-faced, sunken-eyed, hair plastered lank to drooping head, he found her lovely.

"Aren't you through, darling?" Her tone was dull but her hand sought his. "We're better off in the main room. Mohandas' punkah arrangement does help."

"Yes, I'm coming."

"Kiss me first. Share the salt on me."

Afterward she looked over his report. "Do you believe they will try any further?" she asked. "Materials so scarce and expensive since the war—"

"If they don't," he answered, "I have a feeling—oh, crazy, I know, but why should we not be crazy?—I think if they don't, more than our bones will stay here. Our souls will, waiting for the ships that never come."

She actually shivered, and urged him toward their comrades.

Maybe I should go back inside. Mother might need me. She cries a lot, still. Crying, all alone in our little apartment. But maybe she'd rather not have me around. What can a gawky, pimply-faced fourteen-year-old boy do?

What can he do when he grows up?

Oh Dad, big brave Dad, I want to follow you. Even to Murphy's . . . Hold?

Director Saburo Murakami had stood behind the table in the commons and met their eyes, pair by pair. For a while silence had pressed inward. The bright colors and amateurish figures in the mural that Georgios Efthimakis had painted for pleasure—beings that never were, nymphs and fauns and centaurs frolicking beneath an unsmoky sky, beside a bright river, among grasses and laurel trees and daisies of an Earth that no longer was—became suddenly grotesque, infinitely alien. He heard his heart knocking. Twice he must swallow before he had enough moisture in his mouth to move his wooden tongue.

But when he began his speech, the words came forth steadily, if a trifle flat and cold. That was no surprise. He had lain awake the whole night rehearsing them.

"Yousouf Yacoub reports that he has definitely succeeded in checking the pseudovirus. This is not a cure; such must await laboratory research. Our algae will remain scant and sickly until the next supply ship brings us a new stock. I will radio Cosmocontrol, explaining the need. They will have ample time on Earth to prepare. You remember the ship is scheduled to leave at . . . at a date to bring it here in about nine months. Meanwhile we are guaranteed a rate of oxygen renewal sufficient to keep us alive, though weak, if we do not exert ourselves. Have I stated the matter correctly, Yousouf?"

The Arab nodded. His own Spanish had taken on a denser accent, and a tic played puppet master with his right eye. "Will you not request a special ship?" he demanded.

"No," Saburo told them. "You are aware how expensive

anything but an optimum Hohmann orbit is. That alone would wipe out the profit from this station—permanently, I fear, because of financing costs. Likewise would our idleness for nine months."

He leaned forward, supporting his weight easily on finger-tips in the low Martian gravity. "That is what I wish to discuss today," he said. "Interest rates represent competition for money. Money represents human labor and natural resources. This is true regardless of socioeconomic arrangements. You know how desperately short they are of both labor and resources on Earth. Yes, many billions of hands—but because of massive poverty, too few educated brains. Think back to what a political struggle the Foundation had before this base could be established.

"We know what we are here for. To explore. To learn. To make man's first permanent home outside Earth and Luna. In the end, in the persons of our great-grandchildren, to give Mars air men can breathe, water they can drink, green fields and forests where their souls will have room to grow." He gestured at the mural, though it seemed more than ever jeering. "We cannot expect starvelings on Earth, or those who speak for them, to believe this is good. Not when each ship bears away metal and fuel and engineering skill that might have gone to keep *their* children alive a while longer. We justify our continued presence here solely by mining the fissionables. The energy this gives back to the tottering economy, over and above what we take out, is the profit."

He drew a breath of stale, metallic-smelling air. Anoxia made his head whirl. Somehow he stayed erect and continued:

"I believe we, in this tiny solitary settlement, are the last hope for man remaining in space. If we are maintained until we have become fully self-supporting, Syrtis Harbor will be the seedbed of the future. If not—"

He had planned more of an exhortation before reaching the climax, but his lungs were too starved, his pulse too fluttery. He gripped the table edge and said through flying rags of darkness: "There will be oxygen for half of us to keep on after a fashion. By suspending their other projects and working exclusively in the mines, they can produce enough uranium and thorium that the books at least show no net economic loss. The sacrifice will . . . will be . . . of propaganda value. I call for male volunteers, or we can cast lots, or—Naturally, I myself am the first."

—That had been yesterday.

Saburo was among those who elected to go alone, rather than in a group. He didn't care for hymns about human solidarity; his dream was that someday those who bore some of his and Alice's chromosomes would not need solidarity. It was perhaps well that she had already died in a cinderslip. The scene with their children had been as much as he could endure.

He crossed Weinbaum Ridge but stopped when the dome-cluster was out of sight. He must not make the searchers come too far. If nothing else, a quick dust storm might cover his tracks, and he might never be found. Someone could make good use of his airsuit. Almost as good use as the alga tanks could of his body.

For a time, then, he stood looking. The mountainside ran in dark scaurs and fantastically carved pinnacles, down to the softly red-gold-ocher-black-dappled plain. A crater on the near horizon rose out of its own blue shadow like a challenge to the deep purple sky. In this thin air—he could just hear the wind's ghostly whistle—Mars gave to his gaze every aspect of itself, diamond sharp, a beauty strong, subtle, and abstract as a torii gate before a rock garden. When he glanced away from the shrunken but dazzling-bright sun, he could see stars.

He felt at peace, almost happy. Perhaps the cause was simply that now, after weeks, he had a full ration of oxygen.

I oughtn't to waste it, though, he thought. He was pleased by the steadiness of his fingers when he closed the valve.

Then he was surprised that his unbelieving self bowed over both hands to the Lodestar and said, *"Namu Amida Butsu."*

He opened his faceplate.

That is a gentle death. You are unconscious within thirty seconds.

—He opened himself and did not know where he was. An enormous room whose doorways framed a night heaven riotous with suns, galaxies, the green mysterious shimmer of nebulae? Or a still more huge ship, outward bound so fast that it was as if the Milky Way foamed along the bow and swirled aft in a wake of silver and planets?

Others were here, gathered about a high seat at the far end of where-he-was, vague in the twilight cast by sheer distance. Saburo rose and moved in their direction. Maybe, maybe Alice was among them.

But was he right to leave Mother that much alone?

I remember her when we got the news. On a Wednesday, when I was free, and I'd been out by the dump playing ball. I may as well admit to myself, I don't like some of the guys. But you have to take whoever the school staggering throws up for you. Or do you want to run around by yourself (remember, no, don't remember what the Hurricane Gang did to Danny) or stay always by yourself in the patrolled areas? So Jake-Jake does throw his weight around, so he does set the dues too high, his drill and leadership sure paid off when the Weasels jumped us last year. They won't try that again—we killed three, count 'em, three!—and I sort of think no other bunch will either.

She used to be real pretty, Mother did. I've seen pictures. She's gotten kind of scrawny, worrying about Dad, I guess, and about how to get along after that last pay cut they screwed the spacefolk with. But when I came in and saw her sitting, not on the sofa but on the carpet, the dingy gray carpet, crying— She hung onto that sofa the way she'd hung on Dad.

But why did she have to be so angry at him too? I mean, what happened wasn't his fault.

"Fifty billion munits!" she screamed when we'd got trying to talk about the thing. "That's a hundred, two hundred billion meals for hungry children! But what did they spend it on? Killing twelve men!"

"Aw, now, wait," I was saying, "Dad explained that. The resources involved, uh, aren't identical," when she slapped me and yelled:

"You'd like to go the same way, wouldn't you? Thank God, it almost makes his death worthwhile that you won't!"

I shouldn't have got mad. I shouldn't have said, "Y-y-you want me to become . . . a desk pilot, a food engineer, a doctor . . . something nice and safe and in demand . . . and keep you the way you wanted he should keep you?"

I better stop beating this rail. My fist'll be no good if I don't. Oh, someday I'll find how to make up those words to her.

I'd better not go in just yet.

But the trouble *wasn't* Dad's fault. If things had worked out right, why, we'd be headed for Alpha Centauri in a couple of years. Her and him and me— The planets yonderward, sure, they're the real treasure. But the ship itself! I remember Jake-Jake telling me I'd be dead of boredom inside six months. "Bored aboard, haw, haw, haw!" He really is a lardbrain. A good leader, I guess, but a lardbrain at heart— hey, once Mother would have laughed to hear me say that— How could you get tired of Dad's ship? A million books and tapes, a hundred of the brightest and most alive people who ever walked a deck—

Why, the trip would be like the revels in Elf Hill that Mother used to read me about when I was small, those old, old stories, the flutes and fiddles, bright clothes, food, drink, dancing, girls sweet in the moonlight. . . .

Murphy's Hill?

From Ganymede, Jupiter shows fifteen times as broad as Luna seen from Earth; and however far away the sun, the king planet reflects so brilliantly that it casts more than fifty times the radiance that the brightest night of man's home will ever know.

"*Here* is man's home," Catalina Sanchez murmured.

Arne Jensen cast her a look which lingered. She was fair to see in the goldenness streaming through the conservatory's clear walls. He ventured to put an arm about her waist. She sighed and leaned against him. They were scantily clad—the colony favored brief though colorful indoor garments—and he felt the warmth and silkiness of her. Among the manifold perfumes of blossoms (on plants everywhere to right and left and behind, extravagantly tall stalks and big flowers of every possible hue and some you would swear were impossible, dreamlike catenaries of vines and labyrinths of creepers) he caught her summery odor.

The sun was down and Jupiter close to full. While the terraforming project was going rapidly ahead, as yet the moon had too little air to blur vision. Tawny shone that shield, emblazoned with slowly moving cloud bands that were green, blue, orange, umber, and with the jewel-like Red Spot. To know that a single one of the storms raging there could swallow Earth whole added majesty to beauty and serenity; to know that, without the magnetohydronamic satellites men had orbited around this globe, its surface would be drowned in lethal radiation, added triumph. A few stars had the brilliance to pierce the luminousness, down by the rugged horizon. The gold poured soft across crags, cliffs, craters, glaciers, and the machinery of the conquest.

Outside lay a great quietness, but here music lilted from the ballroom. Folk had reason to celebrate. The newest electrolysis plant had gone into operation and was releasing oxygen at a rate 15 percent above estimate. However, low-weight or no, you got tired dancing—since Ganymedean steps took advantage, soaring and bounding aloft—mirth bubbled like champagne and the girl you admired said yes, she was in a mood for Jupiter watching—

"I hope you're right," Arne said. "Less on our account—

we have a good, happy life, fascinating work, the best of company—than on our children's." He squeezed a trifle harder.

She didn't object. "How can we fail?" she answered. "We've become better than self-sufficient. We produce a surplus, to trade to Earth, Luna, Mars, or plow directly back into development. The growth is exponential." She smiled. "You must think I'm awfully professorish. Still, really, what can go wrong?"

"I don't know," he said. "War, overpopulation, environmental degradation—"

"Don't be a gloomy," Catalina chided him. The lambent light struck rainbows from the tiara of native crystal that she wore in her hair. "People can learn. They needn't make the same mistakes forever. We'll build paradise here. A strange sort of paradise, yes, where trees soar into a sky full of Jupiter, and waterfalls tumble slowly, slowly down into deep-blue lakes, and birds fly like tiny bright-colored bullets, and deer cross the meadows in ten-meter leaps . . . but paradise."

"Not perfect," he said. "Nothing is."

"No, and we wouldn't wish that," she agreed. "We want some discontent left to keep minds active, keep them hankering for the stars." She chuckled. "I'm sure history will find ways to make them believe things could be better elsewhere. Or nature will— Oh!"

Her eyes widened. A hand went to her mouth. And then, frantically, she was kissing him, and he her, and they were clasping and feeling each other while the waltz melody sparkled and the flowers breathed and Jupiter's glory cataracted over them uncaring whether they existed.

He tasted tears on her mouth. "Let's go dancing," she begged. "Let's dance till we drop."

"Surely," he promised, and led her back to the ballroom.

It would help them once more forget the giant meteoroid, among the many which the planet sucked in from the Belt, that had plowed into grim and marginal Outpost Ganymede precisely half a decade before the Martian colony was discontinued.

Well, I guess people don't learn. They breed, and fight, and devour, and pollute, till:

Mother: "We can't afford it."

Dad: "We can't not afford it."

Mother: "Those children—like goblins, like ghosts, from starvation. If Tad were one of them, and somebody said never mind him, we have to build an interstellar ship . . . I wonder how you would react."

Dad: "I don't know. But I do know this is our last chance. We'll be operating on a broken shoestring as is, compared to what we need to do the thing right. If they hadn't made that breakthrough at Lunar Hydromagnetics Lab, when the government was on the point of closing it down— Anyway, darling, that's why I'll have to put in plenty of time aboard myself, while the ship is built and tested. My entire gang will be on triple duty."

Mother: "Suppose you succeed. Suppose you do get your precious spacecraft that can travel almost as fast as light. Do you imagine for an instant it can—an armada can erase life an atom's worth for mankind?"

Dad: "Well, several score atoms' worth. Starting with you and Tad and me."

Mother: "I'd feel a monster, safe and confortable en route to a new world while behind me they huddled in poverty by the billions."

Dad: "My first duty is to you two. However, let's leave that aside. Let's think about man as a whole. What is he? A beast that is born, grubs around, copulates, quarrels, and dies. Uh-huh. But sometimes something more in addition. He does breed his occasional Jesus, Leonardo, Bach, Jefferson, Einstein, Armstrong, Olveida—whoever you think best justifies our being here—doesn't he? Well, when you huddle people together like rats, they soon behave like rats. What then of the spirit? I tell you, if we don't make a fresh start, a

bare handful of us but free folk whose descendants may in the
end come back and teach—if we don't, why, who cares
whether the two-legged animal goes on for another million
years or becomes extinct in a hundred? Humanness will be
dead."

Me: "And gosh, Mother, the fun!"

Mother: "You don't understand, dear."

Dad: "Quiet. The man-child speaks. He understands better than you."

Quarrel: till I run from them crying. Well, eight or nine
years old. That night, was that the first night I started telling
myself stories about Murphy's Hall?

It *is* Murphy's Hall. I say that's the right place for Dad to
be.

When Hoo Fong, chief engineer, brought the news to the
captain's cabin, the captain sat still for minutes. The ship
thrummed around them; they felt it faintly, a song in their
bones. And the light fell from the overhead, into a spacious
and gracious room, furnishings, books, a stunning photograph of the Andromeda galaxy, an animation of Mary and
Tad; and weight was steady underfoot, a full gee of acceleration, one light-year per year per year, though this would
become more in shipboard time as you started to harvest the
rewards of relativity . . . a mere two decades to the center of
this galaxy, three to the neighbor whose portrait you
adored. . . . How hard to grasp that you were dead!

"But the ramscoop is obviously functional," said the
captain, hearing his pedantic phrasing.

Hoo Fong shrugged. "It will not be, after the radiation has
affected electronic parts. We have no prospect of decelerating and returning home at low velocity before both we and the
ship have taken a destructive dose."

Interstellar hydrogen, an atom or so in a cubic centimeter,
raw vacuum to Earthdwellers at the bottom of their ocean of
gas and smoke and stench and carcinogens. To spacefolk,

fuel, reaction mass, a way to the stars, once you're up to the modest pace at which you meet enough of those atoms per second. However, your force screens must protect you from them, else they strike the hull and spit gamma rays like a witch's curse.

"We've hardly reached one-fourth c," the captain protested. "Unmanned probes had no trouble at better than 99 percent."

"Evidently the system is inadequate for the larger mass of this ship," the engineer answered. "We should have made its first complete test flight unmanned too."

"You know we didn't have funds to develop the robots for that."

"We can send our data back. The next expedition—"

"I doubt there'll be any. Yes, yes, we'll beam the word home. And then, I suppose, keep going. Four weeks, did you say, till the radiation sickness gets bad? The problem is not how to tell Earth, but how to tell the rest of the men."

Afterward, alone with the pictures of Andromeda, Mary, and Tad, the captain thought: *I've lost more than the years ahead. I've lost the years behind, that we might have had together.*

What shall I say to you? That I tried and failed and am sorry? But am I? At this hour I don't want to lie, most especially not to you three.

Did I do right?

Yes.

No.

Oh God, oh, shit, how can I tell? The Moon is rising above the soot-clouds. I might make it that far. Commissioner Wenig was talking about how we should maintain the last Lunar base another few years, till industry can find a substitute for those giant molecules they make there. But wasn't the Premier of United Africa saying those industries ought to be forbidden, they're too wasteful, and any country that keeps them going is an enemy of the human race?

Gunfire rattles in the streets. Some female voice somewhere is screaming.

I've got to get Mother out of here. That's the last thing I can do for Dad.

After ten years of studying to be a food engineer or a doctor, I'll probably feel too tired to care about the Moon. After another ten years of being a desk pilot and getting fat, I'll probably be outraged at any proposal to spend my tax money—

—except maybe for defense. In Siberia they're preaching that strange new missionary religion. And the President of Europe has said that if necessary, his government will denounce the ban on nuclear weapons.

The ship passed among the stars bearing a crew of dead bones. After a hundred billion years it crossed the Edge—not the edge of space or time, which does not exist, but the Edge—and came to harbor at Murphy's Hall.

And the dust which the cosmic rays had made began to stir, and gathered itself back into bones; and from the radiation-corroded skeleton of the ship crept atoms which formed into flesh; and the captain and his men awoke. They opened themselves and looked upon the suns that went blazing and streaming overhead.

"We're home," said the captain.

Proud at the head of his men, he strode uphill from the dock, toward the hall of the five hundred and forty doors. Comets flitted past him, novae exploded in dreadful glory, planets turned and querned, the clinker of a once living world drifted by, new life screamed its outrage at being born.

The roofs of the house lifted like mountains against night and the light-clouds. The ends of rafters jutted beyond the eaves, carved into dragon heads. Through the doorway toward which the captain led his crew, eight hundred men could have marched abreast. But a single form waited to greet them; and beyond him was darkness.

When the captain saw who that was, he bowed very deeply.

The other took his hand. "We have been waiting," he said.

The captain's heart sprang. "Mary too?"

"Yes, of course. Everyone."

Me. And you. And you. And you in the future, if you exist. In the end, Murphy's Law gets us all. But we, my friends, must go to him the hard way. Our luck didn't run out. Instead, the decision that could be made was made. It was decided for us that our race—among the trillions which must be out there wondering what lies beyond their skies—is not supposed to have either discipline or dreams. No, our job is to make everybody nice and safe and equal, and if this happens to be impossible, then nothing else matters.

If I went to that place—and I'm glad that this is a lie—I'd keep remembering what we might have done and seen and known and been and loved.

Murphy's Hell.

THE
PIRATE

Here we return for a while to standard science fiction, indeed to space opera—but, I hope, with a difference. Again the basic plot idea came from John Campbell: what might be the effect of a supernova, a gigantic exploding star, within a few light-years of an inhabited planet? But as soon as I started work, I realized that the story couldn't really be about that. Instead, it had to be about—

Well, you decide for yourself. Of readers who have commented on it to me, the young have generally confessed to being a bit puzzled, while the older have instantly seen what was going on. However, this dichotomy probably isn't complete. What do you yourself make of it?

WE GUARD the great Pact; but the young generations, the folk of the star frontier, so often do not understand.

They avail themselves of our ordinary work. (*Ship* Harpsong *of Nerthus, out of Highsky for David's Landing, is long overdue. . . . Please forecast the competition which a cybernation venture on Oasis would probably face after the older firms elsewhere learned that a market had been established. . . . Bandits reported. . . . How shall we deal with this wholly strange race of beings we have come upon?*) But then we step in their own paths and say, "Thou shalt not." And suddenly we are the Cordys, the enemy.

The case of the slain world named Good Luck is typical. Now that the Service is ready, after a generation, to let the truth be known, I can tell you about Trevelyan Micah, Murdoch Juan, Smokesmith, red Faustina, and the rest, that you may judge the rights or wrongs for yourself.

In those days Trevelyan spent his furloughs on Earth. He said its quiet, its intellectuality, were downright refreshing, and he could get all the rowdiness he wanted elsewhere. But of course his custom put him at the nerve center of the Service, insofar as an organization operating across a fraction of the galaxy can have one. He got a larger picture than most of his colleagues of how it fared with the Pact. This made him more effective. He was a dedicated man.

I suspect he also wanted to renew his humanity at the wellspring of humankind, he who spent most of his life amidst otherness. Thus he was strengthened in his will to be a faithful guardian.

Not that he was a prig. He was large and dark, with aquiline features and hard aquamarine eyes. But his smile was ready, his humor was dry, his tunic and culottes were always in the latest mode, he enjoyed every aspect of life from Bach to beer.

When the machine summoned him to the Good Luck affair, he had been living for a while at Laugerie Haute, which is in the heart of the steep, green, altogether beautiful Dordogne country. His girl of the moment had a stone house that was built in the Middle Ages against an overhanging cliff. Its interior renovation did not change its exterior ancientness, which made it seem a part of the hills or they a part of it. But in front grew bushes, covering a site excavated centuries ago, where flint-working reindeer hunters lived for millennia while the glacier covered North Europe. And daily overhead through the bright sky glided a spear that was the Greenland-Algeria carrier; and at night, across the stars where men now traveled, moved sparks that were spaceships lifting out of Earth's shadow. In few other parts of the planet could you be more fully in the oneness of time.

"You don't have to go, not yet," Braganza Diane said, a little desperately because she cared for him and our trumpeter blows too many Farewells each year.

" 'Fraid I do," he said. "The computer didn't ring me up for fun. In fact, it's a notoriously sober-sided machine." When she didn't answer his grin, he explained: "The data banks show I'm the only person available who's dealt with, uh, a certain individual before. He's a slippery beast, with sharp teeth, and experience might make the critical quantum of difference."

"It better!" She curbed the tears that could have caused him to think her immature and bent her lips upward. "You will add . . . the rest of this leave . . . to your next, and spend it with me. Won't you?"

"I'd love to," he said, carefully making no promises. He kissed her, where they stood in the hay scent of summer. They went back to the house for a while.

After he packed his kit and phoned good-bye to some neighbors—landholders, friendly folk whose ancestors had dwelt here for generations beyond counting—she flew him to Aerogare Bordeaux. Thence he took a carrier to Port Nevada. The computer had briefed him so well that he could go straight to work and he wanted to catch Murdoch Juan at ease if possible.

His timing was good. Sunset was slanting across western North America and turning the mountains purple when he arrived. The city walled him off from that serenity as he entered. It shouldered big square buildings above streets in which traffic clamored; the growl of machines perpetually underlay the shrill of voices; frantically flickering signs drowned out the stars; humans and nonhumans hustled, jostled, chiseled, brawled, clashed, stole, evangelized, grew rich, grew poor, came, went, and were forgotten, beneath a tawdry front was that heedless vigor which the cargo ships bring from their homes to enclaves like this. Trevelyan allowed himself a brief "Phew!" when the stinks rolled around him.

He knew this town, on a hundred different worlds. He knew how to make inquiries of chance-met drinking companions. Eventually he found one of Murdoch's crew who could tell him where the boss was this evening. It turned out to be no dive, with the smoke of a dozen drugs stinging the eyes, but the discreet and expensive Altair House.

There a headwaiter, live though extraterrestrial, would not conduct him to his man. Captain Murdoch had requested privacy for a conference. Captain Murdoch was entitled to— Trevelyan showed his identification. It gave him no legal prerogative; but a while ago the Service had forestalled a war on the headwaiter's native planet.

Upstairs, he chimed for admittance to the room. He had been told that Captain Murdoch's dinner guest had left, seemingly well pleased, while Captain Murdoch and his female companion stayed behind with a fresh order of champagne, vigorator, and other aids to celebration. "Come in, come in!" boomed the remembered hearty voice. The door dilated and Trevelyan trod through.

"Huh? I thought you were— Sunglaze! You again!" Murdoch surged to his feet. Briefly he stood motionless, among drapes and paintings, sparkling glassware, drift of music and incense. Then, tiger softly, he came around the table to a fist's reach of Trevelyan.

He was as tall, and broader in the shoulders. His features were rugged, deeply weathered, blond hair and a sweeping blond moustache. His clothes were too colorful to be stylish on Earth, but he wore them with such panache that you didn't notice.

The woman remained seated. She was as vivid in her way as he in his, superbly formed, the classicism of her face brought to life by the nearly Asian cheekbones; and she owned the rare combination of pure white skin and fox-red hair. Yet she was no toy. When she saw Murdoch thus taken aback, Trevelyan read shock upon her. It was followed by unflinching enmity.

He bowed to her. "Forgive me if I intrude," he said.

Murdoch relaxed in a gust of laughter. "Oh, sure, sure, Mike, you're forgiven. If you don't stay too mugthundering long." He clapped hands on the agent's shoulders. "How've you been, anyway? How many years since last?"

"Five or six." Trevelyan tried to smile back. "I'm sorry to bother you, but I understand you're shipping out day after tomorrow, which no doubt means you'll be busy for the prior twenty-four hours."

"Right, buck," Murdoch said. "This here tonight is our lift-off party. However, it began with business—lining up a financial backer for later on—so it may as well continue that way a few microseconds." The tone stayed genial, but the gaze was pale and very steady. "Got to be business, don't it? You didn't track me down just to wish an old sparring partner a bony voyage."

"Not really," Trevelyan admitted.

Murdoch took his arm and led him to the table. "Well, sit yourself and hang a glug with us. Faustina, meet Trevelyan Micah of the Stellar Union Co-ordination Service."

"Juan has spoken of you," the woman said distantly.

Trevelyan eased into a chair. His muscles relaxed, one by one, that his brain might be undistracted in the coming duel. "I hope he used language suitable to a lady," he said.

"I'm from New Mars," she snapped. "We don't have time for sex distinctions in our manners."

I might have guessed, he thought. There aren't as many unclaimed planets habitable by man as is popularly believed; so the marginal ones get settled too. He could imagine scarring poverty in her background, and Murdoch Juan as the great merry beloved knight who took her from it and would bear her on his saddlebow to the castle he meant to conquer for them.

"I did my duty as I saw it, which happened to conflict with Captain Murdoch's rights as he saw them," Trevelyan said.

"I was making a fortune off fur and lumber on Vanaheim," the other man said.

"And disrupting the ecology of a continent," Trevelyan replied.

"You didn't have to come in and talk them into changing the laws on me," Murdoch said without rancor. He rinsed a glass from the water carafe and filled it with champagne. "Hope you don't mind this being used first by a financier."

"No. Thank you." Trevelyan accepted.

"And then, when he was honorably engaged as a mercenary—" Faustina's tone held venom.

"Bringing modern weapons in against primitives who were no menace," Trevelyan said. "That's universally illegal. Almost as illegal as dispossessing autochthons or prior colonists."

"Does your precious Union actually claim jurisdiction over the entire cosmos?"

"Ease off, Faustina," Murdoch said.

"The Union is not a government, although many governments support it," Trevelyan said to the woman. "This galaxy alone is too big for any power to control. But we do claim the right to prevent matters from getting out of hand, as far as we're able. That includes wrongdoing by our own citizens anywhere."

"The Cordys never jailed me," Murdoch said. "They only scuppered my operation. I got away in time and left no usable evidence. No hard feelings." He raised his glass. Unwillingly, Trevelyan clinked rims with him and drank. "In fact," Murdoch added, "I'm grateful to you, friend. You showed me the error of my ways. Now I've organized a thing that'll not only make me rich, but so respectable that nobody can belch in my presence without a permit."

Faustina ignited a cigarette and smoked in hard puffs.

"I've been asked to verify that," Trevelyan said.

"Why, everything's open and honest," Murdoch said. "You know it already. I got me a ship, never mind how, and went exploring out Eridanus way. I found a planet, uninhabited but colonizable, and filed for a discoverer's patent.

The Service inspection team verified that Good Luck, as I'm calling it, is a lawfully exploitable world. Here I am on Earth, collecting men and equipment for the preliminary work of making a defined area safe for humans. You remember." His manner grew deliberately patronizing. "Check for dangerous organisms and substances in the environment, establish the weather and seismic patterns, et cetera. When we're finished, I'll advertise my real estate and my ferry service to it. For the duration of my patent, I can set the terms of immigration, within limits. Most discoverers just charge a fee. But I am to supply everything—transportation there, a functioning physical community built in advance, whatever people need to make a good start. That's why I've been discussing financial backing."

"Your approach has been tried," Trevelyan warned, "but never paid off. The cost per capita of a prefabricated settlement is more than the average would-be immigrant' can afford. So he stays home, and puff goes the profit. Eventually, the entrepreneur is glad to sell out for a millo on the credit."

"Not this one," Murdoch said. "I'll be charging irresistibly little—about half what it'd cost 'em to buy unimproved land and make their own homes and highways and such out of local materials. They'll come." He tossed off the rest of his glass and refilled it. "But why are you curious, you Cordys? I haven't told you anything that isn't on file. If you wanted to snoop, why didn't you come see me earlier?"

"Because we have too much else on file," Trevelyan said bitterly. "Our computer didn't get around to correlating certain facts until yesterday. We're trying to keep the galaxy livable, but it's too much for us, too diverse—"

"Good!" Faustina said.

He gave her a grave look. "Be careful, my lady," he said, "or one day a piece of that diversity may kill you."

Murdoch scowled. "That'll do," he said. "I've been nice, but this is my evening out with my girl and you're obviously on a fishing expedition. You haven't got a thing against me, legally, have you? Very well, get out.''

Trevelyan tensed where he sat.

''Or good night, if you prefer,'' Murdoch said in friendlier wise.

Trevelyan rose, bowed, murmured the polite formulas, and left. Inwardly he felt cold. There had been more than a gloat in his enemy's manner; there had been the expectation of revenge.

It looks as if I'd better take direct action, he thought.

The *Campesino* cleared from orbit, ran out of the Solar System on gravs, and went into hyperdrive in the usual fashion. She was a long-range cruiser with boats and gear for a variety of conditions. Aboard were Murdoch, Faustina, half a dozen spacemen, and a score of technicians.

The Service speedster *Genji* followed, manned by Trevelyan and that being whose humanly unpronounceable name was believed to mean something like Smokesmith. To shadow another vessel is more art than science and more witchcraft than either. *Campesino* could easily be tracked while in the normale mode—by amplified sight, thermal radiation, radar, neutrinos from the powerplant. But once she went over to the tachyon mode, only a weak emission of superlight particles was available. And Murdoch also had detectors, surely kept wide open.

With skill and luck, *Genji* could stay at the effective edge of the field she was observing, while it masked her own. For this to be possible, however, she must be much smaller as well as much faster than the other craft. Therefore nothing more formidable than her could be used. She did have a blast cannon, a couple of heavy slugthrowers, and several one-meter dirigible missiles with low-yield nuclear warheads. But Trevelyan would have been surprised if Murdoch's people didn't build themselves huskier weapons en route.

He sat for hours at the conn, staring into the jeweled

blackness of its star simulacrum, while the ship murmured around him and the subliminal beat of drive energies wove into his bones. At last he said, "I think we've done it." He pointed to the instruments. A hunter's exultation lifted within him. "They are definitely sheering off the Eridanus course."

"They may have become aware of us, or they may do so later, and attack," replied the flat artificial voice of Smokesmith.

"We take that chance," Trevelyan agreed. "I can't quite believe it of Murdoch, though. He plays rough, but I don't know about any cold-blooded murders he's done."

"Our information concerning his world line is fragmentary, and zero about its future segment. Furthermore, available data indicate that his companions are quite unintegrate."

"M-m-m, yes, hard cases, none Earth-born, several nonhumans from raptor cultures among them. That was one fact which alerted us."

"What else? We departed too hurriedly for me to obtain entire background, I being ignorant of the biological and social nuances among your species."

Trevelyan considered his shipmate. Chief Rodionov had had to assign the first and presumably best agent he could, and there were never many nonhumans at Australia Center. Homo Sapiens is a wolfish creature; two of him can end with ripping each other apart, on an indefinitely long voyage in as cramped a shell as this. But even when our agents have gentler instincts, we try to make up teams out of diverse breeds. The members must be compatible in their physical requirements but, preferably, different enough in psychologies and abilities that they form a whole which is more than its parts.

The trouble was, Trevelyan had never before encountered a being from the planet men called Reardon's. He had heard of them, but space is too full of life for us to remember it all, let alone meet it.

Smokesmith's barrel-like body stood about 140 centimeters high on four stumpy, claw-footed legs. Four tentacles ringed the top of it, each ending in three boneless fingers whose grip was astonishing. The head was more like a clump of fleshy blue petals than anything else; patterns upon them were the outward signs of sense organs, though Trevelyan didn't know how these worked. Withal, Smokesmith was handsome in his (?) fashion. Indeed, the mother-of-pearl iridescence on his rugose torso was lovely to watch.

The man decided on a straightforward approach. "Well," he said, "the fact that Murdoch is involved was in itself suspicious. He probably came to Earth to outfit, rather than some colonial world where he isn't known, because he wouldn't attract attention."

"I should extrapolate otherwise, when few commercial ventures originate on Earth."

"But the average Terrestrial hasn't got the average colonist's lively interest in such matters. The port cities are mostly ignored by the rest of the planet, a regrettable necessity to be kept within proper bounds. Then too, Murdoch would have a better chance of getting substantial but close-mouthed—uh, that means secretive—money help on Earth, which is still the primary banker of the human species. And finally, though it's true that Service reports from everywhere go to the molecular file at Center . . . that fact makes the data flow so huge that Murdoch might well have completed his business and departed before the continuous search-and-correlation noticed him."

"What was smelled, then, to excite suspicion? I do not hypothesize that the initial stimulus was the composition of his crew."

"No. We checked that out later. Nor did the economics of his project look especially interesting. Doubtless his ready-built community will be a wretched clutter of hovels; but *caveat emptor*, he'll be within the law, and word will soon get around not to buy from him.

"No, the real anomaly is the equipment he ordered. The report on this Good Luck of his is complete enough that you can fairly well predict what a ground-preparation gang will need. The planet's smaller than Earth, relatively cold and arid, relatively thin atmosphere. But it has a magnetic field and a weak sun; hence the radiation background is low."

"What is required would depend on what race is to colonize."

"Sure. Murdoch will sell to humans. Not Earth humans, naturally. Colonial ones, from all over. We won't be able to monitor every embarkation and debarkation, any except a tiny fraction. Not when we are as few as we are, with so much else to do. And local authorities won't care. They'll be too glad to get rid of excess population. Besides, most colonials are anarchic oriented; they won't stand for official inquiries into their business." Trevelyan blinked in surprise. "What started me off on that?"

"Conceivably an element of your mentation has sensed a thought."

"If so, it's a hunch too faint to identify. Well. Why doesn't he have water-finding gear with him, drills and explosives to start forming lakes, that kind of stuff? Why does he have a full line of radiation spotters and protective suits? The biological laboratory he's assembled isn't right for Good Luck either; it's meant to study life forms a lot more terrestroid. I could go on, but you get the idea."

"And now he has changed course." Smokesmith considered the indicators with whatever he used to see. "A geodesic, which will bring him in the direction of Scorpius."

"Huh? You don't have to ask the computer? . . . Trouble is, no law says he must go to his announced destination, or tell us why he didn't." Trevelyan smiled with shut lips. "Nor does any law say we can't tail along."

A keening broke from Smokesmith, made not with his vocoder but with his own tympani. It wavered up and down the scale; a brief shakenness in his nerves told Trevelyan it entered the subsonic. Odors rolled up the air, pungencies like blood and burnt sulfur and others men do not know.

"Good Cosmos, what're you doing?" he exclaimed.

"It is an old communication of my infraculture. Of whetted winds, frost, a mountain that is a torch, beneath iron moons, a broken night, and the will to pursue that which has poison fangs. . . . Enough.''

Five hundred and twenty-eight light-years from Sol, the sky ahead suddenly blazed.

Trevelyan had been meditating upon his philosophy. That, and reading, and listening to music tapes, and tinkering with handicrafts, and physical exercises, had been his refuge from the weary weeks. Smokesmith was a decent being in his way, but too alien for games or conversation. When asked how he passed the time, with no apparent motion save of his end-lessly interweaving arms, he replied: ''I make my alternate life. Your language lacks the necessary concepts.''

The blossoming of what had been merely another, slowly waxing blue star, jerked Trevelyan to alertness. He sat up, clenched hands on chair arms, and stared at the simulacrum until his vision seemed to drown in those glittering dark depths. The star climbed in brilliance even as he watched, for *Genji* passed the wave front of the initial explosion and entered that which had come later. It dominated the whole sky before Trevelyan could shout:

''Supernova!''

And still it flamed higher, until its one searing point gave fifty times the light that full Luna does to Earth, ten million times the light of the next most luminous—and nearby—sun. Although the screens throttled down that terrible whiteness, Trevelyan could not look close to it, and his vision was fogged with shining spots for minutes after the glimpse he had first gotten.

Smokesmith's claws clicked on the deck of the conn section as the Reardonite entered. Trevelyan caught a hackle-raising whiff from him and knew he was equally awed. Perhaps his expressionless phrasing was a defense:

''Yes, a supernova of Type II, if the theoretical accounts I have witnessed are correct. They are estimated to occur at the rate of one every fifty-odd years in the galaxy. The remnants of some have been investigated, but to date no outburst has been observed within the range of recorded explorations."

"We've gone beyond that range already," the man whispered. He shook himself. "Is Murdoch headed toward it?"

"Approximately. No change in course."

"Can't be coincidence. He must have traveled far, looking for game the Cordys wouldn't take from him, and—" Roughly: "Let's get some readings."

Instruments, astrophysical files carried on every Service vessel, and computation produced a few answers. The star was about 150 parsecs away, which meant it had died five centuries ago. It had been a blue giant, with a mass of some ten Sols, an intrinsic luminosity of perhaps 50,000; but the Scorpian clouds had hidden it from early Terrestrial astronomers, and modern scientists were as yet too busy to come this far afield.

So wild a burning could not go on for many million years. Instabilities built up until the great star shattered itself. At the peak of its explosion, it flooded forth energy equal to the output of the rest of the galaxy.

That could last for no more than days, of course. Racing down the light-years, Trevelyan saw the lurid splendor fade. A mistiness began to glow, a nebula born of escaped gases, rich in new nuclei of the heavier elements, destined at last to enter into the formation of new suns and planets. Instruments picked out the core of the star: whitely shining, fiercer still in the X-ray spectrum, lethal to come near. But it collapsed rapidly beneath its own monstrous gravitation, to the size of a dwarf, a Jupiter, an Earth. At the end it would be so dense that nothing, not even light, could leave; and it would have vanished from the universe.

Trevelyan said with bleak anger: "He didn't report it. The information that's already been lost as the wave front swelled—"

"Shall we return at once?" the Reardonite asked.

"Well . . . no, I suppose not. If we let Murdoch go, Cosmos knows what deviltry might happen. There'll be other supernovas, but a dead sentience doesn't come back.''

"We have a strong indication of his goal."

"What?" Trevelyan set down the pipe he had been nervously loading.

"Examine the photomultiplier screen, and next these." Fingertendrils snaked across dial faces. "The star to which I point is an ordinary G3 sun within a hundred light-years of the supernova. Proper motions show that it was somewhat closer at the time of the eruption. Our study object is on an unmistakable intercept track. It is plausible that this is meant to terminate there.''

"But—No!" Trevelyan protested. "What can he want?"

"The dosage received by any planet of the lesser sun, through the cosmic rays given off by the larger at its maximum, was in the thousands of roentgens, delivered in a period of days. Atmosphere and magnetic field would have provided some shielding, but the effect must nonetheless have been biologically catastrophic. Presumably, though, most lower forms of life would survive, especially vegetable and marine species. A new ecological balance would soon be struck, doubtless unstable and plagued by a high mutation rate but converging upon stability. Probably the infall of radionuclides, concentrated in certain areas by natural processes, would make caution advisable to the present time. But on the whole, this hypothetical planet could now be salubrious for your race or mine, if it otherwise resembles our homes sufficiently. I might add that it has been conjectured that accidents of this sort were responsible for periods of massive extinction on numerous worlds, including, I have absorbed, your own home sphere.''

Trevelyan scarcely heard the flat words. All at once he was confronting horror.

When the yellow sun was a disk, too lightful for bare eyes but softly winged with corona and zodiacal glow in a step-down screen: then the supernova nebula, thirty parsecs off, was only an irregular blur, a few minutes across, among the constellations opposite, as if a bit of the Milky Way had drifted free. One had trouble imagining how it had raged in these skies four hundred years ago. Nor did interplanetary space any longer have an unusual background count; nor did the seven attendant worlds that *Genji*'s cameras identified seem in any way extraordinary.

That was a false impression, Trevelyan knew. Every world is a wilderness of uncountably many uniquenesses. But the third one out, on which his attention focused, resembled Earth.

He was confined to optical means of study. Beams and probes might be detected aboard *Campesino*. Murduch had gone out of hyper into normal mode several millions of kilometers back. His shadowers necessarily followed suit. Then—lest he spot their neutrino emission, as they were now tracking him by his—they stopped the fusion generators and orbited free at their considerable distance, drawing power from the accumulators.

"The study object is in the final phase of approach to atmosphere of the terrestroid planet," Smokesmith announced.

"I'm scarcely surprised," Trevelyan answered. He looked up from his meters and notes. "Apparently it is as terrestroid as any you'll ever find, too. Air, irradiation, size, mass as gotten from the satellites—nearly identical. Those are two small, fairly close-in moons, by the way; so the tide patterns must be complicated, but the oceans will be kept from stagnation. Twenty-eight-hour spin, twelve-degree tilt. Mean temperature a touch higher than Earth's, no polar caps, somewhat less land area . . . an interglacial macroclimate, I'd guess. In short, aside from pockets of leftover radioactivity, idyllic."

"And possible ecological difficulties," the Reardonite said.

Trevelyan winced. "Damn, did you have to remind me?" He left off peering, leaned back in his chair, held his chin, and scowled. "Question is, what do we do about Murdoch? He doesn't seem to have committed any violation except failure to register a discovery. And we probably couldn't prove this isn't his own first time here, that he didn't come this way on impulse. Besides, the offense is trivial."

"Do methods not exist of compelling humans to speak truth?"

"Yes. Electronic brainphasing. Quite harmless. But our species has rules against involuntary self-incrimination. So it's mainly used to prove the honesty of prosecution witnesses. And as I said, I've no real case against him."

"Need we do more than report back? Authorized expeditions could then be dispatched."

" 'Back' is a mighty long ways. What might he do here meanwhile? Of course—hm—if Murdoch doesn't suspect we're on to him, he may proceed leisurely with his preparations, giving us a chance to—"

"The study object has ceased to emit."

"What?" Trevelyan surged from his chair. He abraded his arm on his companion's integument, so fast did he brush by to look for himself. The indications were subtle, because the normal neutrino count is always high. But this tracer included a computer which identified engine sign amidst noise and put its volume on a single dial. That needle had fallen to zero.

Chilled, Trevelyan said: "He's going down on accumulators and aerodynamics. By the time we come in range for a different tracking method, he can be wherever on the surface."

Smokesmith's tone was unchanging, but an acrid odor jetted from him and the petals of his face stirred. "Apparently he does not fear detection from the ground. We observe no trace of atomic energy, hence doubtless no one capable of locating it. The probability is that he desires to remove us and none else from his trail."

"Yeh." Trevelyan began to pace, back and forth between the caging bulkheads. "We half expected he'd tag us somewhere along the line, when I'd already put him on the *qui vive* in Port Nevada. But why's he telling us unequivocally that he has?''

''In my race, messages are always intended as vectors on the world line of the percipient.''

''In mine too, sort of.'' Trevelyan's strides lengthened. ''What does Murdoch hope to get us to do by thumbing his nose at us? We have two alternatives. We can go straight back, or we can land first for a closer look.''

''The latter would not add significantly to the interval before we can have returned.''

''That's the black deuce of it, my friend. The very nearest Service base where we could originate any kind of investigatory expedition is, um, Lir, I suppose, if they aren't still too busy with the Storm Queen affair. There are frontier planets closer than that, full of men who'll gladly swarm here for a chance of striking it rich. And if they can also do the Cordys one in the eye, why, fine.''

''Furthermore,'' Smokesmith pointed out, ''we have no clear proof that anything is involved sufficiently important to justify a long-range mission. The supernova, yes. That is a scientific treasure. But here we have merely a seemingly uninhabited planet. Why should a base commander who does not know Murdoch's past—especially a nonhuman base commander who cannot ingest its significance—assume he has an unlawful purpose? Will he not expect Murdoch to request an inspection team, that a patent of discovery may be issued?''

Trevelyan nodded. We are scattered so thinly, we who guard the great Pact. Often we must pass by tracks that may well lead toward a hidden evil, because we *know* about another beast elsewhere. Or we learn of something that was wrong at the beginning and should have been stopped, but whose amendment now would be a worse wrong. We have Nerthus, for example, always before us: a human colony founded and flourishing, then learning that native intelligent life did exist. We are fortunate that in that case the interests of the two species are reconcilable, with endless difficulty.

"Does Murdoch wish us to return in alarm bearing data inadequate to provoke prompt official action?" Smokesmith queried. "That seems plausible. Coming as he lately did from the Union's Scorpian march, he must be better informed than we about current situations there. Thus, he might know we can get no help at Lir."

"We can—we can even commandeer civilian ships and personnel—if yonder planet has sentient beings on it. Clear and present danger of territorial conquest. Or Murdoch might simply be plundering them."

"It is improbable that such are alive."

"True. But if dead—"

Trevelyan stopped. He looked long outward. Unmagnified, the world was a point of light, a clear and lovely blue. But close in would be mapless immensity. The other crew would have had ample chance to conceal their vessel. They could be anywhere, preparing anything. They surely outnumbered and outgunned him. He hated to imagine big, bluff Murdoch Juan as planning murder. On the other hand, Faustina might, and she had had this entire voyage in which to be the only human female. . . .

Resolution crystallized. "We're going in," he said.

They approached slowly, both to observe in detail and to make certain preparations. Circling in the fringes of atmosphere, they confirmed the thing they had guessed at.

This had been a peopled world. The people had been slain.

Were there survivors, there would be evidence of them. Civilization might well have gone under in mass death, panic, anarchy, and famine after crops perished in fields now brushland or desert. But savage descendants of a city-building race would live in villages. *Genji*'s sensors would register their very campfires. Besides, it was more reasonable that some comeback would have been made, however weak. For the sleet of cosmic radiation harmed no buildings, no tools or machines, no books, little, indeed, except what was alive.

Gazing into a viewscreen, where clouds parted briefly to show high towers by a lake, Trevelyan said: "Populous, which means they had efficient agriculture and transportation, at least in their most advanced regions. I can identify railway lines and the traces of roads. Early industrial, I'd guess, combustion engines, possible limited use of electricity. . . . But they had more aesthetic sense, or something, than most cultures at that technological level. They kept beauty around them." He hauled his thoughts away from what that implied. If he did not stay impersonal, he must weep.

"Did they succumb to radiation effects alone?" Smokesmith wondered. He appeared to have no trouble maintaining detachment. But then, he did not feel humanlike emotions, as Trevelyan judged the dead beings had. "Shelter was available."

"Maybe they didn't know about radioactivity. Or maybe the escapers were too few, too scattered, too badly mutated. Anyhow, they're gone— Hold!"

Trevelyan's hands danced over the board. *Genji* swung about, backtracked, and came to hover.

Atmosphere blurred the magnified view, but beams, detectors, and computer analysis helped. A town stood on an island in a wide river. Thus, despite the bridges that soared from bank to bank, it was not thickly begrown by vegetation. What had entered was largely cleared away: recent work, the rawness identifiable. The job had been done by machines, a couple of which stood openly in a central plaza. Trevelyan couldn't spot details, but never doubted they were Earthmade robotic types. Several buildings had been blasted, either as too ruinous or as being in the way, and the rubble shoved aside. He got no indications of current activity, but strong electronic resonance suggested that a modern power network was partly completed.

"Murdoch," Trevelyan said like a curse.

"Can you obtain indications of his ship?" the Reardonite asked.

"No. When he detected us approaching, he must have moved her, and screened as well as camouflaged the hull. Maybe he hoped we wouldn't chance to notice what he's been up to, or maybe this is another gibe. Certainly he must've gotten busy here the instant he landed, after choosing the site on his first visit."

Trevelyan put the speedster back into orbit. For a while the conn held only a humming silence. The planet filled half the sky with clouds, seas, sunrises and sunsets; the other half was stars.

"No autochthons left," Smokesmith mused at last. "Their relics are of limited scientific interest. Will this be adjudged grounds for sending armed craft, that are badly needed elsewhere, to make him stop?"

"Supposing it is—that's uncertain, as you say, but supposing it is—*can* they stop him?" Trevelyan seized the controls again. The power hum deepened. "Prepare for descent."

He chose a city near the edge of morning, that he might have a long daylight. A mole jutted from the waterfront into an emerald-and-sapphire bay. Sonic beams declared it to be of reinforced concrete, as firm as the day it was dedicated. He landed there, and presently walked forth. A grav sled would have taken him faster and easier, but part of his aim was to get to know somewhat about those who were departed. His ship, all systems on standby, fell behind him like a coppery cenotaph.

He didn't worry about the safety of the environment. Murdoch had proven that for him. What had still to be learned was mere detail: for instance, what imported crops would do well?

Any number, Trevelyan felt sure. It was a rich and generous planet. No doubt it had been more so before the catastrophe, but it remained wonderful enough, and nature was fast healing the wounds.

The bay glittered and chuckled between golden-green hills. At its entrance began an ocean; coming down, he had identified fantastically big shoals of marine plants and animals. No wings rode the wind that rumpled his hair. Most, perhaps all vertebrates were extinct. But lower forms had survived the disaster. Insects, or their equivalent, swarmed on delicate membranes that often threw back the sunlight in rainbows. Silvery forms leaped from the water. The wind smelled of salt, iodine, and life.

Overhead wandered some clouds, blue-shadowed in a dazzlingly blue heaven. At this season, the supernova was aloft by day, invisible. Dis-aster, Trevelyan thought with a shudder. How little had Earth's ancient astrologers known of how terrible a word they were shaping!

But the day was sunny, cool, and peaceful. He walked shoreward, looking.

The watercraft had sunk or drifted free of their rotted lines. However, the shallower water inshore was so clear that he could see a few where they lay, somewhat preserved. The gracious outlines of the sailboats did not astonish him; that demand was imposed by natural law. But his eyes stung to think that the dead had loved sloops and yawls as much as he did. And they had put bronze figureheads on many, whose green-corroded remnants hinted at flowers. wings, flames, anything fair and free. A large ship had drifted aground. It had been iron-hulled and, judging from the stacks, steam-propelled. But it, no, she had also been designed to look like a dancer on the waves.

He neared the quay. A row of wooden warehouses (?) was partly moldered away, partly buried under vines. Nevertheless he could make out how roofs once swept in high curves that the doorways matched. A rusting machine, probably a crane, was decorated at the end of its lifting arm with a merry animal face.

He stood for some while before an arch at the head of the

mole. Here the dwellers had represented themselves.

Their art was not photographic. It had a swing of line and mass that woke a pulse in Trevelyan, it was not quite like anything he had ever seen before. But the bipeds with their long slim six-fingered hands, long necks, and long-beaked heads, came through to him as if still alive. He almost thought he could hear their stone cloaks flap in the wind.

Walking farther into the city, he began to find their bones.

Carrion eaters had seldom or never disturbed them. Dust blew in, settled on pavement, became soil; seeds followed, struck frail roots that gradually crumbled brick and concrete; bushes and vines grew over that first carpet and up the walls; those kinds of trees that survived extended their range into the domains of trees that had not, and beyond that into farm and town. But the invasion was slow. The wilderness had all the time in the world. It was in full occupation of the shoreward edges of this city, and reducing the next line, but as yet just a few forerunners and (Trevelyan thought with a hurtful smile) sappers had won this near the waterfront.

The buildings of granite, marble, and masonry rose tall, washed by rain and sunlight, little damaged by weather, only occasional creepers blurring their outlines. Like the relief sculpture on their walls, they leaped and soared, not as man-built skyscrapers do but in that peculiar rhythm which made their heights seem to fly. They were colonnaded, balustraded, many-windowed, and kept some of the coloring that once softened their austerity.

Trevelyan wondered at the absense of parks or gardens. His observations from altitude had suggested a deep-reaching love of landscape and care for it. And floral motifs were about the commonest decorations. Well, the dwellers had not been human; it would take long to get some insight into what their race psyche might have been. Maybe they enjoyed the contrast of art and openness. If this place was typical, every city was a delight to live in. At some economic sacrifice, the dwellers had avoided filling their air and water with noise, dirt, and poison. To be sure, they were lucky that no heating was required. But as far as Trevelyan had been able to ascertain, industrial plants were widely scattered outside urban limits, connected by railways. There were no automobiles, though that was probably within the technological capabilities. Instead, he found the depictions, and some bones, of large quadrupeds that served like horses; he also identified the hulks of what appeared to have been public vehicles with primitive electric motors. It was hard to tell after four hundred years, but he at least got the impression that, while theirs was a productive and prosperous civilization, the dwellers had not created overly much trash either. They could have foreseen the problem and taken steps. He'd like to know.

Not that they were saints. He came upon statues and dimmed murals which showed combat. Twice, above inscriptions he would never interpret, he saw a being dressed in rags bursting chains off himself; no doubt somebody put those chains on in the first place. But oftenest he found imagery which he read as of affection, gentleness, work, teaching, discovery, or the sheer splendor of being alive.

He entered courtyards, walked past dried pools and fountains, on into the buildings. Few had elevators, which was suggestive since the culture could have supplied them. He noted that the shafts of the wide circular staircases would easily accommodate grav lifts. The murals indoors were scarcely faded; their vividness took some of the grief off him. Nevertheless, and although he was not superstitious or even especially religious, he knocked on the first door he came to.

Every door was sliding or folding, none bore locks or latches, which again implied unusual traits. The majority of apartments had been deserted. Cloth had decayed, metal tarnished, plaster cracked, and dust fallen centimeters thick. But the furnishings remained usable by humans, who were formed quite like the dwellers. Clean and patch up; restore the water supply; make do with the airily shaped oil lanterns, if need be, and a camp stove since the original owners didn't seem to have cooked anything; throw padding over chairs, divans, beds, intricately grained floors: and you would be altogether comfortable. Soon power would become available, and you could change the place around at your leisure until it was ideal.

Early in the game, though, you'd better get rid of those pictures, papers, enigmatic tools, and shelves full of books. They could be disturbing to live with.

As the hours passed, Trevelyan did find skeletons in a few apartments. Either these individuals had died by surprise, like those he infrequently noticed in the streets, or they desired privacy for their final day. One lay in a kind of chaise longue, with a book upon what had been the lap. Twice he found small skeletons covered by a large one. Did the mother understand that death was coming from the sky? Yes, she could see it up there, a point of radiance too brilliant to look near, surrounded by the auroras it evoked in this atmosphere. Probably she knew the death was everywhere. But she was driven by the instinct of Niobe.

When he discovered the ossuary, Trevelyan decided there must be several, and this was how the average dweller had elected to go. It was in a large hall—theater? auditorium? temple? The most susceptible must already have died, and radiation sickness be upon the rest. In man it approaches its terminus with nausea, vomiting, hair coming out, internal bleeding, blood from the orifices and eyes, strengthlessness, fever, and delirium. Doubtless it was similar for the dwellers.

Outside were the remnants of several improvised coal furnaces. Their pipes fed into the sealed hall, carbon monoxide generators. Bones and rusted weaons nearby suggested the operators had finished their task and then themselves. The door was the single tightly fastened one Trevelyan had encountered, but being wooden it yielded to his boot in a cloud of punk. Beyond lay the skeletons of adults, hundreds of them, and many more young, and toys, games, cups, banners, musical instruments—*I don't know what they did at that party,* Trevelyan thought, *but if we humans had the same guts, we'd tell the children that Carnival came early this year.*

He walked back out into the bright quiet. Something like a butterfly went past, though its wings were fairer than anything evolved on Earth. Being a little of an antiquarian, he said aloud: "The Lord giveth and the Lord taketh away; I will not bless the name of the Lord. But I will remember. Oh, yes, I will remember."

He had not gone much farther toward the middle of town when he heard a thunder rumble. Looking up past the towertops, he saw the great shining form of *Campesino* descend. She came between him and the sun and covered him with her shadow.

Reflexively, he took shelter in a doorway. One hand dropped to his pistol. With a sour grin at himself, he activated the tiny radio transceiver in his tunic pocket. On the standard band, he heard Murdoch's voice: "Cordy ahoy! Respond!"

The empty speedster made no reply. A drone and a quivering went through the air as *Campesino* balanced on her gravs.

"You!" Murdoch barked. "We picked up your tachyons halfway to here. We followed you down by your neutrinos. Don't try bluffing us about having a friend in reserve. You're alone, and we've got a cyclic blast zeroed in, and I want to speak with you."

More silence in the receivers. Trevelyan felt the sweat on his ribs, under his arms, and smelled it. He could not foretell what would happen. At best, he had sketched behavior patterns Murdoch might adopt and responses he might make. His plan amounted to creating a situation where he could improvise . . . whether successfully or not.

A barely distinguishable background growl: "No one inside, I'd guess. Exploring the city?"

"Could be," Murdoch said. "Odd they'd leave their boat unguarded."

"A trap?"

"Well—maybe. Don't seem Cordy style, but maybe we better keep clear."

Trevelyan did in fact wish *Campesino* to set down elsewhere, making *Genji* less of a hostage. He decided to push matters, trod forth, and shot a flash from his gun into the air. It crackled. Ozone touched his nostrils.

"Look! Below! You, d'you read us?"

Trevelyan saw no sense in giving away the fact that he could listen. He might gain some slight advantage thereby; and Cosmos knew, with that metal storm cloud hanging above him, he needed whatever help he could get. He waved and jogged off toward the city center, where he had noticed a plaza from above.

After a conference he couldn't make out, the others did what he would have done in their place. *Campesino* opened a hatch and discharged a grav sled with a man or two aboard. Not carrying missiles, she could give them no effective armament. But they would hover near *Genji* and cry warning of anything suspicious. The ship herself dropped behind the towers. When she landed, the ground trembled and echoes boomed slowly from wall to wall.

Trevelyan switched off his radio speaker, turned on the transmitter, and hastened his trot. Once he accidentally kicked a skull. It rolled aside with a dry clatter. *I'm sorry*, he thought to it. That being not altogether alien to him had felt this street underfoot, sunwarmth reflected off cataract-like façades, muscle movement, heartbeat, breath. The city had lived around the being, with friends, loves, traffic, music, pleasure . . . did the race laugh? *I may be joining you soon*, he added, and scorned himself for the juvenilism.

He emerged not on a square but a golden rectangle. Grassy growth was thrusting up and apart those blocks which had paved it, but the rains of four centuries had not quite washed out the grooves worn by generations of feet. The enclosing buildings were lower here. Their lines bespoke tranquility rather than excitement, though three of them held the fragments of dazzling stained-glass windows. Numerous skeletons lay prostrated before one. *Campesino* rose brutal from the plaza center.

Several men and not-men waited, guns at the ready. They were a hard-looking gang. Murdoch stood at ease, Faustina tensed beside him. Both wore black coveralls with silver ornamentation. Her hair glowed in the light. Trevelyan approached at a reduced pace, hands well away from his pistol.

"Mike!" the adventurer bawled. He threw back his head in laughter that made his moustaches vibrate. "Why the chaos didn't I expect you'd be the one?"

"Who else with you?" Faustina said.

Trevelyan shrugged. "Who with you?" he countered.

"You've seen our roster," Murdoch said. "I figured you'd refuse to board, afraid we'd grab you, so I came out." He jerked a thumb at the sheer hull behind. "Got a full compliment inside at alert stations."

Trevelyan achieved a smile. "What makes you expect trouble, Juan?" he asked in his mildest voice.

Murdoch blinked. "Why . . . you dogged us clear from Earth—"

"No, think," Trevelyan said. "Space is free. The Coordination Service investigates where it can, but forbids violence to its agents except under extreme necessity. You know that as well as I do."

The guards around shifted stance, muttered among themselves, flicked eyes from side to side. Trevelyan virtually felt the unease in them.

"For example," he drawled, "you're breaking the law here, first by not reporting a discovery—"

"We've only just made it!" Fausina said. Red stained the white cheekbones. Her fists were clenched. He studied her for a moment, thinking with compassion: *She's afraid I'll take away her glory—her chance to rake in money until she can lose the fear of being poor that was ground into her,* and with caution: *In an aggressive human personality, fear begets ruthlessness.*

"Please let me finish," he said. "I'm not interested in lodging charges, nor would my superiors be. The offense probably occurs hundreds of times a year, and seldom matters. Out of necessity, the Service operates on the old principle that the law should not concern itself with trifles."

She stepped back, breathing hard, lips pulled away from teeth, but plainly bemused. Murdoch's massive features had grown immobile. "Continue," he said.

"You've committed a more important breach of law by tampering with and destroying material of scientific value." Trevelyan kept his tone amiable and a faint smile on his mouth. "I refer to that island city. But the planet is such an archaeological and biological Golconda that we'll overlook your indiscretion, we'll put it down to an amateur's forgivable enthusiasm, in exchange for the service you've done to civilization by bringing this world to our knowledge. You'll remember an agent like me has authority to issue pardons in minor cases. I'll write you one today, if you wish, and recommend you for next year's Polaris Medal into the bargain."

He offered his hand. "Stop worrying," he said. "Let's have a drink and go home together."

Murdoch did not take the hand. The big man stood for a while, staring, and the silence of the dead grew and grew. He broke it with a whisper: "Are you serious?"

Trevelyan dropped pretense. He said in a hardened voice, while his nerves felt the surrounding guns: "It's an honest offer. You already have Good Luck to make your living off. Be content with that."

"Good Luck?" Faustina cried. She swept one arm in a taloned arc. "You incredible idiot! *This* is Good Luck!"

"I kept hoping it wasn't," Trevelyan said low.

"What do you figure I had in mind?" Murdoch demanded.

"Obvious," Trevelyan sighed. "Here was your real discovery. But how to exploit it? You couldn't get a patent, because the Union would forbid colonization until the scientists finished their researches. Considering the distance, and the shortage of personnel, and the vast amount there is to study, that would take at least a hundred years, probably longer. In fact, the odds are we'd put a secrecy seal on the co-ordinates for a decade or two, to keep unqualified visitors away until a big enough enterprise got started that the scientists could do their own guarding."

"Scientists!" Faustina nearly shrieked. Murdoch laid a warning grip on her arm. His predator's gaze stayed on Trevelyan.

"What a means to a fortune, though!" the Co-ordinator said. "You could offer an utterly desirable home, complete with every facility for hundreds of millions of people, at a price the ordinary colonial can afford. You stood to become one of the wealthiest humans that ever lived.

"Well, you went looking for a world we wouldn't disallow. What you turned up isn't particularly good. But it's no worse than some which have been settled, and at least doesn't have a population already squeezing its meager resources. People would buy your real estate there, if the preliminary work had been done for them and the cost was not beyond their means.

"Some you actually would take to the marginal planet—say when an agent like me happened to be around. You'd lose money on them. But it wouldn't matter, because most would be shipped here, where entire cities cost you practically nothing. They'd write home. Your ships would carry the overjoyed mail, maybe censoring it a wee bit to keep us Cordys from getting wind of your enterprise too soon. Not that we'd be likely to, when we're run off our feet with urgent cases, and when few people on those thousands of entire worlds give us any active co-operation. You could carry on for a number of years, I'm sure, before the discrepancies got so glaring that we investigated.''

"What'd you do after you learned?'' Murdoch asked.

"Nothing,'' Trevelyan said. "How could we displace tens of thousands, maybe millions of men, women, and children, who'd come in good faith, started a good new life, put down roots, begun bringing forth a new generation? It'd be a political impossibility, a moral one, maybe a physical one. They'd fight for their homes, and we couldn't bomb them, could we?

"You personally would be subject to—in theory, confiscation of your properties and imprisonment of your body. In practice, you'd have put both where we couldn't touch them without more effort and killing than it was worth. You'd have rigged the colonial government and its constitution early in the game to make you something like the Founding Father president of Good Luck. They'd fight for you too. So, rather than violate its own prohibition on conquest—for the sake of scientific and aesthetic values that'd already been ruined—the Union would accept what you'd done to it.''

Trevelyan closed his mouth. He felt hoarse and tired and wanted a smoke, but didn't dare reach for his pipe under those guns.

Murdoch nodded. "You read me good.'' He chuckled. "Thanks for the Founding Father title. I hadn't thought of that. Sounds like what I need.''

"I can't allow it, you know,'' Trevelyan said.

"Why not?'' Murdoch grew curiously earnest. "What's here, really? A worldful of bones. I'm sorry it happened, but dead's dead. And they were, well, one more race among millions. What can we learn from them that matters? Oh, I suppose you can hope for a few technique or art form or whatever, that'll revolutionize civilization. But you prob'ly understand better than me how small that chance is. Meanwhile, yonder we've got people who're alive, and hurting, now.''

"The planet will be opened for settlement, region by

region, in due course.''

"How long is due course? How many'll die during it, that could've lived happier?''

"Emigrants are always replaced at home by fresh births. In the long run, the exact time of migration makes no difference.''

"Forget the long run and think about flesh and blood.''

Trevelyan's anger broke his control. "Don't hand me that guff, Murdoch,'' he snapped. "You're about as altruistic as a blast cannon.''

"And you,'' Faustina spat, "you're a machine. I look forward to killing you—dismantling you!''

"Wait, wait, there,'' Murdoch said. "Ease off and let's talk sane.''

He regarded the ground for a moment before he straightened, faced Trevelyan squarely, and said:

"I'll tell you how it lies. When we knew we were being dogged, we decided to lead you on, because once the supernova got reported, this sector 'ud be swarmed and somebody else might find our Good Luck.

"You could've skited for home without landing. If you'd done that, we'd've made for the nearest human planets to here. We'd've rallied a lot of men, transported 'em free, gotten well dug in before you could raise any action at headquarters. It might've been enough to stop you from doing anything.''

"I assumed that was your plan,'' Trevelyan said. "On my way back, I'll visit every Scorpian world and announce, without specifying location too closely, that this planet is interdicted to preserve cultural values. To come here then, knowingly, will justify and require violence by the Service. We do have to maintain the precedent.''

"What makes you think you're going back?'' asked Faustina. She grinned with hatred.

"Ease off,'' Murdoch repeated. To Trevelyan: "I did hope you'd land, like you have. Waved a large red flag at you, didn't I? You see, I knew you must have less beef than my ship. Now I've got you.''

"What will you do with me?" the Co-ordinator replied.

"Well, uh, I'll admit some of my mates got a little, uh, vehement," Murdoch said. "But I don't see any point in killing you. I sure don't want to. You're not a bad osco, Mike, for a Cordy. And they can't have any idea on Earth which way we headed. I'm not about to return there; I've done my credit arranging. If they ask me about you later on, why, I never had any notion you were trying to follow me. You must've come to grief somehow, and I'm awful sorry. Maybe I'll use your boat to fake some clues."

His mask of bashfulness fell away. He beamed. "Tell you what, Mike," he said. "Let's find you a nice island out in mid-ocean. We'll leave you tools and supplies and show you what's safe to eat. You Cordys are supposed to be philosophers. You should be glad of a few years for thinking. If you want, I'll try to get you a woman. And soon's I can, I'll flit you to our spaceport we'll've built. How's that for a fair proposition?"

Trevelyan savored the breath he drew, the light he saw, the will rising within him like a physical tide. "Let me be sure I understand you," he said. "Do you seriously intend to maroon me in order that I won't report the facts of this case?"

"Too good for you," Faustina said. "But if Juan's that tender-spirited, yes."

"Do you realize that this involves grave violations of personal integrity?" Trevelyan asked. "Do you realize that it involves direct interference with an officer of the Union in the performance of his duty?"

Murdoch flushed. "Obscenity your duty!"

"I demand you let me go back to my spacecraft and depart unmolested," Trevelyan said.

Faustina snickered.

"You will not?" Trevelyan asked. He waited. A breeze whispered.

"Very well," he said. "I can now testify under brainphasing that you are guilty of attempted crimes sufficient to justify your arrest. Will you come quietly with me?"

"Have you lost your orbit?" Murdoch exclaimed.

"Since you resist arrest in addition," Trevelyan said, "the necessity of applying force becomes incontestable."

The guards jabbered, swore, and brought their weapons to bear. Faustina hissed. Murdoch's hand streaked to his own pistol.

Trevelyan ostentatiously folded his arms and said: "If my Service does not respect your rights, civilization is worthless. But civilization has rights of its own. I admit I led your thoughts away from my partner"—he heard a gasp and an oath—"but that scarcely constitutes entrapment. He's under a roof in this city, on an accumulator-powered grav sled, along with several nuclear missiles. Through a miniradio in my pocket, he's been listening to our conversation. If you don't surrender yourselves, he'll destroy you."

He paid scant attention to the uproar of the guards. His focus was entirely on their leaders.

Murdoch yanked a transceiver from his jacket to speak an order. "Give them a demonstration, Smokesmith," Trevelyan said.

No one saw the torpedo rise. It went too fast. Momentarily the sky was bedazzled with hell-colored flame. Concussion smote, not unduly hard from that altitude, but it shook men where they stood and bellowed in their ears. The bones before the temple shuddered.

"A bit close," Trevelyan said. He was aware that his own body quivered and went dry in the mouth. A remote part of him decided this was an unintegrate reaction and he needed more training. Speech and reasoning mind, though, were steel cool. "We may want antirad shots. I think you'll agree, Juan, the next can drop right here. Afterward my Reardonite friend won't have trouble picking off your watchmen."

"You'll be dead too," Murdoch groaned.

"I don't want to be," Trevelyan said, "but rather more is at stake than what I want."

Faustina whipped around behind Murdoch. She snatched

his gun from the holster, flung herself forward, and rammed the muzzle into Trevelyan's belly. "Oof!" he choked. *I don't exactly cut a heroic figure, do I?* flashed through him. *But the beings here only had what dignity they could make for themselves, after heaven's meaningless anger fell on them.*

"I'll kill you myself!" she raved.

He knew tricks for knocking the weapon aside and taking it from her. But others were trained on him. He met her eyes, from which the tears went flooding, and said: "If you do, why should my partner not destroy you?"

Murdoch wrenched the gun from her. She raked at his face. He knocked her down. Panting, sweat a-river on his skin, he said: "What do you want?"

"If you know something about Reardonites," Trevelyan said, and saw that Murdoch did, "you'll realize it won't bother Smokesmith to annihilate me along with you. But he agrees it's undesirable. So is the destruction of this beautiful plaza. Let's compromise."

"I asked what do you want, you devil?"

"Safe conduct back to my vessel. Smokesmith will monitor me by radio. Your ship will stay put. At the first sign of any ill faith whatsoever, he shoots. At worst, you see, he must eliminate both ships and hope this world gets rediscovered by someone who'll respect it. Once aloft, I'll quickly drop down again and pick him up, too quickly for you to rise. At that point you'll be helpless; but have no fears. With a head start and a faster craft, I'll be on the frontier planets before you, issuing prohibitions. No one's going to follow you when he knows it'll bring warships down on him. I suggest you find an obscure place and lie low."

Murdoch beat fist into palm, again and again. For a minute he looked old and hollowed out.

Then his mirth awoke. "You win this 'un, too, Mike," he said. "I'll escort you to your boat personal. Here." He offered his pistol. Trevelyan accepted it.

Faustina sat up. A bruise was spreading on her slim jaw

where her lover's fist had smitten. She looked at them both, through tears and matted locks, and was no longer anything except a bewildered beaten child.

"Why?" she pleaded. "Why can't we have a patent—when w-w-we found the supernova for you? You'd do this—wreck everything for . . . two, three hundred s-s-specialists—and their *curiosity*?"

Trevelyan hunkered down before her. He took both her hands in one of his. The other pointed around, ending at the temple. "No," he said most gently. "For these. Have they no rights? That someone shall come to know them, and they won't be lost from us."

But she did not understand. We guard the great Pact, which is the heart of civilization, of society, and ultimately of life itself: the unspoken Pact between the living, the dead, and the unborn, that to the best of poor mortal abilities they shall all be kept one in the oneness of time. Without it, nothing would have meaning and it may be that nothing would survive. But the young generations so often do not understand.

GOAT
SONG

By way of contrast to the foregoing, here is a story which on the one hand uses ancient motifs in the fantasy tradition, and on the other hand is strict science fiction in the sense of using no concept that the most conservative scientist could say is theoretically impossible. As a matter of fact, I don't think anything in it is even technologically impossible. That scares me.

THREE WOMEN: one is dead; one is alive; One is both and neither, and will never live and never die, being immortal in SUM.

On a hill above that valley through which runs the highroad, I await Her passage. Frost came early this year, and the grasses have paled. Otherwise the slope is begrown with blackberry bushes that have been harvested by men and birds, leaving only briars, and with certain apple trees. They are very old, those trees, survivors of an orchard raised by generations which none but SUM now remembers (I can see a few fragments of wall thrusting above the brambles)— scattered crazily over the hillside and as crazily gnarled. A little fruit remains on them. Chill across my skin, a gust shakes loose an apple. I hear it knock on the earth, another stroke of some eternal clock. The shrubs whisper to the wind.

Elsewhere the ridges around me are wooded, afire with scarlets and brasses and bronzes. The sky is huge, the westering sun wanbright. The valley is filling with a deeper blue, a haze whose slight smokiness touches my nostrils. This is Indian summer, the funeral pyre of the year.

There have been other seasons. There have been other lifetimes, before mine and hers; and in those days they had words to sing with. We still allow ourselves music, though, and I have spent much time planting melodies around my rediscovered words. *"In the greenest growth of the May-time—"* I unsling the harp on my back, and tune it afresh, and sing it to her, straight into autumn and the waning day.

> "—You came, and the sun came after,
>   And the green grew golden above:
> And the flag-flowers lightened with laughter,
>   And the meadowsweet shook with love."

A footfall stirs the grasses, quite gently, and the woman says, trying to chuckle, "Why, thank you."

Once, so soon after my one's death that I was still dazed by it, I stood in the home that had been ours. This was on the hundred and first floor of a most desirable building. After dark the city flamed for us, blinked, glittered, flung immense sheets of radiance forth like banners. Nothing but SUM could have controlled the firefly dance of a million aircars among the towers: or, for that matter, have maintained the entire city, from nuclear powerplants through automated factories, physical and economic distribution networks, sanitation, repair, services, education, culture, order, everything as one immune immortal organism. We had gloried in belonging to this as well as to each other.

But that night I told the kitchen to throw the dinner it had made for me down the waste chute, and ground under my heel the chemical consolations which the medicine cabinet extended to me, and kicked the cleaner as it picked up the mess, and ordered the lights not to go on, anywhere in our suite. I stood by the vieWall, looking out across megalopolis, and it was tawdry. In my hands I had a little clay figure she had fashioned herself. I turned it over and over and over.

But I had forgotten to forbid the door to admit visitors. It recognized this woman and opened for her. She had come with the kindly intention of teasing me out of a mood that seemed to her unnatural. I heard her enter, and looked around through the gloom. She had almost the same height as my girl did, and her hair chanced to be bound in a way that my girl often favored, and the figurine dropped from my grasp and shattered, because for an instant I thought she was my girl. Since then I have been hard put not to hate Thrakia.

This evening, even without so much sundown light, I would not make that mistake. Nothing but the silvery bracelet about her left wrist bespeaks the past we share. She is in wildcountry garb: boots, kilt of true fur and belt of true leather, knife at hip and rifle slung on shoulder. Her locks are matted and snarled, her skin brown from weeks of weather; scratches and smudges show beneath the fantastic zigzags she has painted in many colors on herself. She wears a necklace of bird skulls.

Now that one who is dead was, in her own way, more a child of trees and horizons than Thrakia's followers. She was so much at home in the open that she had no need to put off clothes or cleanliness, reason or gentleness, when we sickened of the cities and went forth beyond them. From this trait I got many of the names I bestowed on her, such as Wood's Colt or Fallow Hind or, from my prowlings among ancient books, Dryad and Elven. (She liked me to choose her names, and this pleasure had no end, because she was inexhaustible.)

I let my harpstring ring into silence. Turning about, I say to Thrakia, "I wasn't singing for you. Not for anyone. Leave me alone."

She draws a breath. The wind ruffles her hair and brings me an odor of her: not female sweetness, but fear. She clenches her fists and says, "You're crazy."

"Wherever did you find a meaningful word like that?" I gibe; for my own pain and—to be truthful—my own fear must strike out at something, and here she stands. "Aren't you content any longer with 'untranquil' or 'disequilibrated'?"

"I got it from you," she says defiantly, "you and your damned archaic songs. There's another word, 'damned.' And how it suits you! When are you going to stop this morbidity?"

"And commit myself to a clinic and have my brain laundered nice and sanitary? Not soon, darling." I use *that* last word aforethought, but she cannot know what scorn and sadness are in it for me, who know that once it could also have been a name for my girl. The official grammar and pronunciation of language is as frozen as every other aspect of our civilization, thanks to electronic recording and neuronic teaching; but meanings shift and glide about like subtle serpents. (O adder that stung my Foalfoot!)

I shrug and say in my driest, most city-technological voice, "Actually, I'm the practical, nonmorbid one. Instead of running away from my emotions—via drugs, or neuroadjustment, or playing at savagery like you, for that matter—I'm about to implement a concrete plan for getting back the person who made me happy."

"By disturbing Her on Her way home?"

"Anyone has the right to petition the dark Queen while she's abroad on earth."

"But this is past the proper time—"

"No law's involved, just custom. People are afraid to meet Her outside a crowd, a town, bright flat lights. They won't admit it, but they are. So I came here precisely not to be part of a queue. I don't want to speak into a recorder for subsequent computer analysis of my words. How could I be sure She was listening? I want to meet Her as myself, a unique being, and look in Her eyes while I make my prayer.''

Thrakia chokes a little. "She'll be angry.''

"Is She able to be angry, anymore?''

"I . . . I don't know. What you mean to ask for is so impossible, though. So absurd. That SUM should give you back your girl. You know It never makes exceptions.''

"Isn't She Herself an exception?''

"That's different. You're being silly. SUM has to have a, well, a direct human liaison. Emotional and cultural feedback, as well as statistics. How else can It govern rationally? And She must have been chosen out of the whole world. Your girl, what was she? Nobody!''

"To me, she was everybody.''

"You—'' Thrakia catches her lip in her teeth. One hand reaches out and closes on my bare forearm, a hard hot touch, the grimy fingernails biting. When I make no response, she lets go and stares at the ground. A V of outbound geese passes overhead. Their cries come shrill through the wind, which is loudening in the forest.

"Well,'' she says, "you are special. You always were. You went to space and came back, with the Great Captain. You're maybe the only man alive who understands about the ancients. And your singing, yes, you don't really entertain, your songs trouble people and can't be forgotten. So maybe She will listen to you. But SUM won't. It can't give special resurrections. Once that was done, a single time, wouldn't it have to be done for everybody? The dead would overrun the living.''

"Not necessarily,'' I say. "In any event, I mean to try.''

"Why can't you wait for the promised time? Surely, then, SUM will re-create you two in the same generation.''

"I'd have to live out this life, at least, without her,'' I say, looking away also, down to the highroad which shines through shadow like death's snake, the length of the valley. "Besides, how do you know there ever will be any resurrections? We have only a promise. No, less than that. An announced policy.''

She gasps, steps back, raises her hands as if to fend me off.
Her soul bracelet casts light into my eyes. I recognize an
embryo exorcism. She lacks ritual; every "superstition" was
• patiently scrubbed out of our metal-and-energy world, long
ago. But if she has no word for it, no concept, nevertheless
she recoils from blasphemy.

So I say, wearily, not wanting an argument, wanting only
to wait here alone: "Never mind. There could be some
natural catastrophe, like a giant asteroid striking, that wiped
out the system before conditions had become right for resurrections to commence."

"That's impossible," she says, almost frantic. "The ho-
meostats, the repair functions—"

"All right, call it a vanishingly unlikely theoretical con-
tingency. Let's declare that I'm so selfish I want Swallow
Wing back now, in this life of mine, and don't give a curse
whether that'll be fair to the rest of you. "

You won't care either, anyway, I think. None of you. You
don't grieve. It is your own precious private consciousnesses
that you wish to preserve; no one else is close enough to you
to matter very much. Would you believe me if I told you I am
quite prepared to offer SUM my own death in exchange for It
releasing Blossom-in-the-Sun?

I don't speak that thought, which would be cruel, nor
repeat what is crueller: my fear that SUM lies, that the dead
never will be disgorged. For (I am not the All-Controller, I
think not with vacuum and negative energy levels but with
ordinary begotten molecules; yet I can reason somewhat
dispassionately, being disillusioned) consider—

The object of the game is to maintain a society stable, just,
and sane. This requires satisfaction not only of somatic, but
of symbolic and instinctual needs. Thus children must be
allowed to come into being. The minimum number per generation is equal to the maximum: that number which will
maintain a constant population.

It is also desirable to remove the fear of death from men.

Hence the promise: At such time as it is socially feasible, SUM will begin to refashion us, with our complete memories but in the pride of our youth. This can be done over and over, life after life across the millennia. So death is, indeed, a sleep.

—in that sleep of death, what dreams may come— No. I myself dare not dwell on this. I ask merely, privately: Just when and how does SUM expect conditions (in a stabilized society, mind you) to have become so different from today's that the reborn can, in their millions, safely be welcomed back?

I see no reason why SUM should not lie to us. We, too, are objects in the world that It manipulates.

"We've quarreled about this before, Thrakia," I sigh. "Often. Why do you bother?"

"I wish I knew," she answers low. Half to herself, she goes on: "Of course I want to copulate with you. You must be good, the way that girl used to follow you about with her eyes, and smile when she touched your hand, and— But you can't be better than everyone else. That's unreasonable. There are only so many possible ways. So why do I care if you wrap yourself up in silence and go off alone? Is it that that makes you a challenge?"

"You think too much," I say. "Even here. You're a pretend primitive. You visit wildcountry to 'slake inborn atavistic impulses' . . . but you can't dismantle that computer inside yourself and simply feel, simply be."

She bristles. I touched a nerve there. Looking past her, along the ridge of fiery maple and sumac, brassy elm and great dun oak, I see others emerge from beneath the trees. Women exclusively, her followers, as unkempt as she; one has a brace of ducks lashed to her waist, and their blood has trickled down her thigh and dried black. For this movement, this unadmitted mystique has become Thrakia's by now: that not only men should forsake the easy routine and the easy pleasure of the cities, and become again, for a few weeks

each year, the carnivores who begot our species; women too
should seek out starkness, the better to appreciate civilization
when they return.

I feel a moment's unease. We are in no park, with laid-out
trails and campground services. We are in wildcountry. Not
many men come here, ever, and still fewer women; for the
region is, literally, beyond the law. No deed done here is
punishable. We are told that this helps consolidate society, as
the most violent among us may thus vent their passions. But I
have spent much time in wildcountry since my Morning Star
went out—myself in quest of nothing but solitude—and I
have watched what happens through eyes that have also read
anthropology and history. Institutions are developing; ceremonies, tribalisms, acts of blood and cruelty and acts
elsewhere called unnatural are becoming more elaborate and
more expected every year. Then the practitioners go home to
their cities and honestly believe they have been enjoying
fresh air, exercise, and good tension-releasing fun.

Let her get angry enough and Thrakia can call knives to her
aid.

Wherefore I make myself lay both hands on her shoulders,
and meet the tormented gaze, and say most gently, "I'm
sorry. I know you mean well. You're afraid She will be
annoyed and bring misfortune on your people."

Thrakia gulps. "No," she whispers. "That wouldn't be
logical. But I'm afraid of what might happen to you. And
then—" Suddenly she throws herself against me. I feel arms,
breasts, belly press through my tunic, and smell meadows in
her hair and musk in her mouth. "You'd be gone!" she
wails. "Then who'd sing to us?"

"Why, the planet's crawling with entertainers," I
stammer.

"You're more than that," she says. "So much more. I
don't like what you sing, not really—and what you've sung
since that stupid girl died, oh, meaningless, horrible!—but, I
don't know why, I *want* you to trouble me."

Awkward, I pat her back. The sun now stands very little

above the treetops. Its rays slant interminably through the booming, frosting air. I shiver in my tunic and buskins and wonder what to do.

A sound rescues me. It comes from one end of the valley below us, where further view is blocked off by two cliffs; it thunders deep in our ears and rolls through the earth into our bones. We have heard that sound in the cities, and been glad to have walls and lights and multitudes around us. Now we are alone with it, the noise of Her chariot.

The women shriek, I hear them faintly across wind and rumble and my own pulse, and they vanish into the woods. They will seek their camp, dress warmly, build enormous fires; presently they will eat their ecstatics, and rumors are uneasy about what they do after that.

Thrakia seizes my left wrist, above the soul bracelet, and hauls. "Harper, come with me!" she pleads. I break loose from her and stride down the hill toward the road. A scream follows me for a moment.

Light still dwells in the sky and on the ridges, but as I descend into that narrow valley I enter dusk, and it thickens. Indistinct bramblebushes whicker where I brush them, and claw back at me. I feel the occasional scratch on my legs, the tug as my garment is snagged, the chill that I breathe, but dimly. My perceived-outer-reality is overpowered by the rushing of Her chariot and my blood. My inner-universe is fear, yes, but exaltation too, a drunkenness which sharpens instead of dulling the senses, a psychedelia which opens the reasoning mind as well as the emotions; I have gone beyond myself, I am embodied purpose. Not out of need for comfort, but to voice what Is, I return to words whose speaker rests centuries dust, and lend them my own music. I sing:

> "—Gold is my heart, and the world's golden,
>   And one peak tipped with light;
> And the air lies still about the hill
>   With the first fear of night;

Till mystery down the soundless valley
　　Thunders, and dark is here;
And the wind blows, and the light goes,
　　And the night is full of fear.

And I know one night, on some far height,
　　In a tongue I never knew,
I yet shall hear the tidings clear
　　From them that were friends of you.

They'll call the news from hill to hill,
　　Dark and uncomforted,
Earth and sky and the winds; and I
　　Shall know that you are dead.—"

But I have reached the valley floor, and She has come in sight.

Her chariot is unlit, for radar eyes and inertial guides need no lamps, nor sun nor stars. Wheel-less, the steel tear rides on its own roar and thrust of air. The pace is not great, far less than any of our mortals' vehicles are wont to take. Men say the Dark Queen rides thus slowly in order that She may perceive with Her own senses and so be the better prepared to counsel SUM. But now Her annual round is finished; She is homeward bound; until spring She will dwell with It Which is our lord. Why does She not hasten tonight?

Because Death has never a need of haste? I wonder. And as I step into the middle of the road, certain lines from the yet more ancient past rise tremendous within me, and I strike my harp and chant them louder than the approaching car:

"I that in heill was and gladnèss
　　Am trublit now with great sickness
　　And feblit with infirmitie:—
　　　Timor mortis conturbat me."

The car detects me and howls a warning. I hold my ground.

The car could swing around, the road is wide and in any event a smooth surface is not absolutely necessary. But I hope, I believe that She will be aware of an obstacle in Her path, and tune in Her various amplifiers, and find me abnormal enough to stop for. Who, in SUM's world—who, even among the explorers that It has sent beyond in Its unappeasable hunger for data—would stand in a cold wildcountry dusk and shout while his harp snarls

> "Our pleasance here is all vain glory,
> This fals world is but transitory,
> The flesh is bruckle, the Feynd is slee:—
> > *Timor mortis conturbat me.*
>
> The state of man does change and vary,
> Now sound, now sick, now blyth, now sary,
> No dansand mirry, now like to die:—
> > *Timor mortis conturbat me.*
>
> No state in Erd here standis sicker;
> As with the wynd wavis the wicker
> So wannis this world's vanitie:—
> > *Timor mortis conturbat me.—?*"

The car draws alongside and sinks to the ground. I let my strings die away into the wind. The sky overhead and in the west is gray-purple; eastward it is quite dark and a few early stars peer forth. Here, down in the valley, shadows are heavy and I cannot see very well.

The canopy slides back. She stands erect in the chariot, thus looming over me. Her robe and cloak are black, fluttering like restless wings; beneath the cowl Her face is a white blur. I have seen it before, under full light, and in how many thousands of pictures; but at this hour I cannot call it back to my mind, not entirely. I list sharp-sculptured profile and pale lips, sable hair and long green eyes, but these are nothing more than words.

"What are you doing?" She has a lovely low voice; but is it, as oh, how rarely since SUM took Her to Itself, is it the least shaken? "What is that you were singing?"

My answer comes so strong that my skull resonates; for I am borne higher and higher on my tide. "Lady of Ours, I have a petition."

"Why did you not bring it before Me when I walked among men? Tonight I am homebound. You must wait till I ride forth with the new year."

"Lady of Ours, neither You nor I would wish living ears to hear what I have to say."

She regards me for a long while. Do I indeed sense fear also in Her? (Surely not of me. Her chariot is armed and armored, and would react with machine speed to protect Her should I offer violence. And should I somehow, incredibly, kill Her, or wound Her beyond chemosurgical repair, She of all beings has no need to doubt death. The ordinary bracelet cries with quite sufficient radio loudness to be heard by more than one thanatic station, when we die; and in that shielding the soul can scarcely be damaged before the Winged Heels arrive to bear it off to SUM. Surely the Dark Queen's circlet can call still further, and is still better insulated, than any mortal's. And She will most absolutely be re-created. She has been, again and again; death and rebirth every seven years keep Her eternally young in the service of SUM. I have never been able to find out when She was first born.)

Fear, perhaps, of what I have sung and what I might speak?

At last She says—I can scarcely hear through the gusts and creakings in the trees—"Give me the Ring, then."

The dwarf robot which stands by Her throne when She sits among men appears beside Her and extends the massive dull-silver circle to me. I place my left arm within, so that my soul is enclosed. The tablet on the upper surface of the Ring, which looks so much like a jewel, slants away from me; I cannot read what flashes onto the bezel. But the faint glow picks Her features out of murk as She bends to look.

Of course, I tell myself, the actual soul is not scanned. That would take too long. Probably the bracelet which contains the soul has an identification code built in. The Ring sends this to an appropriate part of SUM, Which instantly sends back what is recorded under that code. I hope there is nothing more to it. SUM has not seen fit to tell us.

"What do you call yourself at the moment?" She asks.

A current of bitterness crosses my tide. "Lady of Ours, why should You care? Is not my real name the number I got when I was allowed to be born?"

Calm descends once more upon Her. "If I am to evaluate properly what you say, I must know more about you than these few official data. Name indicates mood."

I too feel unshaken again, my tide running so strong and smooth that I might not know I was moving did I not see time recede behind me. "Lady of Ours, I cannot give You a fair answer. In this past year I have not troubled with names, or with much of anything else. But some people who knew me from earlier days call me Harper."

"What do you do besides make that sinister music?"

"These days, nothing, Lady of Ours. I've money to live out my life, if I eat sparingly and keep no home. Often I am fed and housed for the sake of my songs."

"What you sang is unlike anything I have heard since—" Anew, briefly, that robot serenity is shaken. "Since before the world was stabilized. You should not wake dead symbols, Harper. They walk through men's dreams."

"Is that bad?"

"Yes. The dreams become nightmares. Remember: Mankind, every man who ever lived, was insane before SUM brought order, reason, and peace."

"Well, then," I say, "I will cease and desist if I may have my own dead wakened for me."

She stiffens. The tablet goes out. I withdraw my arm and the Ring is stored away by Her servant. So again She is faceless, beneath flickering stars, here at the bottom of this shadowed valley. Her voice falls cold as the air: "No one can be brought back to life before Resurrection Time is ripe.''

I do not say, "What about You?" for that would be
vicious. What did She think, how did She weep, when SUM
chose Her of all the young on earth? What does She endure in
Her centuries? I dare not imagine.

Instead, I smite my harp and sing, quietly this time:

> "Strew on her roses, roses,
> And never a spray of yew.
> In quiet she reposes:
> Ah! Would that I did too."

The Dark Queen cries, "What are you doing? Are you
really insane?" I go straight to the last stanza.

> "Her cabin'd, ample Spirit
> It flutter'd and fail'd for breath.
> To-night it doth inherit
> The vasty hall of Death."

I know why my songs strike so hard: because they bear
dreads and passions that no one is used to—that most of us
hardly know could exist—in SUM's ordered universe. But I
had not the courage to hope She would be as torn by them as I
see. Has She not lived with more darkness and terror than the
ancients themselves could conceive? She calls, "Who has
died?"

"She had many names, Lady of Ours," I say. "None was
beautiful enough. I can tell You her number, though."

"Your daughter? I . . . sometimes I am asked if a dead
child cannot be brought back. Not often, anymore, when they
go so soon to the crèche. But sometimes. I tell the mother she
may have a new one; but if ever We started re-creating dead
infants, at what age level could We stop?"

"No, this was my woman."

"Impossible!" Her tone seeks to be not unkindly but is,
instead, well-nigh frantic. "You will have no trouble finding

others. You are handsome, and your psyche is, is, is extraordinary. It burns like Lucifer."

"Do You remember the name Lucifer, Lady of Ours?" I pounce. "Then You are old indeed. So old that You must also remember how a man might desire only one woman, but her above the whole world and heaven."

She tries to defend Herself with a jeer: "Was that mutual, Harper? I know more of mankind than you do, and surely I am the last chaste woman in existence."

"Now that she is gone, Lady, yes, perhaps You are. But we— Do you know how she died? We had gone to a wild-country area. A man saw her, alone, while I was off hunting gem rocks to make her a necklace. He approached her. She refused him. He threatened force. She fled. This was desert land, viper land, and she was barefoot. One of them bit her. I did not find her till hours later. By then the poison and the unshaded sun— She died quite soon after she told me what had happened and that she loved me. I could not get her body to chemosurgery in time for normal revival procedures. I had to let them cremate her and take her soul away to SUM."

"What right have you to demand her back, when no one else can be given their own?"

"The right that I love her, and she loves me. We are more necessary to each other than sun or moon. I do not think You could find another two people of whom this is so, Lady. And is not everyone entitled to claim what is necessary to his life? How else can society be kept whole?"

"You are being fantastic," She says thinly. "Let me go."

"No, Lady, I am speaking sober truth. But poor plain words won't serve me. I sing to You because then maybe You will understand." And I strike my harp anew; but it is more to her than Her that I sing.

> "If I had thought thou couldst have died,
>   I might not weep for thee:
> But I forgot, when by thy side,
>   That thou couldst mortal be:

It never through my mind had past
    The time would e'er be o'er,
And I on thee should look my last,
    And thou shouldst smile no more!''

"I cannot—'' She falters. "I do not know—any such feelings—so strong—existed any longer.''

"Now You do, Lady of Ours. And is that not an important datum for SUM?''

"Yes. If true.'' Abruptly She leans toward me. I see Her shudder in the murk, under the flapping cloak, and hear Her jaws clatter with cold. "I cannot linger here. But ride with Me. Sing to Me. I think I can bear it.''

So much have I scarcely expected. But my destiny is upon me. I mount into the chariot. The canopy slides shut and we proceed.

The main cabin encloses us. Behind its rear door must be facilities for Her living on earth; this is a big vehicle. But here is little except curved panels. They are true wood of different comely grains: so She also needs periodic escape from our machine existence, does She? Furnishing is scant and austere. The only sound is our passage, muffled to a murmur for us; and, because their photomultipliers are not activated, the scanners show nothing outside but night. We huddle close to a glower, hands extended toward its fieriness. Our shoulders brush, our bare arms, Her skin is soft and Her hair falls loose over the thrown-back cowl, smelling of the summer which is dead. What, is She still human?

After a timeless time, She says, not yet looking at me: "The thing you sang, there on the highroad as I came near—I do not remember it. Not even from the years before I became what I am.''

"It is older than SUM,'' I answer, "and its truth will outlive It.''

"Truth?'' I see Her tense Herself. "Sing Me the rest.''

My fingers are no longer too numb to call forth chords.

"—Unto the Death gois all Estatis,
Princis, Prelattis, and Potestatis,
Baith rich and poor of all degree:—
　Timor mortis conturbat me.

He takis the knichtis in to the field
Enarmit under helm and scheild;
Victor he is at all mellie:—
　Timor mortis conturbat me.

That strong unmerciful tyrand
Takis, on the motheris breast sowkand,
The babe full of benignitie:—
　Timor mortis conturbat me.

He takis the campion in the stour,
The captain closit in the tour,
The ladie in bour full of bewtie:—"

(There I must stop a moment.)

　"Timor mortis conturbat me.

He sparis no lord for his piscence,
Na clerk for his intelligence;
His awful straik may no man flee:—
　Timor mortis conturbat me."

She breaks me off, clapping hands to ears and half shriek-
ing, "No!"

I, grown unmerciful, pursue Her: "You understand now,
do You not? You are not eternal either. SUM isn't. Not
Earth, not sun, not stars. We hid from the truth. Every one of
us. I too, until I lost the one thing which made everything
make sense. Then I had nothing left to lose, and could look
with clear eyes. And what I saw was Death."

"Get out! Let Me alone!"

"I will not let the whole world alone, Queen, until I get her back. Give me her again, and I'll believe in SUM again. I'll praise It till men dance for joy to hear Its name."

She challenges me with wildcat eyes. "Do you think such matters to It?"

"Well," I shrug, "songs could be useful. They could help achieve the great objective sooner. Whatever that is. 'Optimization of total human activity'—wasn't that the program? I don't know if it still is. SUM has been adding to Itself so long. I doubt if You Yourself understand Its purposes, Lady of Ours."

"Don't speak as if It were alive," She says harshly. "It is a computer-effector complex. Nothing more."

"Are You certain?"

"I—yes. It thinks, more widely and deeply than any human ever did or could; but It is not alive, not aware, It has no consciousness. That is one reason why It decided It needed Me."

"Be that as it may, Lady," I tell Her, "the ultimate result, whatever It finally does with us, lies far in the future. At present I care about that; I worry; I resent our loss of self-determination. But that's because only such abstractions are left to me. Give me back my Lightfoot, and she, not the distant future, will be my concern. I'll be grateful, honestly grateful, and You Two will know it from the songs I then choose to sing. Which, as I said, might be helpful to It."

"You are unbelievably insolent," She says without force.

"No, Lady, just desperate," I say.

The ghost of a smile touches Her lips. She leans back, eyes hooded, and murmurs, "Well, I'll take you there. What happens then, you realize, lies outside My power. My observations, My recommendations, are nothing but a few items to take into account, among billions. However . . . we have a long way to travel this night. Give me what data you think will help you, Harper."

I do not finish the Lament. Nor do I dwell in any other

fashion on grief. Instead, as the hours pass, I call upon those who dealt with the joy (not the fun, not the short delirium, but the joy) that man and woman might once have of each other.

Knowing where we are bound, I too need such comfort.

And the night deepens, and the leagues fall behind us, and finally we are beyond habitation, beyond wildcountry, in the land where life never comes. By crooked moon and waning starlight I see the plain of concrete and iron, the missiles and energy projectors crouched like beasts, the robot aircraft wheeling aloft: and the lines, the relay towers, the scuttling beetle-shaped carriers, that whole transcendent nerve-blood-sinew by which SUM knows and orders the world. For all the flitting about, for all the forces which seethe, here is altogether still. The wind itself seems to have frozen to death. Hoarfrost is gray on the steel shapes. Ahead of us, tiered and mountainous, begins to appear the castle of SUM.

She Who rides with me does not give sign of noticing that my songs have died in my throat. What humanness She showed is departing; Her face is cold and shut, Her voice bears a ring of metal. She looks straight ahead. But She does speak to me for a little while yet:

"Do you understand what is going to happen? For the next half year I will be linked with SUM, integral, another component of It. I suppose you will see Me, but that will merely be My flesh. What speaks to you will be SUM."

"I know." The words must be forced forth. My coming this far is more triumph than any man in creation before me has won; and I am here to do battle for my Dancer-on-Moonglades; but nonetheless my heart shakes me, and is loud in my skull, and my sweat stinks.

I manage, though, to add: "You *will* be a part of It, Lady of Ours. That gives me hope."

For an instant She turns to me, and lays Her hand across mine, and something makes Her again so young and untaken that I almost forget the girl who died; and she whispers, "If you knew how I hope!"

The instant is gone, and I am alone among machines.

We must stop before the castle gate. The wall looms sheer above, so high and high that it seems to be toppling upon me against the westward march of the stars, so black and black that it does not only drink down every light, it radiates blindness. Challenge and response quiver on electronic bands I cannot sense. The outer-guardian parts of It have perceived a mortal aboard this craft. A missile launcher swings about to aim its three serpents at me. But the Dark Queen answers— She does not trouble to be peremptory—and the castle opens its jaws for us.

We descend. Once, I think, we cross a river. I hear a rushing and hollow echoing and see droplets glitter where they are cast onto the viewports and outlined against dark. They vanish at once: liquid hydrogen, perhaps, to keep certain parts near absolute zero?

Much later we stop and the canopy slides back. I rise with Her. We are in a room, or cavern, of which I can see nothing, for there is no light except a dull bluish phosphorescence which streams from every solid object, also from Her flesh and mine. But I judge the chamber is enormous, for a sound of great machines at work comes very remotely, as if heard through dream, while our own voices are swallowed up by distance. Air is pumped through, neither warm nor cold, totally without odor, a dead wind.

We descend to the floor. She stands before me, hands crossed on breast, eyes half shut beneath the cowl and not looking at me nor away from me. "Do what you are told, Harper," She says in a voice that has never an overtone, "precisely as you are told." She turns and departs at an even pace. I watch Her go until I can no longer tell Her luminosity from the formless swirlings within my own eyeballs.

A claw plucks my tunic. I look down and am surprised to see that the dwarf robot has been waiting for me this whole time. How long a time that was, I cannot tell.

Its squat form leads me in another direction. Weariness crawls upward through me, my feet stumble, my lips tingle, lids are weighted and muscles have each their separate aches.

Now and then I feel a jag of fear, but dully. When the robot indicates *Lie down here*, I am grateful.

The box fits me well. I let various wires be attached to me, various needles be injected which lead into tubes. I pay little attention to the machines which cluster and murmur around me. The robot goes away. I sink into blessed darkness.

I wake renewed in body. A kind of shell seems to have grown between my forebrain and the old animal parts. Far away I can feel the horror and hear the screaming and thrashing of my instincts; but awareness is chill, calm, logical. I have also a feeling that I slept for weeks, months, while leaves blew loose and snow fell on the upper world. But this may be wrong, and in no case does it matter. I am about to be judged by SUM.

The little faceless robot leads me off, through murmurous black corridors where the dead wind blows. I unsling my harp and clutch it to me, my sole friend and weapon. So the tranquility of the reasoning mind which has been decreed for me cannot be absolute. I decide that It simply does not want to be bothered by anguish. (No; wrong; nothing so humanlike; It has no desires; beneath that power to reason is nullity.)

At length a wall opens for us and we enter a room where She sits enthroned. The self-radiation of metal and flesh is not apparent here, for light is provided, a featureless white radiance with no apparent source. White, too, is the muted sound of the machines which encompass Her throne. White are Her robe and face. I look away from the multitudinous unwinking scanner eyes, into Hers, but She does not appear to recognize me. Does She even see me? SUM has reached out with invisible fingers of electromagnetic induction and taker Her back into Itself. I do not tremble or sweat—I cannot—but I square my shoulders, strike one plangent chord, and wait for It to speak.

It does, from some invisible place. I recognize the voice It has chosen to use: my own. The overtones, the inflections are true, normal, what I myself would use in talking as one reasonable man to another. Why not? In computing what to

do about me, and in programming Itself accordingly, SUM
must have used so many billion bits of information that
adequate accent is a negligible sub-problem.

No . . . there I am mistaken again . . . SUM does not do
things on the basis that It might as well do them as not. This
talk with myself is intended to have some effect on me. I do
not know what.

"Well," It says pleasantly, "you made quite a journey,
didn't you? I'm glad. Welcome."

My instincts bare teeth to hear those words of humanity
used by the unfeeling unalive. My logical mind considers
replying with an ironic "Thank you," decides against it, and
holds me silent.

"You see," SUM continues after a moment that whirrs,
"you are unique. Pardon Me if I speak a little bluntly. Your
sexual monomania is just one aspect of a generally atavistic,
superstition-oriented personality. And yet, unlike the ordinary misfit, you're both strong and realistic enough to cope
with the world. This chance to meet you, to analyze you
while you rested, has opened new insights for Me on human
psychophysiology. Which may lead to improved techniques
for governing it and its evolution."

"That being so," I reply, "give me my reward."

"Now look here," SUM says in a mild tone, "you if
anyone should know I'm not omnipotent. I was built origi-
nally to help govern a civilization grown too complex.
Gradually, as My program of self-expansion progressed, I
took over more and more decision-making functions. They
were *given* to Me. People were happy to be relieved of
responsibility, and they could see for themselves how much
better I was running things than any mortal could. But to this
day, My authority depends on a substantial consensus. If I
started playing favorites, as by re-creating your girl, well, I'd
have troubles."

"The consensus depends more on awe than on reason," I
say. "You haven't abolished the gods, You've simply absorbed them into Yourself. If You choose to pass a miracle

for me, your prophet singer—and I will be Your prophet if You do this—why, that strengthens the faith of the rest."

"So you think. But your opinions aren't based on any exact data. The historical and anthropological records from the past before Me are unquantitative. I've already phased them out of the curriculum. Eventually, when the culture's ready for such a move, I'll order them destroyed. They're too misleading. Look what they've done to you."

I grin into the scanner eyes. "Instead," I say, "people will be encouraged to think that before the world was, was SUM. All right. I don't care, as long as I get my girl back. Pass me a miracle, SUM, and I'll guarantee You a good payment."

"But I have no miracles. Not in your sense. You know how the soul works. The metal bracelet encloses a pseudo-virus, a set of giant protein molecules with taps directly to the bloodstream and nervous system. They record the chromosome pattern, the synapse flash, the permanent changes, everything. At the owner's death, the bracelet is dissected out. The Winged Heels bring it here, and the information contained is transferred to one of My memory banks. I can use such a record to guide the growing of a new body in the vats: a young body, on which the former habits and recollections are imprinted. But you don't understand the complexity of the process, Harper. It takes Me weeks, every seven years, and every available biochemical facility, to re-create My human liaison. And the process isn't perfect, either. The pattern is affected by storage. You might say that this body and brain you see before you remembers each death. And those are short deaths. A longer one—man, use your sense. Imagine."

I can; and the shield between reason and feeling begins to crack. I had sung, of my darling dead,

> "No motion has she now, no force;
>   She neither hears nor sees;
> Roll'd round in earth's diurnal course,
>   With rocks, and stones, and trees."

Peace, at least. But if the memory-storage is not permanent
but circulating; if, within those gloomy caverns of tubes and
wire and outerspace cold, some remnant of her psyche must
flit and flicker, alone, unremembering, aware of nothing but
having lost life— No!

I smite the harp and shout so the room rings: "Give her
back! Or I'll kill you!"

SUM finds it expedient to chuckle; and, horribly, the smile
is reflected for a moment on the Dark Queen's lips, though
otherwise She never stirs. "And how do you propose to do
that?" It asks me.

It knows, I know, what I have in mind, so I counter: "How
do You propose to stop me?"

"No need. You'll be considered a nuisance. Finally
someone will decide you ought to have psychiatric treatment.
They'll query My diagnostic outlet. I'll recommend certain
excisions."

"On the other hand, since You've sifted my mind by now,
and since You know how I've affected people with my
songs—even the Lady yonder, even Her—wouldn't you
rather have me working for You? With words like, *'O taste,
and see, how gracious the Lord is; blessed is the man that
trusteth in him. O fear the Lord, ye that are his saints; for
they that fear him lack nothing.'* I can make You into God."

"In a sense, I already am God."

"And in another sense not. Not yet." I can endure no
more. "Why are we arguing? You made Your decision
before I woke. Tell me and let me go!"

With an odd carefulness, SUM responds: "I'm still studying you. No harm in admitting to you, My knowledge of the
human psyche is as yet imperfect. Certain areas won't yield
to computation. I don't know precisely what you'd do,
Harper. If to that uncertainty I added a potentially dangerous
precedent—"

"Kill me, then." Let my ghost wander forever with hers,
down in Your cryogenic dreams.

"No, that's also inexpedient. You've made yourself too

conspicuous and controversial. Too many people know by now that you went off with the Lady." Is it possible that, behind steel and energy, a nonexistent hand brushes across a shadow face in puzzlement? My heartbeat is thick in the silence.

Suddenly It shakes me with decision: "The calculated probabilities do favor your keeping your promises and making yourself useful. Therefore I shall grant your request. However—"

I am on my knees. My forehead knocks on the floor until blood runs into my eyes. I hear through storm winds:

"—testing must continue. Your faith in Me is not absolute; in fact, you're very skeptical of what you call My goodness. Without additional proof of your willingness to trust Me, I can't let you have the kind of importance which your getting your dead back from Me would give you. Do you understand?"

The question does not sound rhetorical. "Yes," I sob.

"Well, then," says my civilized, almost amiable voice, "I computed that you'd react much as you have done, and prepared for the likelihood. Your woman's body was re-created while you lay under study. The data which make personality are now being fed back into her neurones. She'll be ready to leave this place by the time you do.

"I repeat, though, there has to be a testing. The procedure is also necessary for its effect on you. If you're to be My prophet, you'll have to work pretty closely with Me; you'll have to undergo a great deal of reconditioning; this night we begin the process. Are you willing?"

"Yes, yes, yes, what must I do?"

"Only this: Follow the robot out. At some point, she, your woman, will join you. She'll be conditioned to walk so quietly you can't hear her. Don't look back. Not once, until you're in the upper world. A single glance behind you will be an act of rebellion against Me, and a datum indicating you can't really be trusted . . . and that ends everything. Do you understand?"

"Is that all?" I cry. "Nothing more?"

"It will prove more difficult than you think," SUM tells me. My voice fades, as if into illimitable distances: "Farewell, worshipper."

The robot raises me to my feet, I stretch out my arms to the Dark Queen. Half blinded with tears, I nonetheless see that She does not see me. "Good-bye," I mumble, and let the robot lead me away.

Our walking is long through those mirk miles. At first I am in too much of a turmoil, and later too stunned, to know where or how we are bound. But later still, slowly, I become aware of my flesh and clothes and the robot's alloy, glimmering blue in blackness. Sounds and smells are muffled; rarely does another machine pass by, unheeding of us. (What work does SUM have for them?) I am so careful not to look behind me that my neck grows stiff.

Though it is not prohibited, is it, to lift my harp past my shoulder, in the course of strumming a few melodies to keep up my courage, and see if perchance a following illumination is reflected in this polished wood?

Nothing. Well, her second birth must take time—O SUM, be careful of her!—and then she must be led through many tunnels, no doubt, before she makes rendezvous with my back. Be patient, Harper.

Sing. Welcome her home. No, these hollow spaces swallow all music; and she is as yet in that trance of death from which only the sun and my kiss can wake her; if, indeed, she has joined me yet. I listen for other footfalls than my own.

Surely we haven't much farther to go. I ask the robot, but of course I get no reply. Make an estimate. I know about how fast the chariot traveled coming down. . . . The trouble is, time does not exist here. I have no day, no stars, no clock but my heartbeat and I have lost the count of that. Nevertheless, we must come to the end soon. What purpose would be served by walking me through this labyrinth till I die?

Well, if I am totally exhausted at the outer gate, I won't

make undue trouble when I find no Rose-in-Hand behind me.

No, now that's ridiculous. If SUM didn't want to heed my plea, It need merely say so. I have no power to inflict physical damage on Its parts.

Of course, It might have plans for me. It did speak of reconditioning. A series of shocks, culminating in that last one, could make me ready for whatever kind of gelding It intends to do.

Or It might have changed Its mind. Why now? it was quite frank about an uncertainty factor in the human psyche. It may have reevaluated the probabilities and decided: better not to serve my desire.

Or It may have tried, and failed. It admitted the recording process is imperfect. I must not expect quite the Gladness I knew; she will always be a little haunted. At best. But suppose the tank spawned a body with no awareness behind the eyes? Or a monster? Suppose, at this instant, I am being followed by a half-rotten corpse?

No! Stop that! SUM would know, and take corrective measures.

Would It? *Can It?*

I comprehend how this passage through night, where I never look to see what follows me, how this is an act of submission and confession. I am saying, with my whole existent being, that SUM is all-powerful, all-wise, all-good. To SUM I offer the love I came to win back. Oh, It looked more deeply into me than ever I did myself.

But I shall not fail.

Will SUM, though? If there has indeed been some grisly error . . . let me not find it out under the sky. Let her, my only, not. For what then shall we do? Could I lead her here again, knock on the iron gate, and cry, ''Master, You have given me a thing unfit to exist. Destroy it and start over.''—? For what might the wrongness be? Something so subtle, so pervasive, that it does not show in any way save my slow, resisted discovery that I embrace a zombie? Doesn't it make better sense to look—make certain while she is yet drowsy with death—use the whole power of SUM to correct what may be awry?

No, SUM wants me to believe that It makes no mistakes. I agreed to that price. And to much else . . . I don't know how much else, I am daunted to imagine, but that word "recondition" is ugly. . . . Does not my woman have some rights in the matter too? Shall we not at least ask her if she wants to be the wife of a prophet; shall we not, hand in hand, ask SUM what the price of her life is to her?

Was that a footfall? Almost, I whirl about. I check myself and stand shaking; names of hers break from my lips. The robot urges me on.

Imagination. It wasn't her step. I am alone. I will always be alone.

The halls wind upward. Or so I think; I have grown too weary for much kinesthetic sense. We cross the sounding river and I am bitten to the bone by the cold which blows upward around the bridge, and I may not turn about to offer the naked newborn woman my garment. I lurch through endless chambers where machines do meaningless things. She hasn't seen them before. Into what nightmare has she risen; and why don't I, who wept into her dying senses that I loved her, why don't I look at her, why don't I speak?

Well, I could talk to her. I could assure the puzzled mute dead that I have come to lead her back into sunlight. Could I not? I ask the robot. It does not reply. I cannot remember if I may speak to her. If indeed I was ever told. I stumble forward.

I crash into a wall and fall bruised. The robot's claw closes on my shoulder. Another arm gestures. I see a passageway, very long and narrow, through the stone. I will have to crawl through. At the end, at the end, the door is swinging wide. The dear real dusk of Earth pours through into this darkness. I am blinded and deafened.

Do I hear her cry out? Was that the final testing; or was my own sick, shaken mind betraying me; or is there a destiny which, like SUM with us, makes tools of suns and SUM? I don't know. I know only that I turned, and there she stood. Her hair flowed long, loose, past the remembered face from which the trance was just departing, on which the knowing and the love of me had just awakened—flowed down over the body that reached forth arms, that took one step to meet me and was halted.

The great grim robot at her own back takes her to it. I think it sends lightning through her brain. She falls. It bears her away.

My guide ignores my screaming. Irresistible, it thrusts me out through the tunnel. The door clangs in my face. I stand before the wall which is like a mountain. Dry snow hisses across concrete. The sky is bloody with dawn; stars still gleam in the west, and arc lights are scattered over the twilit plain of the machines.

Presently I go dumb. I become almost calm. What is there left to have feelings about? The door is iron, the wall is stone fused into one basaltic mass. I walk some distance off into the wind, turn around, lower my head, and charge. Let my brains be smeared across Its gate; the pattern will be my hieroglyphic for hatred.

I am seized from behind. The force that stops me must needs be bruisingly great. Released, I crumple to the ground before a machine with talons and wings. My voice from it says, "Not here. I'll carry you to a safe place."

"What more can You do to me?" I croak.

"Release you. You won't be restrained or molested on any orders of Mine."

"Why not?"

"Obviously you're going to appoint yourself My enemy forever. This is an unprecedented situation, a valuable chance to collect data."

"You tell me this, You warn me, deliberately?"

"Of course. My computation is that these words will have the effect of provoking your utmost effort."

"You won't give her again? You don't want my love?"

"Not under the circumstances. Too uncontrollable. But your hatred should, as I say, be a useful experimental tool."

"I'll destroy You," I say.

It does not deign to speak further. Its machine picks me up and flies off with me. I am left on the fringes of a small town farther south. Then I go insane.

I do not much know what happens during that winter, nor care. The blizzards are too loud in my head. I walk the ways of Earth, among lordly towers, under neatly groomed trees, into careful gardens, over bland, bland campuses. I am unwashed, uncombed, unbarbered; my tatters flap about me and my bones are near thrusting through the skin; folk do not like to meet these eyes sunken so far into this skull, and perhaps for that reason they give me to eat. I sing to them.

> "From the hag and hungry goblin
> That into rags would rend ye
> And the spirit that stan' by the naked man
> In the Book of Moons defend ye!
> That of your five sound senses
> You never be forsaken
> Nor travel from yourselves with Tom
> Abroad to beg your bacon."

Such things perturb them, do not belong in their chrome-edged universe. So I am often driven away with curses, and sometimes I must flee those who would arrest me and scrub my brain smooth. An alley is a good hiding place, if I can find one in the oldest part of a city; I crouch there and yowl with the cats. A forest is also good. My pursuers dislike to enter any place where any wildness lingers.

But some feel otherwise. They have visited parklands, preserves, actual wildcountry. Their purpose was overconscious—measured, planned savagery, and a clock to tell them when they must go home—but at least they are not afraid of silences and unlighted nights. As spring returns, certain among them begin to follow me. They are merely curious, at first. But slowly, month by month, especially among the younger ones, my madness begins to call to something in them.

> "With an host of furious fancies
> Whereof I am commander
> With a burning spear, and a horse of air,
> To the wilderness I wander.
> By a knight of ghosts and shadows
> I summoned am to tourney
> Ten leagues beyond the wild world's edge.
> Me thinks it is no journey."

They sit at my feet and listen to me sing. They dance, crazily, to my harp. The girls bend close, tell me how I fascinate them, invite me to copulate. This I refuse, and when I tell them why they are puzzled, a little frightened maybe, but often they strive to understand.

For my rationality is renewed with the hawthorn blossoms. I bathe, have my hair and beard shorn, find clean raiment, and take care to eat what my body needs. Less and less do I rave before anyone who will listen; more and more do I seek solitude, quietness, under the vast wheel of the stars, and think.

What is man? Why is man? We have buried such questions; we have sworn they are dead—that they never really existed, being devoid of empirical meaning—and we have dreaded that they might raise the stones we heaped on them, rise and walk the world again of nights. Alone, I summon them to me. They cannot hurt their fellow dead, among whom I now number myself.

I sing to her who is gone. The young people hear and wonder. Sometimes they weep.

> "Fear no more the heat o' the sun,
>   Nor the furious winter's rages;
> Thou thy worldly task hast done,

Home art gone, and ta'en thy wages:
Golden lads and girls all must
As chimney-sweepers, come to dust.''

"But this is not so!" they protest. "We will die and sleep a while, and then we will live forever in SUM.''

I answer as gently as may be: "No. Remember I went there. So I know you are wrong. And even if you were right, it would not be right that you should be right.''

"What?''

"Don't you see, it is not right that a thing should be the lord of man. It is not right that we should huddle through our whole lives in fear of finally losing them. You are not parts in a machine, and you have better ends than helping the machine run smoothly.''

I dismiss them and stride off, solitary again, into a canyon where a river clangs, or onto some gaunt mountain peak. No revelation is given me. I climb and creep toward the truth. Which is that SUM must be destroyed, not in revenge, not in hate, not in fear, simply because the human spirit cannot exist in the same reality as It.

But what, then, is our proper reality? And how shall we attain to it?

I return with my songs to the lowlands. Word about me has gone widely. They are a large crowd who follow me down the highroad until it has changed into a street.

"The Dark Queen will soon come to these parts,'' they tell me. "Abide till She does. Let Her answer those questions you put to us, which make us sleep so badly.''

"Let me retire to prepare myself,'' I say. I go up a long flight of steps. The people watch from below, dumb with awe, till I vanish. Such few as were in the building depart. I walk down vaulted halls, through hushed high-ceilinged rooms full of tables, among shelves made massive by books. Sunlight slants dusty through the windows.

The half memory has plagued me of late: once before, I know not when, this year of mine also took place. Perhaps in this library I can find the tale that—casually, I suppose, in my abnormal childhood—I read. For man is older than SUM: wiser, I swear; his myths hold more truth than Its mathematics. I spend three days and most of three nights in my search. There is scant sound but the rustling of leaves between my hands. Folk place offerings of food and drink at the door. They tell themselves they do so out of pity, or curiosity, or to avoid the nuisance of having me die in an unconventional fashion. But I know better.

At the end of the three days I am little further along. I have too much material; I keep going off on sidetracks of beauty and fascination. (Which SUM means to eliminate.) My Education was like everyone else's, science, rationality, good sane adjustment. (SUM writes our curricula, and the teaching machines have direct connections to It.) Well, I can make some of my lopsided training work for me. My reading has given me sufficient clues to prepare a search program. I sit down before an information retrieval console and run my fingers across its keys. They make a clattery music.

Electron beams are swift hounds. Within seconds the screen lights up with words, and I read who I am.

It is fortunate that I am a fast reader. Before I can press the Clear button, the unreeling words are wiped out. For an instant the screen quivers with formlessness, then appears

I HAD NOT CORRELATED THESE DATA WITH THE FACTS CONCERNING YOU. THIS INTRODUCES A NEW AND INDETERMINATE QUANTITY INTO THE COMPUTATIONS.

The nirvana which has come upon me (yes, I found that word among the old books, and how portentous it is) is not passiveness, it is a tide more full and strong than that which bore me down to the Dark Queen those ages apast in wildcountry. I say, as coolly as may be, "An interesting coincidence. If it is a coincidence." Surely sonic receptors are emplaced hereabouts.

EITHER THAT, OR A CERTAIN NECESSARY CONSEQUENCE OF THE LOGIC OF EVENTS.

The vision dawning within me is so blinding bright that I

cannot refrain from answering, "Or a destiny, SUM?"

MEANINGLESS. MEANINGLESS. MEANINGLESS.

"Now why did You repeat Yourself in that way? Once would have sufficed. Thrice, though, makes an incantation. Are You by any chance hoping Your words will make me stop existing?"

I DO NOT HOPE. YOU ARE AN EXPERIMENT. IF I COMPUTE A SIGNIFICANT PROBABILITY OF YOUR CAUSING SERIOUS DISTURBANCE, I WILL HAVE YOU TERMINATED.

I smile. "SUM," I say, "I am going to terminate You." I lean over and switch off the screen. I walk out into the evening.

Not everything is clear to me yet, that I must say and do. But enough is that I can start preaching at once to those who have been waiting for me. As I talk, others come down the street, and hear, and stay to listen. Soon they number in the hundreds.

I have no immense new truth to offer them: nothing that I have not said before, although piecemeal and unsystematically; nothing they have not felt themselves, in the innermost darknesses of their beings. Today, however, knowing who I am and therefore why I am, I can put these things in words. Speaking quietly, now and then drawing on some forgotten song to show my meaning, I tell them how sick and starved their lives are; how they have made themselves slaves; how the enslavement is not even to a conscious mind, but to an insensate inanimate thing which their own ancestors began; how that thing is not the centrum of existence, but a few scraps of metal and bleats of energy, a few sad stupid patterns, adrift in unbounded space-time. Put not your faith in SUM, I tell them. SUM is doomed, even as you and I. Seek out mystery; what else is the whole cosmos but mystery? Live bravely, die and be done, and you will be more than any machine. You may perhaps be God.

They grow tumultuous. They shout replies, some of which are animal howls. A few are for me, most are opposed. That doesn't matter. I have reached into them, my music is being played on their nervestrings, and this is my entire purpose.

The sun goes down behind the buildings. Dusk gathers. The city remains unilluminated. I soon realize why. She is coming, the Dark Queen Whom they wanted me to debate with. From afar we hear Her chariot thunder. Folk wail in terror. They are not wont to do that either. They used to disguise their feelings from Her and themselves by receiving Her with grave sparse ceremony. Now they would flee if they dared. I have lifted the masks.

The chariot halts in the street. She dismounts, tall and shadowy cowled. The people make way before Her like water before a shark. She climbs the stairs to face me. I see for the least instant that Her lips are not quite firm and Her eyes abrim with tears. She whispers, too low for anyone else to hear, "Oh, Harper, I'm sorry."

"Come join me," I invite. "Help me set the world free."

"No. I cannot. I have been too long with It." She straightens. Imperium descends upon Her. Her voice rises for everyone to hear. The little television robots flit close, bat shapes in the twilight, that the whole planet may witness my defeat. "What is this freedom you rant about?" She demands.

"To feel," I say. "To venture. To wonder. To become men again."

"To become beasts, you mean. Would you demolish the machines that keep us alive?"

"Yes. We must. Once they were good and useful, but we let them grow upon us like a cancer, and now nothing but destruction and a new beginning can save us."

"Have you considered the chaos?"

"Yes. It too is necessary. We will not be men without the freedom to know suffering. In it is also enlightenment. Through it we travel beyond ourselves, beyond earth and stars, space and time, to Mystery."

"So you maintain that there is some undefined ultimate vagueness behind the measurable universe?" She smiles into the bat eyes. We have each been taught, as children, to laugh on hearing sarcasms of this kind. "Please offer me a little proof."

"No," I say. "Prove to me instead, beyond any doubt, that there is *not* something we cannot understand with words and equations. Prove to me likewise that I have no right to seek for it.

"The burden of proof is on You Two, so often have You lied to us. In the name of rationality, You resurrected myth. The better to control us! In the name of liberation, You chained our inner lives and castrated our souls. In the name of service, You bound and blinkered us. In the name of achievement, You held us to a narrower round than any swine in its pen. In the name of beneficence, You created pain, and horror, and darkness beyond darkness." I turn to the people. "I went there. I descended into the cellars. I know!"

"He found that SUM would not pander to his special wishes, at the expense of everyone else," cries the Dark Queen. Do I hear shrillness in Her voice? "Therefore he claims SUM is cruel."

"I saw my dead," I tell them. "She will not rise again. Nor yours, nor you. Not ever. SUM will not, cannot raise us. In Its house is death indeed. We must seek life and rebirth elsewhere, among the mysteries."

She laughs aloud and points to my soul bracelet, glimmering faintly in the gray-blue thickening twilight. Need She say anything?

"Will someone give me a knife and an ax?" I ask.

The crowd stirs and mumbles. I smell their fear. Streetlamps go on, as if they could scatter more than this corner of the night which is rolling upon us. I fold my arms and wait. The Dark Queen says something to me. I ignore Her.

The tools pass from hand to hand. He who brings them up the stairs comes like a flame. He kneels at my feet and lifts what I have desired. The tools are good ones, a broad-bladed hunting knife and a long double-bitted ax.

Before the world, I take the knife in my right hand and slash beneath the bracelet on my left wrist. The connections

to my inner body are cut. Blood flows, impossibly brilliant
under the lamps. It does not hurt; I am too exalted.

The Dark Queen shrieks. "You meant it! Harper, Harper!"

"There is no life in SUM," I say. I pull my hand through
the circle and cast the bracelet down so it rings.

A voice of brass: *"Arrest that maniac for correction. He is
deadly dangerous."*

The monitors who have stood on the fringes of the crowd
try to push through. They are resisted. Those who seek to
help them encounter fists and fingernails.

I take the ax and smash downward. The bracelet crumples.
The organic material within, starved of my secretions,
exposed to the night air, withers.

I raise the tools, ax in right hand, knife in bleeding left. "I
seek eternity where it is to be found," I call. "Who goes with
me?"

A score or better break loose from the riot, which is already
calling forth weapons and claiming lives. They surround me
with their bodies. Their eyes are the eyes of prophets. We
make haste to seek a hiding place, for one military robot has
appeared and others will not be long in coming. The tall
engine strides to stand guard over Our Lady, and this is my
last glimpse of Her.

My followers do not reproach me for having cost them all
they were. They are mine. In me is the godhead which can do
no wrong.

And the war is open, between me and SUM. My friends
are few, my enemies many and mighty. I go about the world
as a fugitive. But always I sing. And always I find someone
who will listen, will join us, embracing pain and death like a
lover.

With the Knife and the Ax I take their souls. Afterward we
hold for them the ritual of rebirth. Some go thence to become
outlaw missionaries; most put on facsimile bracelets and
return home, to whisper my word. It makes little difference to
me. I have no haste, who own eternity.

For my word is of what lies beyond time. My enemies say I
call forth ancient bestialities and lunacies; that I would bring
civilization down in ruin; that it matters not a madman's
giggle to me whether war, famine, and pestilence will again
scour the earth. With these accusations I am satisfied. The
language of them shows me that here, too, I have reawakened
anger. And that emotion belongs to us as much as any other.
More than the others, maybe, in this autumn of mankind. We
need a gale, to strike down SUM and everything It stands for.
Afterward will come the winter of barbarism.

And after that the springtime of a new and (perhaps) more
human civilization. My friends seem to believe this will come
in their very lifetimes: peace, brotherhood, enlightenment,
sanctity. I know otherwise. I have been in the depths. The
wholeness of mankind, which I am bringing back, has its
horrors.

When one day
    the Eater of the Gods returns
    the Wolf breaks his chain
    the Horsemen ride forth
    the Age ends
    the Beast is reborn
then SUM will be destroyed; and you, strong and fair, may go
back to earth and rain.

I shall await you.

My aloneness is nearly ended, Daybright. Just one task
remains. The god must die, that his followers may believe he
is raised from the dead and lives forever. Then they will go on
to conquer the world.

There are those who say I have spurned and offended
them. They too, borne on the tide which I raised, have torn
out their machine souls and seek in music and ecstasy to find a
meaning for existence. But their creed is a savage one, which
has taken them into wildcountry, where they ambush the
monitors sent against them and practice cruel rites. They
believe that the final reality is female. Nevertheless, messen-

gers of theirs have approached me with the suggestion of a mystic marriage. This I refused; my wedding was long ago, and will be celebrated again when this cycle of the world has closed.

Therefore they hate me. But I have said I will come and talk to them.

I leave the road at the bottom of the valley and walk singing up the hill. Those few I let come this far with me have been told to abide my return. They shiver in the sunset; the vernal equinox is three days away. I feel no cold myself. I stride exultant among briars and twisted ancient apple trees. If my bare feet leave a little blood in the snow, that is good. The ridges around are dark with forest, which waits like the skeleton dead for leaves to be breathed across it again. The eastern sky is purple, where stands the evening star. Overhead, against blue, cruises an early flight of homebound geese. Their calls drift faintly down to me. Westward, above me and before me, smolders redness. Etched black against it are the women.

THE
VISITOR

And now we move further toward fantasy—or do we? Though occasionally employing "psionics" in stories, I was skeptical about its validity in the real world . . . until I watched a demonstration of water dowsing (which did not work for me) and soon afterward John Campbell made me try conduit dowsing (which did work for me). I still don't believe anything occult is involved. Rather, I think, along with such researchers as Rocard, that it's a matter of our having sensitivities we had not officially suspected until lately, to variations in quantities like terrestrial magnetism. However, in a universe which includes things like black holes and their nonconservation properties, it's foolish to be dogmatic. When an Edward Mitchell sees fit to found a school of noetics, I pay respectful attention. He's been on the Moon.

The body of this tale originated in a dream I had. When I told my wife about it, she suggested the framework which makes it a story. The writing was one of the hardest jobs I have ever undertaken.

AS WE DROVE up between lawns and trees, Ferrier warned me, "Don't be shocked at his appearance."

"You haven't told me anything about him," I answered. "Not to mention."

"For good reason," Ferrier said. "This can never be a properly controlled experiment, but we can at least try to keep down the wild variables." He drummed fingers on the steering wheel. "I'll say this much. He's an important man in his field, investment counseling and brokerage."

"Oh, you mean he's a partner in— Why, I've done some business with them myself. But I never met him."

"He doesn't see clientele. Or very many people ever. He works the research end. Mail, telephone, teletype, and reads a lot."

"Why aren't we meeting in his office?"

"I'm not ready to explain that." Ferrier parked the car and we left it.

The hospital stood well out of town. It was a tall clean block of glass and metal which somehow fitted the Ohio countryside rolling away on every side, green, green, and green, here and there a whitesided house, red-sided barn, blue-blooming flax field, motley of cattle, to break the corn and woodlots, fence lines and toning telephone wires. A warm wind soughed through birches and flickered their leaves; it bore scents of a rose bed where bees querned.

Leading me up the stairs to the main entrance, Ferrier said, "Why, there he is." A man in a worn and outdated brown suit waited for us at the top of the flight.

No doubt I failed to hide my reaction, but no doubt he was used to it, for his handclasp was ordinary. I couldn't read his face. Surgeons must have expended a great deal of time and skill, but they could only tame the gashes and fill in the holes, not restore an absolute ruin. That scar tissue would never move in human fashion. His hair did, a thin flutter of gray in the breeze; and so did his eyes, which were blue behind glasses. I thought they looked trapped, those eyes, but it could be only a fancy of mine.

When Ferrier had introduced me, the scarred man said, "I've arranged for a room where we can talk." He saw a bit of surprise on me and his tone flattened. "I'm pretty well known here." His glance went to Ferrier. "You haven't told me

what this is all about, Carl. But''—his voice dropped—
''considering the place—''

The tension in my friend had hardened to sternness.
''Please, let me handle this my way,'' he said.

When we entered, the receptionist smiled at our guide. The
interior was cool, dim, carbolic. Down a hall I glimpsed
somebody carrying flowers. We took an elevator to the
uppermost floor.

There were the offices, one of which we borrowed. Ferrier
sat down behind the desk, the scarred man and I took chairs
confronting him. Though steel filing cabinets enclosed us, a
window at Ferrier's back stood open for summer to blow in.
From this level I overlooked the old highway, nowadays a
mere picturesque side road. Occasional cars flung sunlight at
me.

Ferrier became busy with pipe and tobacco. I shifted
about. The scarred man waited. He had surely had experience
in waiting.

''Well,'' Ferrier began. ''I apologize to both you gentle-
men. This mysteriousness. I hope that when you have the
facts, you'll agree it was necessary. You see, I don't want to
predispose your judgments or . . . or imaginations. We're
dealing with an extraordinarily subtle matter.''

He forced a chuckle. ''Or maybe with nothing. I give no
promises, not even to myself. Parapsychological phenomena
at best are''—he paused to search—''fugitive.''

''I know you've made a hobby of them,'' the scarred man
said. ''I don't know much more.''

Ferrier scowled. He got his pipe going before he replied:
''I wouldn't call it a hobby. Can serious research only be
done for an organization? I'm convinced there's a, well, a
reality involved. But solid data are damnably hard to come
by.'' He nodded at me. ''If my friend here hadn't happened
to be in on one of my projects, his whole experience might as
well never have been. It'd have seemed like just another
dream.''

A strangeness walked along my spine. "Probably that's all it was," I said low. "Is."

The not-face turned toward me, the eyes inquired; then suddenly hands gripped tight the arms of the chair, as they do when the doctor warns he must give pain. I didn't know why. It made my voice awkward:

"I don't claim sensitivity, I can't read minds or guess Rhine cards, nothing of that sort works for me. Still, I do often have pretty detailed and, uh, coherent dreams. Carl's talked me into describing them on a tape recorder, first thing when I wake up, before I forget them. He's trying to check on Dunne's theory that dreams can foretell the future." Now I must attempt a joke. "No such luck, so far, or I'd be rich. However, when he learned about one I had a few nights ago—"

The scarred man shuddered. "And you happened to know *me*, Carl," broke from him.

The lines deepened around Ferrier's mouth. "Go on," he directed me, "tell your story, quick," and cannonaded smoke.

I sought from them both to the serenity beyond these walls, and I also spoke fast:

"Well, you see, I'd be.n alone at home for several days. My wife had taken our kid on a visit to her mother. I won't deny; Carl's hooked me on this ESP. I'm not a true believer, but I agree with him the evidence justifies looking further, and into curious places, too. So I was in bed, reading myself sleepy with . . . Berdyaev, to be exact, because I'd been reading Lenau earlier, and he's wild, sad, crazy, you may know he died insane; nothing to go to sleep on. Did he linger anyhow, at the bottom of my mind?"

I was in a formlessness which writhed. Nor had it color, or heat or cold. Through it went a steady sound, whether a whine or drone I cannot be sure. Unreasonably sorrowful, I walked, though there was nothing under my feet, no forward or backward, no purpose in travel except that I could not weep.

The monsters did when they came. Their eyes melted and ran down the blobby heads in slow tears, while matter bubbled from within to renew that stare. They flopped as they floated, having no bones. They wavered around me and their lips made gibbering motions.

I was not afraid of attack, but a horror dragged through me of being forever followed by them and their misery. For now I knew that the nature of hell lies in that it goes on. I slogged, and they circled and rippled and sobbed, while the single noise was that which dwelt in the nothing, and time was not because none of this could change.

Time was reborn in a voice and a splash of light. Both were small. She was barely six years old, I guessed, my daughter's age. Brown hair in pigtails tied by red bows, and a staunch way of walking, also reminded me of Alice. She was more slender (elven, I thought) and more neat than my child—starched white flowerbud-patterned dress, white socks, shiny shoes, no trace of dirt on knees or tip-tilted face. But the giant teddy bear she held, arms straining around it, was comfortably shabby.

I thought I saw ghosts of road and tree behind her, but could not be certain. The mourning was still upon me.

She stopped. Her own eyes widened and widened. They were the color of earliest dusk. The monsters roiled. Then: "Mister!" she cried. The tone was thin but sweet. It cut straight across the hum of emptiness. "Oh, Mister!"

The tumorous beings mouthed at her. They did not wish to leave me, who carried some of their woe. She dropped the bear and pointed. "Go 'way!" I heard. "Scat!" They shivered backward, resurged, clustered close. "Go 'way, I want!" She stamped her foot, but silence responded and I felt the defiance of the monsters. "All right," she said grimly. "Edward, you make them go."

The bear got up on his hind legs and stumped toward me. He was only a teddy, the fur on him worn off in patches by much hugging, a rip in his stomach carefully mended. I never imagined he was alive the way the girl and I were; she just sent him. Nevertheless he had taken a great hammer, which he swung in a fingerless paw, and become the hero who rescues people.

The monsters flapped stickily about. They didn't dare make a stand. As the bear drew close, they trailed off sullenly crying. The sound left us too. We stood in an honest hush and a fog full of sunglow.

"Mister, Mister, Mister!" The girl came running, her arms out wide. I hunkered down to catch her. She struck me in a tumult and joy exploded. We embraced till I lifted her on high, made to drop her, caught her again, over and over, while her laughter chimed.

Finally, breathless, I let her down. She gathered the bear under an elbow, which caused his feet to drag. Her free hand clung to mine. "I'm so glad you're here," she said. "Thank you, thank you. Can you stay?"

"I don't know," I answered. "Are you all by yourself?"

"Yes. 'Cept for Edward and—" Her words died out. At the time I supposed she had the monsters in mind and didn't care to speak of them.

"What's your name, dear?"

"Judy."

"You know, I have a little girl at home, a lot like you. Her name's Alice."

Judy stood mute for a while and a while. At last she whispered, "Could she come play?"

My throat wouldn't let me answer.

Yet Judy was not too dashed. "Well," she said, "I didn't 'spect you, and you came." Happiness rekindled in her and caught in me. Could my presence be so overwhelmingly enough? Now I felt at peace, as though every one of the rat-fears which ride in each of us had fled me. "Come on to my house," she added, a shy invitation, a royal command.

We walked. Edward bumped along after us. The mist vanished and we were on a lane between low hedges.

Elsewhere reached hills, their green a palette for the emerald
or silver of coppices. Cows grazed, horses galloped, across
miles. Closer, birds flitted and sparkled, a robin redbreast, a
chickadee, a mockingbird who poured brook-trills from a
branch, a hummingbird bejeweled among bumblebees in a
surge of honeysuckle. The air was vivid with odors, growth,
fragrance, the friendly smell of the beasts. Overhead lifted an
enormous blue where clouds wandered.

This wasn't my country. The colors were too intense,
crayon-brilliant, and a person could drown in the scents.
Birds, bees, butterflies, dragonflies somehow seemed gigantic, while cattle and horses were somehow unreachably far
off, forever cropping or galloping. The clouds made real
castles and sailing ships. Yet there was rightness as well as
brightness. I felt—maybe not at home, but very welcome.

Oh, infinitely welcome.

Judy chattered, no, caroled. "I'll show you my garden an'
my books an', an' the whole house. Even where Hoo Boy
lives. Would you push me in the swing? I only can pump
myself. I pretend Edward is pushing me, an' he says, 'High,
high, up in the sky, Judy fly, I wonder why,' like Daddy
would, but it's only pretend, like when I play with my dolls or
my Noah's ark animals an' make them talk. Would you play
with me?" Wistfulness crossed her. "I'm not so good at
making up ad-ad*ven*tures for them. Can you?" She turned
merry again and skipped a few steps. "We'll have dinner in
the living room if you make a fire. I'm not s'posed to make
fire, I remember Daddy said, 'cept I can use the stove. I'll
cook us dinner. Do you like tea? We have lots of different
kinds. You look, an' tell me what kind you want. I'll make
biscuits an' we'll put butter an' maple syrup on them like
Grandmother does. An' we'll sit in front of the fire an' tell
stories, okay?" And on and on.

The lane was now a street, shaded by big old elms; but it
was empty save for the dappling of the sunlight, and the
houses had a flatness about them, as if nothing lay behind
their fronts. Wind mumbled in leaves. We reached a gate in a

picket fence, which creaked when Judy opened it.

The lawn beyond was quite real, aside from improbably tall hollyhocks and bright roses and pansies along the edges. So was this single house. I saw where paint had peeled and curtains faded, the least bit, as will happen to any building. (Its neighbors stood flawless.) A leftover from the turn of the century, it rambled in scale-shaped shingles, bays, turrets, and gingerbread. The porch was a cool cavern that resounded beneath our feet. A brass knocker bore the grinning face of a ghome.

Judy pointed to it. "I call him Billy Bungalow because he goes bung when he comes down low," she said. "Do you want to use him? Daddy always did, an' made him go a lot louder than I can. Please. He's waited such a long time." I have too, she didn't add.

I rattled the metal satisfactorily. She clapped her hands in glee. My ears were more aware of stillness behind the little noise. "Do you really live alone, brighteyes?" I asked.

"Sort of," she answered, abruptly going solemn.

"Not even a pet?"

"We had a cat, we called her Elizabeth, but she died an' . . . we was going to get another."

I lifted my brows. "We?"

"Daddy an' Mother an' me. C'mon inside!" She hastened to twist the doorknob.

We found an entry where a Tiffany window threw rainbows onto hardwood flooring. Hat rack and umbrella stand flanked a coat closet, opposite a grandfather clock which broke into triumphant booms on our arrival: for the hour instantly was six o'clock of a summer's evening. Ahead of us swept a staircase; right and left, doorways gave on a parlor converted to a sewing room, and on a living room where I glimpsed a fine stone fireplace. Corridors went high-ceilinged beyond them.

"Such a big house for one small girl," I said. "Didn't you mention, uh, Hoo Boy?"

Both arms hugged Edward close to her. I could barely

hear: "He's 'maginary. They all are."

It never occurred to me to inquire further. It doesn't in dreams.

"But *you're* here, Mister!" Judy cried, and the house was no longer hollow.

She clattered down the hall ahead of me, up the stairs, through chamber after chamber, basement, attic, a tiny space she had found beneath the witch-hat roof of a turret and assigned to Hoo Boy; she must show me everything. The place was bright and cheerful, didn't even echo much as we went around. The furniture was meant for comfort. Down in the basement stood shelves of jelly her mother had put up and a workshop for her father. She showed me a half-finished toy sailboat he had been making for her. Her personal room bulged with the usual possessions of a child, including books I remembered well from years agone. (The library had a large collection too, but shadowy, a party of that home which I cannot catalog.) Good pictures hung on the walls. She had taken the liberty of pinning clippings almost everywhere, cut from the stacks of magazines which a household will accumulate. They mostly showed animals or children.

In the living room I noticed a cabinet-model radio-phonograph, though no television set. "Do you ever use that?" I asked.

She shook her head. "No, nothing comes out of it anymore. I sing for myself a lot." She put Edward on the sofa. "You stay an' be the lord of the manor," she ordered him. "I will be the lady making dinner, an' Mister will be the faithful knight bringing firewood." She went timid. "Will you, please, Mister?"

"Sounds great to me," I smiled, and saw her wriggle for delight.

"Quick!" She grabbed me anew and we ran back to the kitchen. Our footfalls applauded.

The larder was well stocked. Judy showed me her teas and asked my preference. I confessed I hadn't heard of several kinds; evidently her parents were connoisseurs. "So'm I,"

Judy said after I explained that word. "Then I'll pick. An' you tell me, me an' Edward, a story while we eat, okay?"

"Fair enough," I agreed.

She opened a door. Steps led down to the backyard. Unlike the closely trimmed front, this was a wilderness of assorted toys, her swing, and fever-gaudy flowers. I had to laugh. "You do your own gardening, do you?"

She nodded. "I'm not very expert. But Mother promised I could have a garden here." She pointed to a shed at the far end of the grounds. "The firewood's in that. I got to get busy." However firm her tone, the fingers trembled which squeezed mine. "I'm so happy," she whispered.

I closed the door behind me and picked a route among her blossoms. Windows stood wide to a mild air full of sunset, and I heard her start singing.

> "The little red pony ran over the hill
> And galloped and galloped away—"

The horses in those meadows came back to me, and suddenly I stood alone, somewhere, while one of them who was my Alice fled from me for always; and I could not call out to her.

After a time, walking became possible again. But I wouldn't enter the shed at once; I hadn't the guts, when Judy's song had ended, leaving me here by myself. Instead, I brushed on past it for a look at whatever might lie behind for my comfort.

That was the same countryside as before, but long-shadowed under the falling sun and most quiet. A blackbird sat on a blackberry tangle, watched me and made pecking motions. From the yard, straight southward through the land, ran a yellow brick road.

I stepped onto it and took a few strides. In this light the pavement was the hue of molten gold, strong under my feet; here was the kind of highway which draws you ahead one more mile to see what's over the next hill, so you may forget the pony that galloped. After all, don't yellow brick roads lead to, Oz?

"Mister!" screamed at my back. "No, stop, stop!"

I turned around. Judy stood at the border. She shuddered inside the pretty dress as she reached toward me. Her face was stretched quite out of shape. "Not yonder, Mister!"

Of course I made haste. When we were safely in the yard, I held her close while the dread went out of her in a burst of tears. Stroking her hair and murmuring, at last I dared ask, "But where does it go?"

She jammed her head into the curve of my shoulder and gripped me. "T-t-to Grandmother's."

"Why, is that bad? You're making us biscuits like hers, remember?"

"We can't *ever* go there," Judy gasped. Her hands on my neck were cold.

"Well, now, well, now." Disengaging, while still squatted to be at her height, I clasped her shoulder and chucked her chin and assured her the world was fine; look what a lovely evening, and we'd soon dine with Edward, but first I'd better build our fire, so could she help me bring in the wood? Secretly through me went another song I know, Swedish, the meaning of it:

"Children are a mysterious folk, and they live in a wholly strange world—"

Before long she was glad once more. As we left, I cast a final glance down the highway, and then caught a breath of what she felt: less horror than unending loss and grief, somewhere on that horizon. It made me be extra jocular while we took armloads of fuel to the living room.

Thereafter Judy trotted between me and the kitchen, attending to her duties. She left predictable chaos, heaped dishes, scorched pan, strewn flour, smeared butter and syrup and Lord knows what else. I forbore to raise the subject of cleanup. No doubt we'd tackle that tomorrow. I didn't mind.

Later we sat cross-legged under the sofa where Edward presided, ate our biscuits and drank our tea with plenty of milk, and laughed a great deal. Judy had humor. She told me of a Fourth of July celebration she had been at, where there were so many people "I bet just their toes weighed a hundred pounds." That led to a picnic which had been rained out, and—she must have listened to adult talk—she insisted that in any properly regulated universe, Samuel Gompers would have invented rubber boots. The flames whirled red, yellow, blue, and talked back to the ticking, booming clock; shadows played tag across walls; outside stood a night of gigantic stars.

"Tell me another story," she demanded and snuggled into my lap, the calculating little minx. Borrowing from what I had done for Alice, I spun a long yarn about a girl named Judy, who lived in the forest with her friends Edward T. Bear and Billy Bungalow and Hoo Boy, until they built a candy-striped balloon and departed on all sorts of explorations; and her twilight-colored eyes got wider and wider.

They drooped at last, though. "I think we'd better turn in," I suggested, "We can carry on in the morning."

She nodded. "Yesterday they said today was tomorrow," she observed, "but today they know better."

I expected that after those fireside hours the electrics would be harsh to us; but they weren't. We went upstairs, Judy on my right shoulder, Edward on my left. She guided me to a guest room, pattered off, and brought back a set of pajamas. "Daddy wouldn't mind," she said.

"Would you like me to tuck you in?" I asked.

"Oh—" For a moment she radiated. Then the seriousness came upon her. She put finger to chin, frowning, before she shook her head. "No, thanks. I don't think you're s'posed for that."

"All right." My privilege is to see Alice to her bed; but each family has its own tradition. Judy must have sensed my disappointment, because she touched me and smiled at me, and when I stooped she caught me and breathed,

"You're really real, Mister. I love you," and ran down the hall.

My room resembled the others, well and unpretentiously furnished. The wallpaper showed willows and lakes and Chinese castles which I had seen in the clouds. Gauzy white curtains, aflutter in easy airs, veiled away those lantern-big stars. Above the bed Judy had pinned a picture of a galloping pony.

I thought of a trip to the bathroom, but felt no need. Besides, I might disturb my hostess; I had no doubt she brushed her teeth, being such a generally dutiful person. Did she say prayers too? In spite of Alice, I don't really understand little girls, any more than I understand how a mortal could write *Jesu Joy of Man's Desiring*. Boys are different; it's true about the slugs and snails and puppy dogs' tails. I've been there and I know.

I got into the pajamas, lay down in the bed and the breeze, turned off the light, and was quickly asleep.

Sometimes we remember a night's sleep. I spent this one being happy about tomorrow.

Maybe that was why I woke early, in a clear, shadowless gray, cool as the air. The curtains rippled and blew, but there was no sound whatsoever.

Or . . . a rustle? I lay half awake, eyes half open and peace behind them. Someone moved about. She was very tall, I knew, and she was tidying the house. I did not try, then, to look upon her. In my drowsiness, she might as well have been the wind.

After she had finished in this chamber, I came fully to myself, and saw how bureau and chair and the bulge of blankets that my feet made were strangers in the dusk which runs before the sun. I swung legs across bedside, felt hardwood under my soles. My lungs drank odors of grass. Oh, Judy will snooze for hours yet, I thought, but I'll go peek in at her before I pop downstairs and start a surprise breakfast.

When dressed, I followed the hallway to her room. Its door wasn't shut. Beyond, I spied a window full of daybreak.

I stopped. A woman was singing.

She didn't use real words. You often don't, over a small bed. She sang well-worn nonsense,

> "Cloddledy loldy boldy boo,
> Cloddledy lol-dy bol-dy boo-oo,"

to the tenderest melody I have ever heard. I think that tune was what drew me on helpless, till I stood in the entrance.

And she stood above Judy. I couldn't truly see her: a blue shadow, maybe? Judy was as clear to me as she is this minute, curled in a prim nightgown, one arm under her cheek (how long the lashes and stray brown hair), the other around Edward, while on a shelf overhead, Noah's animals kept watch.

The presence grew aware of me.

She turned and straightened, taller than heaven. Why have you looked? she asked me in boundless gentleness. Now you must go, and never come back.

No, I begged. Please.

When even I may do no more than this, she sighed, you cannot stay or ever return, who looked beyond the Edge.

I covered my eyes.

I'm sorry, she said; and I believe she touched my head as she passed from us.

Judy awakened. "Mister—" She lifted her arms, wanting me to come and be hugged, but I didn't dare.

"I have to leave, sweetheart," I told her.

She bolted to her feet. "No, no, no," she said, not loud at all.

"I wish I could stay awhile," I answered. "Can you guess how much I wish it?"

Then she knew. "You . . . were awful kind . . . to come see me," she got out.

She went to me with the same resolute gait as when first we met, and took my hand, and we walked downstairs together and forth into the morning.

"Will you say hello to your daughter from me?" she requested once.

"Sure," I said. Hell, yes. Only how?

We went along the flat and empty street, toward the sun. Where a blackbird perched on an elm bough, and the leaves made darkness beneath, she halted. "Good-bye, you good Mister," she said.

She would have kissed me had I had the courage. "Will you remember me, Judy?"

"I'll play with my remembering of you. Always." She snapped after air; but her head was held bravely. "Thanks again. I do love you."

So she let me go, and I left her. A single time I turned around to wave. She waved back, where she stood under the sky all by herself.

The scarred man was crying. He wasn't skilled in it; he barked and hiccoughed.

Surgically, Ferrier addressed him "The description of the house corresponds to your former home. Am I correct?"

The hideous head jerked a nod.

"And you're entirely unfamiliar with the place," Ferrier declared to me. "It's in a different town from yours."

"Right," I said. "I'd no reason before today to suppose I'd had anything more than a dream." Anger flickered. "Well, God damn your scientific caution, now I want some explanations."

"I can't give you those," Ferrier admitted. "Not when I've no idea how the phenomenon works. You're welcome to what few facts I have."

The scarred man toiled toward a measure of calm. "I, I, I apologize for the scene," he stuttered. "A blow, you realize. Or a hope?" His gaze ransacked me.

"Do you think we should go see her?" Ferrier suggested.

For reply, the scarred man led us out. We were silent in corridor and elevator. When we emerged on the third floor, the hospital smell struck hard. He regained more control over himself as we passed among rubber-tired nurses and views of occupied beds. But his gesture was rickety that, at last, beckoned us through a certain doorway.

Beyond lay several patients in a near-total hush. Abruptly I understood why he, important in the world, went ill-clad. Hospitals don't come cheap.

His voice grated: "Telepathy, or what? The brain isn't gone; not a flat EEG. Could you—" That went as far as he was able.

"No," I said, while my fingers struggled with each other. "It must have been a fluke. And since, I'm forbidden."

We had stopped at a cluster of machinery. "Tell him what happened," Ferrier said without any tone whatsoever.

The scarred man looked past us. His words came steady if a bit shrill. "We were on a trip, my wife and daughter and me. First we meant to visit my mother-in-law in Kentucky."

"You were southbound, then," I foreknew. "On a yellow brick road." They still have that kind, here and there in our part of the country.

"A drunk driver hit our car," he said. "my wife was killed. I became what you see. Judy—" He chopped a hand toward the long white form beneath us. "That was nineteen years ago," he ended.

WOLFRAM

This involves a science and contains a fiction. Therefore it is science fiction. Right?

ADMIRING THE ADS in *Scientific American* a while back—they are always a potent source of wonder—I was pleased to see that the General Dynamics Corporation still refers to element number 74 as tungsten. I strongly disapprove of the arbitrary and high-handed 1949 decree of the International Union of Chemistry, that hereafter everybody shall call it wolfram. Admittedly this squares with the symbol, W. But damn it, "tungsten" was what I learned, and what they make light bulbs with, and if it was good enough for Scheele it's good enough for the International Union of Chemistry. They're probably just an affiliate of the Teamsters anyway. Aye, tear that tattered ensign down!

I growled some such remark to my wife over an evening beer, and she asked where the name "wolfram" came from. Well, I said, it's the German word for tungsten—no harm in that, if only the Germans wouldn't be so aggressive about it—and comes from wolframite, the principal ore. So what's wolframite named for, she wanted to know. I suppose some chemist named Wolfram, who first described it, I shrugged, and got down the American College Encyclopedic Dictionary. It gave the mineral derivation as expected, but said that "wolfram" was of uncert. orig.

I was astonished. Turning to Webster, I found G. *wolf*, meaning "wolf," and *rahm*, meaning "cream, soot." Wolf cream? Wolf soot? Try as I might, I couldn't make sense of it. Webster evidently feels the same way, because his etymology reads "said to be fr.," etc. In other words, he's passing on this ridiculous bit of folklore for lack of anything better, but disclaiming all responsibility. In fact, he's rather badly shaken by the whole episode, so much so that he has forgotten to capitalize the German nouns.

By far the most believable theory is that there was a Wolfram, whose pioneer study of this material won him the honor of having his name bestowed upon it, but who fell into deep posthumous obscurity. Had Webster ransacked enough archives, he would surely have discovered the reference. However, since Wolfram was not a professional chemist (had he been, his name would have gotten into the histories that Webster presumably did consult, if only as a footnote) it's hard to know a priori just where to begin looking.

Nevertheless, I can see him quite clearly, this humble worker in the vineyard of science, altogether overshadowed by his gigantic contemporaries but, perhaps on that very account, shining across time's abyss with a luster of simple humanity and mixed metaphors. Karl Georg Johann Friedrich Augustus Wolfram, born and died in the eighteenth century, court librarian to the Margrave of Oberhaus-Blickstein or whatever the place was called, who occupied his leisure with walks through the countryside and brought back samples of outcroppings in his pockets, to be pored over until the candles guttered low. . . .

He cannot have been even of petty noble birth, or the histories would have paid him some attention. Nor can Oberhaus-Blickstein have been one of the brilliant and intensively studied principalities of that era, like Brandenburg. No, it was undoubtedly a backwater, peaceful, prosperous, a little smug and complacent, inhabited by peasants who tugged their forelocks and said, *"Jawohl Herr Ritterguts-besitzer"* when the squire told them what to do and then went ahead and did the right thing anyway, by artisans and shop-keepers in the villages, and by the bourgeoisie of Shickenburg-g-am-Pfaff. This sleepy old town probably boasted a brick warehouse at the dock where the river barges left cargo twice a month; a pleasant though undistinguished cathedral said, on no very reliable evidence, to have been begun by Henry the Lion; several fine mansions; and of course a small palace.

Even in this idyllic setting there must have been an occasional bit of scandal, especially at court. Not that it mattered if the present Margrave was given to pinching servant girls and spent too much on imported fanciments, notably wine. (Since he really didn't know a thing about wine, the French shippers cheated him shamelessly; in the regional idiom, they took him by the nose and swung him around their heads. But nobody ever told the Margrave, so little harm was done.) Such things were acceptable. In fact, a Margrave with no minor vices would have seemed unnatural. However, in his youth this one had spent a year in Paris and become a liberal. Not too many years ago he had actually corresponded with Voltaire.

Luckily, the phase passed. Voltaire did nothing to encourage the correspondence—the Margrave's letters were incredibly dull—and so his enthusiasm petered out. He settled down to being as cultivated a gentleman as his limited means, his excessive distance from the centers of world civilization, and his not very sharp wits would allow. On the whole he was a good Margrave, well liked by his people. Not at all like his mad grandfather, the one who built that curious castle on the Hochhügel, where the moat was inside the walls to keep the swans safe.

The duties of his librarian were not onerous. Karl Georg Johann Friedrich Augustus Wolfram needed only take care of a generations-old collection of astoundingly unimportant books and documents, work desultorily at cataloging them, and recommend new acquisitions, which his master dutifully ordered but, as a rule, fell asleep over. The pay was not high, but not niggardly either; he could maintain a modest, comfortable house, a couple of servants, and six children. And he had social standing, attended court functions, enjoyed the friendship of other intellectuals like the Kapellmeister. A more dubious privilege was that of playing chess with the Margrave. It took skill and concentration to lose those games, particularly since they had to look hard-fought. Still, this was no major nuisance; and when the Kapellmeister visited the Wolframs, well, then they played real chess, with blood and iron in it.

Altogether, court librarian was quite an eminence for the fourth son of a shopkeeper to have reached. Of course, once when he was a boy, and the schoolmaster said that Karl Georg was the most brilliant Latin pupil he had ever had, and there was talk of sending him to Berlin to study— But that was long ago. Nothing had come of it. Best be content with what God has given one. This is not so little. A secure position; a good, sensible, if somewhat barrel-shaped wife; six fine living children; and, certainly, one's correspondence, one's contacts with the great world beyond the banks of the Pfaff. . . .

Few Schickenburgers had any inkling of their court librarian's other life. The Margrave did, but never really appreciated its significance; the Kapellmeister did, but was never in a position to do anything about it. Outwardly the Herr Hofbibliothekar Karl Georg Johann Friedrich Augustus Wolfram was the most staid and ordinary of men. You could set your watch by the time at which his stocky figure mounted the palace steps on workdays. His clothes were conservative, even a trifle old-fashioned—for Shickenburg, that is, which would have made them ludicrously out-of-date in Paris—and reasonably neat (albeit his wife was once heard to mutter that he was the only man she knew of who could get gravy on his wig). He was a kindly paterfamilias, a bit pompous but not unduly strict by the standards of that day and age; in the evenings he often gathered his family about him and read

aloud from edifying books. Every Sunday morning saw him
in church, every Sunday early afternoon seated at a gargan-
tuan dinner, every Sunday late afternoon fast asleep. He
allowed himself one pipeful of tobacco per diem, though to
be sure it was a very large pipe, whose bowl stood on the
floor. Alcohol was limited to a little beer or wine, except
during Fasching, when he sometimes got mildly tiddly and
recited Latin anacreontics. He did not make financial specu-
lations, frequent the taverns, or pinch servant girls.

As for his nature rambles and his interest in the sciences,
that was nothing unusual in the eighteenth century. What
Oberhaus-Blickstein did not realize was the considerable
actual and the possibly very great potential stature of the man.
He corresponded regularly with Linnaeus, and it seems quite
probable that the suggestions he made, out of his orderly
catalog-oriented mind, had much to do with the evolution of
the Swedish master's taxonomy. In his later years he became
a corresponding member of the Royal Society. There were
men in Paris and London who had never heard of Oberhaus-
Blickstein but who, if the name Wolfram was mentioned,
would nod and say, "Oh, yes, didn't he do something about
minerals?"

We have seen that his description of wolframite, sum-
marizing every reference in the literature and adding keen
original observations by which it could instantly be identified, was honored by the bestowal of his name upon it.
Hitherto every local set of rustics in Europe, if they noticed
the stuff at all, had given it some loutish name of their own,
like "wolf cream," and Chaos was king. But now, once and
forever, scientists around the world could know exactly what
ore was meant and what properties to expect.

His interests were not confined to mineralogy and natural
history. Indeed, he himself considered these his minor hob-
bies. He was quite musical, playing both the violin and the
harpsichord with some skill. A rather charming little hymn,
sung locally to this day on the Eve of St. Odo, is attributed to
Wolfram. He had connections with Leipzig, and one of the

lesser-known Bach sonatas is dedicated to him. (Not *the* Bach—a fourth cousin twice removed.) Much of his time was spent on a ponderous compilation of regional folklore, with commentaries, which he regarded as his life's masterwork. Unfortunately, it is written in so crabbed a style, and is based on so erroneous an identification of every figure in every *Märchen* with something in Classical mythology, that not even Max Müller was able to make any use of it. By contrast, Wolfram's letters are fluent, brilliantly reasoned, lightened by flashes of a wit that few people today are sufficiently well educated to savor.

His life had a normal share of disappointments and blunders. Though he angled for decades to get a patent of nobility, so he might inscribe that magical "von" in front of his name, he never mustered enough influence. In 1768 a young Frenchman wrote to him about certain ideas he had conceived in the field of chemistry. The reply was so disparaging that Lavoisier made no attempt at further correspondence. Wolfram admitted his mistake afterward, in a communication to Linnaeus, but pleaded that the gout which had bothered him of late years had made him irritable that day.

He was quite an old man when Goethe passed through Oberhaus-Blickstein and was the Margrave's guest for a night. Wolfram looked forward to this encounter for months. The diary of his friend the Kapellmeister relates how he spent days rehearsing what he would say, the questions, the comments, the little aphorisms out of a long experience to offer the young titan. He bought an entire new set of clothes, including shoes and wig, for the occasion, though medical bills had been so heavy that he could ill afford to.

Yes, Goethe came; and there was an interminable reception line, followed by an interminable banquet, after which the party repaired to the concert hall and heard a recital by the Margrave's oldest granddaughter and an original composition for voice and wind instruments by the Margrave himself. Geothe's eyes were closed and his head sunken into his chest throughout this entertainment, doubtless so he could concentrate better. Immediately afterward he excused himself, since he must rise betimes to continue his journey in the morning. (However, at the banquet he had sat next to the youngest niece of the Margrave, who was then a widower, and been at his most charming, just beyond earshot of the court librarian. No one inquired where she spent the night.)

As for the Herr Hofbibliothekar Wolfram, he was introduced at the reception, bowed, said, "I am Your Excellency's very admiring servant," and moved on with the line.

He died peacefully just before the Estates General met at Versailles. It was a mercy. His admiration had never extended to the liberal ideas current in his time. Humane by nature, he nonetheless expected nothing but trouble from any upset of a social order which, at least in Oberhaus-Blickstein, worked so well. He would have known his forebodings confirmed, had he lived to witness that last scene of pitiful gallantry, when his old blind Margrave rode forth at the head of the principality's men to meet Napoleon and surrender. Sleep well, Karl Georg Johann Friedrich Augustus Wolfram.

You wouldn't have tried to steal the name off tungsten.

And so we come to the last step of our exploration. The study of prehistory is a science, and "caveman" stories have always been admissible as science fiction, even when they had no additional speculative elements such as "The Long Remembering" does. But archaeology, including the archaeology of what written history somewhat remembers, is a science too.

I wrote "The Peat Bog" for a proposed volume of tales by different authors, all to be set in the first century A.D. Editor Ray Nelson has graciously agreed to its use in the present collection. But would you then call it a historical narrative, or—since it extrapolates from archaeological discoveries—science fiction?

I think you can say either or both, and thus it helps illustrate the artificiality of categories, and that's why I wanted it in this book. Besides, it may persuade you to go someday to Silkeborg in Denmark, and there at the museum visit the Tollund Man. You'll like him.

WE TRAVELED OVERLAND from Massilia to Colonia Agrippina, where we spent the winter while Memmius studied language and gathered intelligence. He required me to join him in the first of these, and said he hoped I could be of value in the second; but I wasn't. That land weighed on me too heavily.

It was not so much that the town was small and raw, most of the streets only hog-wallows twisting between timber houses whose shapes were all wrong, the population a garrison among peasants and barbarians, like a weir staked out in a dark slow river. One expects this on a frontier. In truth, our passage through Gaul had agreeably surprised me by the extent to which civilization had flowed north out of the Narbonnese in the bare hundred or so years since divine Julius opened that sluice gate. Paved roads, orderly fields, neat little cities where one might find not just an amphitheater but men who quoted Euripides or Aristotle as naturally as would a born Greek— When I remarked on this to Memmius, the leather of his face had crinkled upward, and he drawled:

"Look closer, Philon. These people don't even walk like you or me, let alone think the same way. And wait till we get farther north, where the bodies themselves are nothing you'll find anywhere around the Midworld Sea. Rome's spread thinner than I really care to say out loud. New territories like Britain, it's obvious enough there; but here too, here too."

As we came into German country, the alienness grew according to his prediction. In itself, that didn't trouble me. Memmius' enterprises had already taken us as far afield as Mauretania and Pontus. If anything—after I began to catch a bit of the language, which struck me as rather pleasingly resonant, not the harsh gabble it's often called—if anything, I felt less far from home here than in, say, Jerusalem. Here, the attitude did not seem to be shameless importunity and slyness cloaking a resentment which seethed in the marrow. Instead, my impression was of an odd blend of somewhat boorish affability with inward pride. "You beat us in these parts, but we won in the Teutoburg Forest, both fair and square. Now let's see if we can't get along." So their eyes appeared to say. I knew I might be reading what wasn't there into that blueness. Maybe it came from my liking the frank way they strode along, girls almost as big and handsome as boys.

And trees were ablaze with autumn, stubble fields golden, air cool: misty of mornings but star-brilliant at night, by day full of humus odors and wild goose calls. If the fare and accommodations were coarse, beer preferable to what passed locally for wine, the ride long between each pair of stopping places, why, I have never minded that. I expected to find reasonable contentment in Colonia.

What I did not foresee was, first, the confinement, the shrinking of the world to a stockade and fosse. Oh, it was not impossible to go out: even, by prearrangement, across the river, where the unconquered Chatti were milder than the reputation they have in Rome. But there was soon no point in it; I had seen everything the countryside had to offer of human variety that lay within a day's round trip. This was the more true when those days really began to shorten.

The town rated no such name. It was hardly more than a military outpost, set down by Claudius a few years ago upon what had been a marketplace for yeomen, fishers, charcoal burners, woodsrunners. Memmius felt it had great potential. However, that did us no good now. Now was a commandant, the top of the social heap, whose brain was cast iron; a hairy half-educated oaf who grunted us through our language lessons; what few books I had brought along and quickly memorized; chilly rooms, smoky fires, gloom.

Winter cast me far down. It was warmer than I had anticipated, or I should say less cold. But the dankness gnawed into the liver, even as the murk—heavy gray skies above snow and mud, until day's brief glimmer was swallowed by monstrous black—ate at my soul. O islands white against sun-dazzled lapping purple, a temple seen through olive trees as tiny and bright as a star! They danced in my head like the wisps of a dream.

Memmius seemed unaffected, the same deceptively easy-going businessman he had always shown to the world. He studied, fared about, talked, questioned, bargained, bribed, joked, insinuated, did all that a Roman of the equestrian class might do and more besides, but never in a hurry, never letting on that his purpose included anything save a commercial venture. Whether his source of information be the provincial governor passing through or a raggedy crone peddling turnips on an icy corner, an arrogant princely warrior come the whole way from Scandia to see what glory he might pick up or a lout from just across the river, a courtesan who knew everybody or a slave girl rented for a few nights from her horizon-bound rustic owner—he asked, he probed, he learned, he pondered.

I kept records of whatever he chose me to witness or to be told afterward. And, having a gift for tongues, I presently spoke better German than he did. But otherwise I was sad and useless. He tried to jolly me out of it.

One night he even called me to his bed, a thing he had not done for half a dozen years, when I turned fourteen and he laughed that I was getting too angular for his taste. (Then he manumitted me and gave me regular employment. At first I mostly attended his wife; a Greek amaneunsis-cum-factotum is an elegant thing for a Roman lady to have. Later he began using me for real, often confidential work. How burstingly proud I was when he explained: "We're not bound north only to see if we can open new trade. We'll also be on a mission for Caesar." And the characteristically sardonic: "Caesar's ministers, at least; Nero seems to consider other interests more urgent. . . . The fact is, Britain's near the boiling point, Gaul not as quiet as it might be, the Germans beyond the marches moving about—and new powers rising, seaborne, on the far side of the Cimbrian Chersonese. . . . Maybe those chiefs plan no threat to Rome's holdings, no alliances with rebels. Maybe. That's for Rome to find out, and try to influence. We've agents in Scandia and the islands. My task is to find out how things are on the peninsula; if possible, to stiffen those tribes against the easterners. . . ." He, Gnaeus Valerius Memmius, asked me what I, freedman Philon who did not even know my father's name, what I thought about this!)

But that night wasn't what we'd sometimes, earlier had. He was kindly as always, yet—a trifle too abstracted, or too competent?—or had simply too long a while passed? He still

had the hawk profile, but it was grizzled and deeply fur-
rowed. I think he sensed the same as myself, for at length he
raised his leanness on an elbow, stroked my cheek, and said,
smiling a bit through guttering yellow lamplight: "Philon, I
believe you need a girl."

"No, not really." I huddled against him, though mainly
because the room was cold. The breath puffed white from our
lips.

"She'd keep you warm," he said. "And me, for that
matter. In spring, when we leave, I can resell her, maybe for
a profit if she's gotten pregnant."

Her name was Gerda and she was, indeed, quite appealing,
a stocky blonde who was anxious to learn our wishes and,
once she discovered we wouldn't mistreat her, given to
singing little songs while she worked around the house. I
didn't always blow out the flame and pretend she was
Hephaestion to my Alexander; sometimes I enjoyed that she
was Gerda, who demanded no more than I wanted to give.

Not that we often slept together. I wasn't that interested.
And Memmius was: largely because she was a Longobard,
captured in some clasp with the Chatti and passed westward
hand to hand. North of the Longobards dwell the Saxons, and
north of the Saxons are the Cimbrians among others, and it is
from the Cimbrian peninsula that that horde came which
almost overwhelmed Rome, a century and a half ago. The
tribes there are still powerful. It's not strictly true that they
asked for our friendship, when a Roman fleet visited them a
while back. That report was the kind of self-serving which
every delegation to the barbarians makes. They did show our
men hospitality, and they are—like their rivals to the east—
actively trading with us. That's all.

The trade is usually through a long chain of middlemen.
We don't know enough about what's going on in those parts.
Rome has had some catastrophic surprises in the past. On the
other hand, granted sufficient information and connections,
Rome has been able to play one foreign faction off against
another. Like, say, the Cimbrians versus the Scandians. . . .

Gerda didn't greatly brighten my mood, though. Spring-time did, sunlight and greenness, messages from outside, packing up and ho-ha for saddle leather under me again! Lately I've been remembering her, bulge-bellied and weep-ing, when Memmius handed her over to a dealer. At the time, I was too wild with my own freedom to notice.

We jogged through Belgic Gaul to Gesoriacum. I'd done considerable detail work for us, arranging that a ship and crew and trade goods be there when we arrived. The goods were perfectly genuine, silverware, glassware, fine cloth, oils: for those people who dwell between the German and Suebian Seas have a shrewd awareness of the value of their amber, furs, hides, tallow, beeswax. "I am at least as con-cerned," Memmius said, "with establishing a profitable connection as I am with bulwarking the legions."

Beyond the sandy isles and half-drowned marshlands of Frisia, the peninsula thrusts northward. It is also low country, yet not flat; hills rise steep to offer tremendous vistas across moors where only the yellow of gorse breaks the darkling reach of heather. The west coast, like much of the interior, is virtually treeless. What few oaks and evergreens have laid root in its poor soil are stunted, witchily gnarled, bent to the east as if straining from the endless wind. It comes off the sea, that wind, bleak and salt, roaring, steaming; clouds flee before it, their shadows scythe over the earth, sweeps of half-night and half-day like time in the eyes of a god. Nevertheless heaven arches so vast that—save in the frequent rains—the clouds seem lost therein, as do the thousands of waterfowl, storks, herons, hawks, eagles, crows, ravens, every kind of wings aloft.

Our pilot was Eporedorix, a Gaul who had been here often before and led us to a sheltered bay where the amber buyers customarily stop. This merchantman was too deep-bottomed to beach like the light barbarian craft, which depend more on oars or paddles than on sail. Captain Scaubo growled he'd sooner lie at anchor anyway, just in case. "You're a suspicious old Lusitanian, aren't you?" I jested. He looked sour.

Memmius grinned: "That's how he got to be old, Philon."

Nobody was around when the dinghy set us ashore. We were well in advance of the bartering season. For months the tribesmen would be working their farms, chasing deer across the heaths, trapping hares, catching fish and seal and the lesser whales, to replenish larders gone hollow during the winter. Women and children would gather oysters and, after every storm, amber that had been cast on the beaches. "We'll have a short wait, though," Memmius assured me. "Word about us will move around fast." He had deliberately come early, to get settled and begin gathering firsthand information free of the tumult which marts and moots would create.

I stared at enormous manlessness and asked, "How will they know?"

"Oh, natives, they got instincts, like animals," Scaubo grunted.

Memmius shrugged. "It looks simpler to me," he said, "to posit that a herdboy can spy our smoke from ten miles away, and his brothers can lope thirty miles in a day to tell the neighbors." He turned. A red cloak flapped around his tunic. "Let's pitch camp. And unload the horses, especially. I want to be sure they've got their land legs when our yokels arrive."

Soon we had a snug cluster of tents. Scaubo supervised the assembling of a small shrine, and himself made the thank-offering to Neptune for safe passage. Memmius added one to Mercury, since we would be faring along roads now, though I knew he believed in no gods—merely in that dance of blind atoms which Lucretius has written of—and acted pious lest he rouse superstitious fears. This country was so daunting.

Myself, I wandered off. In chilly dusk, in a clump of grass behind a dune, I found a coltsfoot growing, the first frail flower of spring, and knelt to call without words upon Aphrodite. Memmius is wily and learned, he is doubtless right about the absurdity of the myths, very possibly most of the world arises from a play of forces and nothing else; but She is. I have felt Her too often to imagine otherwise.

I am alone—I did not speak to Her—my heart flutters like a snared swallow, I am alike full of grief and of a joy I know will come to me in the future, alike awed and terrified, I feel how tiny are the years of my life but feel too that they are infintely deep, and none of this do I understand. Lady of All, what do You want of me?

Surf growled outside the bay. The tide was coming in, that eternal onslaught we do not know in the Midworld Sea.

I slept poorly, with many dreams.

The next day, however, opened in peace except for a brief, thunderful hailstorm. We explored the area, finding countless traces of former encampments: fire sites, postherds, gnawed bones, crude carvings on boulders which might have been done in idleness or might be sacred. Generations of feet, hoofs, wheels had worn a trail from inland through the brush, so broad and hard-packed it could almost be called a road. Some of the younger sailors and I took weapons and followed it a few miles. Near the end of our venture we came upon a row of great mounds. Though overgrown, several of them had in the course of ages worn down to expose the stone chambers within.

I froze. "But I've seen dolmens like that at home!" I cried.

"You find them everywhere along the coasts, from Caria to here and maybe farther," said Hippodamas, who had become my friend on the sea trip, being a fellow Greek and a bright, good-looking lad. "We saw them when we rounded Armorica, and rows of standing stones too, stark as teeth in a dead giant's jaw."

"Who made them?" I whispered.

"Who knows? I dug into one once. Full of skeletons."

"Tombs—" It came upon me that here was no new land. It was ancient beyond knowing, secret beyond imagining.

Hippodamas saw me shiver and laid a comforting arm around my waist. No fool, he was yet no brooder like me, but lived toughly and merrily in each day as it came. We walked thus awhile, till everybody decided to turn around. Then we found ourselves at the tail of the line. He laid his mouth to my ear and murmured, "You know, Philon, since you shaved this morning, your face could be a girl's."

Beneath the wind, my cheeks heated.

"A touch too strong in the chin, maybe," he went on, a teasing which softened to: "But those're nice lips, and straight nose, curly black hair, fine hazel eyes. . . . How about it?"

"Uh," I mumbled in a wave of confusion.

"We've been warned how chaste the German women are," he laughed. A marvelous interplay of muscles went through his arm where it circled above my hips. "That whore in Gesoriacum is far behind me. Hm?"

"I—I—" It did not seem to be me that stammered, "No, I'm sorry, Hippodamas, but—"

He let go. "Don't tell me you've never, like a Jew."

"No, but—"

"Ah," he said coldly. "Your patron, then. Quite. I understand." He left me and fell into overanimated conversation with a shipmate.

But *I* don't understand! I wanted to cry after him. It's only . . . I don't know what it is. Here, here, She has made something ready for me. I can't imagine how I know—

Staring around: This stern strange country, oh, that must have stirred a thing to life in me, a longing for— But I am already free! A freedman, at least, under the supervision of a kindly and interesting man who . . . who will surely be visiting Greece again, next year or the year after, for a while, and will want me to come along . . . won't he?

Hippodamas, don't be angry because I have fallen into Her hands.

I was outwardly silent the rest of that day. Next noon the dwellers arrived.

We saw them from afar, but were nonetheless surprised.

True, most were locals as expected, on foot, unarmored, bearing spears, axes, long cutting-action swords of soft brown iron, or mere cudgels—about thirty altogether. But at their head came half a dozen riders in helmet and ringmail.

Eporedorix bustled about directing us in how to form up. He wanted no bristling defensive ranks that, by assuming hostility, might provoke it. Rather, we took stances from which we could instantly leap to form a shield-locked square. Memmius donned his toga and advanced in proper Roman dignity. From my post I peered and peered, every thew aquiver, pulse loud in my skull and throat. Were these the terrible Cimbrians?

They averaged taller than men of the Midworld, but not inordinately so, perhaps three or four inches; and their build was more stocky than lean. While some had sun-bleached hair whiter than flax, that of others was brown, red, or black. They cropped it short, like their beards. The only really alien feature was the eyes, sea-pale in those weathered faces. They wore knee-length tunics of coarse wool, to which several added leather cloaks and linen trousers. Fabrics were dyed with woad, madder, and—dimly—berry juices. Their shoes were hairy, strapped around the foot and laced to the ankle.

Such were the walkers: men of this neighborhood, farmers, fishers, hunters, trappers, diggers of peat, who had so little worth stealing that whole lifetimes might pass without a war other than the strife against nature which had no truce. They were brave, hardy, and, I thought then, simple.

The riders, on hammer-headed shaggy-dun ponies, resembled them in many ways, but were a little bigger, much straighter, their hands not misshapen from toil—an upper class. Their conical nose-guarded helmets and knee-length ring-byrnies seemed well made, and might give better protection than a legionary's loricae. The clothes beneath were of good, colorful stuff. They were clean-shaven but wore their hair somewhat longer than the peasants, drawing it into a braid that hung down the left shoulder.

They halted at the edge of the strand. Memmius trod forth,

right arm raised. "Greeting," he said in his German. "We come in peace, as friends, from Rome the Great."

The natives looked nonplussed. One or two snickered. The leading horseman rode from their line, dipped his lance, and, smiling, replied, "Greeting and welcome to the country of the High Jutes"—in accented by comprehensible Latin.

I could only gape. Memmius recovered fast, spoke smooth phrases, told us to lay aside our arms, and invited the barbarians to dine.

"We thank you," said their leader. Beneath his courtesy twinkled the same amusement as before. He had a fine voice, deep and melodious, rising slowly from the depths of the barrel chest. "I am Hesting, son of Beroan, king—or perhaps you'd call me duke—of High Jutland, on whose Weststrands you have landed." Springing to earth with a litheness unusual for his compact build, he clasped Memmius' hand and arm in the Roman manner.

My gaze followed him around. He was not young—past forty, I guessed—though he carried himself so well that this could only be told from the gray in his ruddy locks, furrows and crinkles in his face, unconscious masterfulness in his bearing. Crowsfeet around lightning-blue eyes, lines across broad brow, calipers from strongly curved nose to wide mobile mouth, startling dimples, bespoke years of looking across wide horizons, of thought, and of laughter. Suddenly I imagined Odysseus resembling, not idealized cold marble, but Hesting the Jute.

Through wind and surf, while cloud shadows chilled and the quick wan sun touched me, smelling salt and kelp, feeling sand hiss past my ankles, I watched the chieftain and heard him. He met Scaubo and Eporedorix with easy politeness, as if they were already old comrades. He passed among our crewmen, while heartening his followers with jokes in their own rough tongue, till both groups relaxed and started shyly to mingle.

By then I had discovered that the language here, while akin to what we had studied in Colonia, was sufficiently different

that Memmius and I were lucky to hit on a speaker of Latin.
We had a good foundation, of course, and ought soon to be
reasonably fluent in Jutish; but Hesting could expedite matters for us no end. It made me wonder if Her will had brought
him.

He explained things frankly and amicably while we
showed him around our camp and ship, spread the best repast
we could, made the gifts to him and his men which barbarians
always expect (and Homer's heroes did). We Romans had—
as usual, his eyes if not his lips seemed to chuckle—taken an
overhasty view of a complex situation. (Memmius nodded,
unsurprised. How accurate a picture can you compile from a
few travelers' tales and, otherwise, third- or fourth-hand
rumor?) The Cimbrians proper, whom Hesting called Him-
meri, lived to the north of his own folk. Beyond them were
the Vandals. The High Jutes ("I'd say the name comes less
from boasting, though we get plenty of that, than from our
holding the highest part of the country") occupied the middle
of the peninsula, its major section. South of them dwelt the
Heruls, Angles, and lesser folk.

These were all separate kingdoms, if that is the right word
when a king is, essentially, no more than president at meet-
ings of tribal chieftains, leader in war, and head priest. (Later
I would learn what a clumsy simplification that was too,
which we made at the time out of Hesting's laconic answers
to questions.) But since they were of the same basic stock,
they tended more and more to call themselves, collectively,
Jutes.

This was the easier to do because nowadays they fought
each other far less often than they did the Danes. These were
another set of folk, related but distinct, currently migrating
from Scandia into the islands, driving out or subjugating the
inhabitants. Their swift, many-oared ships had long been
raiding the eastern coast of the peninsula. Hesting expected a
full-scale invasion this summer. It did not seem to perturb
him.

He did not precisely chance to be in our vicinity. Every

spring, after the equinoctial ceremonies at Holy Lake, the Goddess—Whom he called Nerthus while he signed his brow, lips, breast, and loins—traveled around the realm to bless it, as She did in other processions in the other kingdoms. He must accompany Her. Thus he had not been far off when word came of a foreign ship. Though the season was too sacred for combat, it had been only prudent for him and a few of his household warriors to arm themselves and go investigate. They must be back before dark.

As for how he came to know Latin, why, he laughed, that also was reasonable. Rome having conquered the Gauls and certain of the Germans, she was now the greatest power in this part of the world as well as southward. Besides possible diplomatic and military interaction, there was a growing volume of trade, thus far mostly with the mobile Danes. Why should the Jutes not get a bigger share? Furthermore, Danes venturing abroad, even serving hitches in the legions, had picked up quite a lot of knowledge useful in war. Jutes had better bestir themselves likewise.

Therefore Hesting had visited both Roman Germany and northern Gaul as a young man. Later he had acquired a Latin-speaking slave who kept him in practice. The man had lately died of a flux, however.

Hesting had been hoping for the advent of somebody important. He and Memmius traded a glance which lasted for several heartbeats after he said that. Oh, he knew already the Roman was not merely a merchant, and the Roman knew that the Jute knew, and they both smiled the least bit.

Let our leaders follow him on the sacred journey, he invited. It had just a few days left to go. Let them thereafter come dwell as his guests at Owldoon, as long as they wished. That was on the Great Road, an inland trade route which ran many-branched from the Skaw on south through Iron Wood into Germany. We would have no lack of passersby to ask about things. Our goods could be carted there. If we wanted to offer some at the seaside fair, he would arrange for their storage in a nearby community.

"To be honest," Hesting said, "I'm afire to hear what yarns you'll spin!"

I, seated humbly aside, was altogether charmed. Who would have looked for alertness, humor, and curiosity in a northland kinglet? Well, who, in the depths of northland winter, would have looked for the spring to blossom? Hesting suffered from no more than the loneliness of his country, I thought. In heart and brain, he was our kind of man—my kind. I wondered if I would get a chance to recite him lines of Sappho, no, Catullus, or tell him about Socrates and Alexander.

The passage of Nerthus reminded me of the rites of Cybele (and I would stare at the dolmen mounds which brooded everywhere over this landscape, and wonder half shivering what mysteries of a lost past linked the Midworld to the Boreal). Drawn by cows, Her wagon traveled from village to village. At each settlement the folk came forth shouting, singing, dancing, waving newly leaved and flowering branches, the girls garlanded. There followed rites, a feast, and a sacred orgy. Next morning the king and his men went on, to spread Her blessing further that the whole realm might be made fruitful.

Naturally, differences from the south were abundant, starting with those draft cows, which were tough little red beasts. Should one come in heat on the journey, she was bred in the very next place they reached. The bull was afterward killed by young men in a reckless chase and consumed, and great was the rejoicing because this year would surely be good.

The wagon was large, well carpentered, painted, and gold-trimmed; but the figures carved on it were too foreign to a Greek for me to see them as anything except grotesque. Only later would I find the powerful grace in the wood sculptures here. Upon the wagon stood a curtained shrine which housed Her image, that none might look upon save the king. He, white-robed, was the driver. His warriors were acolytes and honor guard, for no one broke the peace of the holy season, when even outlaws might creep from the moors and be given food and shelter.

The king was the priest of all vernal sacrifices and invocations. Those varied from stead to stead. In this thorp one gave a pig at the grave of its founder, in that hamlet a sheaf from the last harvest was burned—he knew each proceeding and conducted it with a dignity that made me, at least, feel Her veritable presence.

But immediately afterward the feast was spread, an extravagance of hoarded meats and breads and fruits, beer and mead and berry wine, for this otherwise lean period; and everybody, from the king on down, bawled in merriment. The jests, songs, and byplay got coarser as hours wore on, until at dark those who were married went by torchlight to a newly plowed field. There they formed a ring; and before their eyes, the king and a maiden chosen by lot disrobed, and he had her virginity; and each man and wife coupled in the furrows.

The girl was considered to be made lucky, a most desirable match. But she would thereafter know none but her husband. We were told that a woman's adultery was punished by her public scalping, clubbing, and living or half-living burial in a bog; she had tainted the blood of the clan. Even the bachelor youths were generally celibate, only a few rich households possessing female slaves whom their scions might enjoy.

"We seed our women upon the earth, that the seed in it may quicken," Hesting explained.

This was the day after we had been allowed to witness such a doing. I myself had been gripped by Her, oh, if only there had been a girl for me! Memmius had whispered dryly in my ear that he was glad this trip would soon be over and that Hesting had promised to include a concubine in his hospitality. I scarcely heard. The blood roared in me.

Now I saw Memmius lift an eyebrow. He knew better than to contradict, but his scoffing was obvious. I grew furious at him. The night before, in Hesting and the maiden I had looked upon raw beauty. That the king spoke in such a matter-of-fact voice did not lessen my respect for him. He went to his gods in the same unafraid way as he went about his daily work, or to war or sea or, at the end, death.

Not that I glorify the Jutes. They are uncivilized, unlettered, stolid save when drunk or in one of the fell rages that can come upon them, as close to the soil and waters as their own animals and therefore almost as far from the loftiest flights of the spirit. Though their craftsmanship is excellent and their art does have that primitive strength, both are limited by crude tools and scanty choice of materials. They think themselves free men, and are in fact the slaves of uncountably many traditions and superstitions. They have no concept of a better life than the labor and danger which are theirs, let alone any dream of a philosophy, a leader, or an empire that could make such betterment possible. They are physically admirable and keep themselves cleaner than I would have imagined after being in grimy Colonia; but their sports are clumsy and unorganized, their music a high-pitched keening, their dances ridiculous.

Typically, a house is a long one-room structure. Within a foundation frame of stones, walls and roof are turf supported by undressed timber, a firetrap if ever I saw any. Oriented east and west, the building has latticework doors but no windows, only a louver through which a little of the smoke off the clay hearth may escape. The gloom is hardly relieved by lamps. The floor is strewn with rushes or, on special occasions, juniper boughs. At one end are clay daises, wooden stools, a weighted loom, cooking gear, food hung from rafters, personal property—living space for the entire large family. The rest of the chamber is divided into stalls for cattle and horses, pens for swine and fowl. The livestock helps keep the place warm, and even I could get used to the stench; but it was disconcerting to rouse at dawn—after a night which had begun with unmistakable sounds of copulation—and see a boy trot past carrying a forkful of manure for the midden outside.

Ten or twenty such houses comprise a village. Around it lie

the ancestral graves and the fields. Each family owns its land, but there is much collective effort, as well as a common. Nearby is a well or stream or other source of water, and usually a boulder or solitary tree or something of that kind to which small offerings are made.

As for religion in the larger sense, the Jutes worship primarily the Goddess, whom they call Nerthus, more in Her aspect of the Great Mother than of that inviolable Aphrodite Whom my heart serves. Her consort is Fro. The rough wooden images of either can be seen everywhere, to my mind grossly sexual until I remembered Diana of Ephesus and the Hermae in Athens. Only the idol which travels in the sacred wagon is forbidden to ordinary view. During the spring procession, the king is considered either to represent or to be Fro—the people are not inclined to draw fine logical distinctions.

They have numberless local divinities, tutelaries, and oracles. In addition, as I began to master the language and converse with folk, I heard about Danish gods and saw propitiations of them. These seemed to be principally the warlike three called by the Romans Mars, Jupiter, and Mercury. The Romans are forever making such naïve identifications. I am far from sure that Tiwu, Thunarr, and Wothen really correspond that closely, not to speak of other deities. At any rate, Nerthus and Fro are the aboriginal Powers of land and sea, fertility and fisheries. The Danes put most of their pantheon in heaven and make them lords of war. As they and the Jutes come increasingly into contact, however hostile, more and more men on either side are deeming it wise to pay respects to the gods associated with the opposition.

This Hesting would not do. "I plain don't aim to truckle to Wothen Psychopompos," he stated. His manner was calm as ever. "Maybe, in time, we can reach an understanding of sorts with the Danes, and thus with their gods. Meanwhile I am Fro's, and Hers, and mainly my people's."

We were riding down the Great Road, approaching Owldoon, his home. The rutted, muddy, rain-puddled path was no legionary highway. Yet it ran for hundreds of miles to join ancient routes in the east of Europe, and along it had gone amber, bronze, furs, glass, slaves, hopes for more centuries than man has kept count of.

Here we were somewhat east of the middle of the peninsula, upon its spine. High banks on either side bore grass, daisies, ferns, dandelions like blobs of gold, briar, crab apple, blackthorn, wild cherry. Above was a thin forest, murky fir, palely budding willow, shuddering aspen. It was good to see trees again after the past days of empty immensity.

A drizzle enclosed my sight; mists smoked over the earth; my garments clung clammy to my skin. Memmius hung back among the guardsmen who followed the wagon and those sailors who accompanied us. The latter were few. They would transport our goods to Owldoon. On their return, the ship would raise anchor—no sense in letting her lie idle—to call for us a year hence. By that time, Memmius hoped to have founded a permanent trading post, with a factor responsible to him. Until then, he and I were the only ones whom it was worth keeping on hand. Wrapped in his cloak, he snuffled and sneezed, miserable from a cold he had caught. "Appreciate your youth while you have it, Philon," he had wheezed to me. Of course I didn't. I was merely not uncomfortable, and fascinated by Hesting's discourse as he drove.

Hoofs plopped, wheels groaned, often an animal puffed a weary snort. I couldn't see many birds but I heard them everywhere around, like an ocean which twittered and fluted. The damp air struck me in the lungs with greenness. Spring does not come this ardently to the Midworld.

"You do expect . . . war, then, . . . sir?" I dared ask.

The blocky eagle-nosed head nodded. "What else? We've had our spies and scouts out. Not that King Knui makes any deep secret of his intentions. He's already gathering ships. Right after hay harvest, we fight."

"But why?"

"Why not? For land, wealth, power, glory—do you Romans fight for anything different?" He turned a wry smile on me. "Except that you don't seem to get much fun out of it."

I thought of kings and heroes on both sides of the gleaming walls of Troy. Roman leaders used to go likewise in the van of their armies. However, Julius Caesar was more a player moving men around from his tent than he was himself a warrior, and as for his recent successors— Heat fluttered in my face, a pulse in my neck, and I cried, "I am no Roman, sir! I am a greek!"

At once I was embarrassed at my outburst. Hesting put me at ease when he said, "Indeed? Well, tell me about that," and I knew his interest was perfectly sincere.

It became a long talk, followed by many more.

Hesting did not go directly home. At a crossroads, the folk of his own region met him, summoned by runners who had waited for sight of us. In a stately and, to me, quite moving ceremony, they bade the Goddess welcome back. Three female slaves were led forth, garlanded and gaily clad, a girl, a mature woman, and a toothless crone. They had obviously been given a great deal to drink. Nonetheless the girl wept ceaselessly and the woman seemed numbed. The granny tried to comfort them both. So did Hesting, who spoke soothing words while he secured them to the wagon by thongs around their wrists. Thus they went along when he drove to Holy Lake, to return the image to its house.

"What will they do?" I tried to ask a guardsman when the solemnities had ended and we pushed on for Owldoon. He had as much trouble getting my meaning as I then had in getting his, but at length I worked out that they would help the king wash and anoint Her, dress Her in new clothes, and set Her in Her place.

Why should that terrify them? Awe? I didn't pursue the

question, my knowledge of local speech being so rudimentary. Anyhow, new impressions were crowding in on me from all sides.

These folk were as intrigued by us outlanders as their kin were, though, living hard by the Great Road, they were more sophisticated. Anticipating a year in their midst, Memmius and I exerted ourselves to make friends. Among such open hearts, that was easy.

Owldoon is the largest village in High Jutland, probably on the entire Cimbrian Chersonese, and really deserves to be called a town. Nearly fifty houses hold a substantial population. That makes the outermost fields pretty far off, but their owners can afford horses, besides having sons who camp out to guard plows and teams or harvested sheaves. A number of men do no farming, being artisans or, in a few cases, full-time widely ranging traders. The latter bring in commodities like charcoal and lumber from distant forests, dried or smoked fish from the seacoast; they manage the annual fair which attracts merchants from as far away as Scrith-Finn Land or Burgundia; could the mucking Danes only be brought to heel, they grumbled, they would build ships.

It surprised me how much the ordinary dweller travels too, on hunting expeditions to areas where game is still plentiful, on visits to relatives or to religiously efficacious sites elsewhere. He works hard at certain times of year, but otherwise he is less homebound and has more leisure than the average Midworld rustic. To be sure, he has no standing army or swarm of officials whom he must sweat to support.

The houses sit in orderly rows. While swine, dogs, chickens, and naked children romp around freely in the unpaved lanes, each family is required to keep its frontage reasonably clean. Nobody minds, because gathered dung is good to spread on the fields. The buildings are not as drab as their turf construction would suggest, for rafter ends and doorposts are carved and gaudily painted, and in summer every sod roof goes wild with flowers. Many bear the nests of storks, a bird sacred to Nerthus. Indoors are apt to be considerable

possessions, including some from Factories in Gaul or Italy
itself. Apart from utilitarian glassware, cheaply made and
cheaply bought, the selections are generally tasteful.

Hesting's home showed little outward distinction. Inside,
however, no animals were admitted save his hounds. Three
hearths provided sufficient winter heating. Their clay had
glass and stones inset, a quite clever imitation of Roman
mosaic. He could be spendthrift with fuel, since a great peat
bog lay nearby and his dwelling, well apart from the rest,
would create no hazard to those if it caught fire. I found that a
peat blaze is remarkably cheery, bright, and smokefree.

Imported tapestries, polished shields and weapons,
shelves full of workaday and ornamental articles, lined the
walls, above benches which ran the length of them. Household members and the frequent guests slept on those or, if
low-ranking, on the floor. In the corners of the east end he
had installed a Danish fashion, beds provided with sliding
panels. They were so short that one must recline half sitting,
but they did offer privacy to the master and mistress, and to
especially favored visitors. Memmius got the spare.

The landscape around is rolling, often rising in stiff-
backed hills or plunging into glens, every road marked by the
burial mounds of a forgotten race. (The Jutes practice inhu-
mation too, but make no dolmens and seldom a very conspicuous grave.) Most of what acreage meets the eye is
intensively cultivated: barley, emmer, spelt, flax, plus plants
we consider weeds such as nettles, black nightshade, butter-
cup, yarrow. Well-nigh treeless, it is dwindled by the sky and
towering clouds, unshielded from the winds which boom
down off a dimly seen northern heath.

In that wet country a well can be sunk almost anywhere, so
men have no need to locate by water. A long lake shines about
three miles southward. Separate from the sacred one, which
is small and whose dense grove is not visible from Owldoon,
this is free to everybody. The ground between it and the town
is a common, where youngsters graze cattle, sheep, goats,
geese throughout the endless summer days. Aspen, beech,

and oak grow abundantly along its shores, making a sun-
flecked rustling shadowiness where I often idled, plucked
berries, chatted with folk, or dreamed by myself. Fishing
boats lie at a dock. In fair weather the people like to go
swimming. Ashore, adults are prudish about covering themselves; but nakedness of both sexes, laughing and romping in
the water, does not count. How beautiful they are!

(My image of Greece—I have seen little of Greece, being
born in Rome, my ancestors slaves since the destruction of
Corinth; Memmius' multifarious businesses have taken him
and me a few times to Athens, where my heart soared among
the pillars of the Acropolis, and once unforgettably through
the islands—my image of the soul of Greece is a boy, seated
on a stone in a forest, beside a chiming stream. He is nude,
deeply browned by the sun, the first signs of manhood barely
upon him. He smiles as he plays a syrinx, whose notes twitter
in tune with the brook's tiny cascade. . . . Since that Jutland
summer, though I know it makes no sense, I see him as
having blue eyes and flax-white hair.)

Barely discernible eastward is another stand of trees,
which grow around the peat bog.

Hesting's wife was a tall woman, her gray-blond tresses
coiled on a head whose face was too heavy and crag-nosed for
my taste, but who greeted us gently. Her name was Ioran.
Beyond his duties as Fro, or a twinkle when a pretty girl
walked by, her husband showed no interest in others. I came
gradually to learn that, in her barbarian fashion, she had a
formidable intellect, including quite a sense of humor.

This was not immediately obvious, and not just because of
my limited command of the language. Except when hostess
at feasts, she was no "queen" in our sense, simply the
hardworking mistress of a large household. For that matter,
when he was not being priest or judge or president or general,
Hesting's attention was on his private affairs. Besides farming and hunting, he had substantial shares in various trading

enterprises. He plowed his own fields, did much of his own carpentry, took the lead in collective labors like threshing, even as did the kings in Homer.

At ceremonial times, Ioran flashed in golden torque and armrings, amber necklace, gown and cape of southland silk. But daily she wore a plain dull-colored dress, not unlike a peplos to which was added a rain hood. She herself took a hand in the numberless tasks she oversaw, milling, baking, brewing, cooking, cleaning, carding, spinning, dying, weaving, sewing, human and veterinary medicine, the rearing of everyone's children and the laying out of everyone's dead.

She and Hesting had six offspring who lived past infancy. The oldest, Walhauk, had become a man with house, wife, and first baby. The youngest was a girl-toddler. In between were two boisterous youths, two maidens quieter but no less independent, they having never been secluded like Midworld women. We fear for the virtue of ours; but those Jutish lasses carry knives just as their brothers do, and know how to use them for weapons as well as tools. I found their company delightful. All those siblings and I became good friends, who savored many an outing or jape or earnest conversation together. But I cannot write of that, it's blurred in my mind, what I remember in hurtful sharpness is their father.

He came home a day after Ioran their mother had received us, and for a while was unwontedly grave and withdrawn. In the complexities of getting better acquainted with him and his, I failed to notice that the three female slaves had not returned.

Memories, memories: they crowd around me, hungry to become real again, like the ghosts around Odysseus when he fared to hell. I too will give a draught of blood, now to this one, now to that one, that it may speak; but I must draw the blood from my heart.

The peat bog will not be denied, it must be first, however gladly I would drown it in its own mire.

I cannot even say that it looked evil (no, looks, far off in Jutland of my ghosts). Truly I clapped my hands and exclaimed when Hesting and I came upon it.

That was soon after our arrival at Owldoon. A spell of rain, day after day and night after night till earth dissolved, plashing broken by flare-ups when wind flung monstrous hailstones, lightning which turned clouds white-hot and thunder which rattled our bones, had driven its chill and damp into the cold Memmius already had. He lay in high fever for a week or more, barely able to get down the broth and herb tea which Ioran made for him. A month passed before he regained his strength. Meanwhile the weather turned good, Hesting went about his affairs, and he invited me along.

"Asrun will be disappointed," Memmius croaked, grinning a bit. She was the slave—taken as a child in a retaliatory raid on the Danes—whom Hesting had told to pleasure us in addition to her usual chores. A plump, freckled, not particularly intelligent redhead, apparently barren but altogether lusty, she routinely got such assignments and made no bones about enjoying them. "I'm scarcely in condition for her, and you're going away. . . . Ah, well, she'll doubtless find plenty of hayricks."

Hesting made numerous journeys, long and short, around his realm in the course of a year. His guardsmen he picked at each village and sent home from the next, for most settlements could not afford to feed many. Certain of the trips were official, to folkmoots where he presided and judged, or to a couple of festivals which the king traditionally attended. More of them were on his own, to look and talk and learn how went the land.

"I've gotten a lot of ideas, you see, mulling over what I saw in Roman territory," he told me. I being anxious to master his tongue, we spoke in it as much as possible; but often it, not I, lacked vocabulary and we resorted to Latin. He squinted across the hills, whose plow-rows were turning emerald as shoots grew forth. Above us the sun was a ball of fire, its light a cataract out of infinite blue. There were no clouds, but uncountable wings, up yonder. A breeze blew odors of earth, flowering, and the warm little horses which trotted between our knees. At our rear jingled the escort. Thrushes caroled, blackbirds whistled.

"My thoughts haven't come easy," Hesting went on. A shadow of struggle passed over the mirth-lined face. "I was a younger son, not expecting to succeed my father. Then he died and my brothers died, and there I was. I'd supposed I, who'd sought out the very Romans, couldn't be taken aback. Wrong. It's overwhelming when it happens."

"I think I can imagine, sir," I said.

He reached over. His fingers brushed lightly across my wrist. " 'Hesting' will do, Philon. We don't go in here for treating a plain leader like a god, the way they seem to southward." After a pause: "And yet, you know, every spring I am a god. It's not just having my image stuck in temples like Caesar's. I *am* the one She needs to quicken the earth, and hasten the sun homeward, and— Well, at the same time, don't you understand, I've been abroad. I've seen how differently things can be done. And times are changing here also. More than the Danes coming in. I think we can handle them. But the trade stuffs, the foreign arts and crafts . . . gods, ways of living, even so innocent-looking a matter as our younger men getting interested in deep-water ships . . . I wonder what it all means, what it'll bring about. I suspect She"—he signed himself—"is readying a new fate for us. She may even intend to have us call Her nothing more than the wife of a he-god, as the Danes do—for Her own ends, for Her chosen centuries. I don't know about that. Yet change of some kind, the house of our fathers torn down and a strange dwelling built, aye, plain to see before us. We Jutes will ride that wave, or we'll be hauled under and drown."

He laughed. "Hoy! You'd call this a, uh, a mixed bag of metaphors, wouldn't you, Philon?" Seriously: "True, though. How glad I am to have somebody around who knows about the whole world." After a moment: "And, what's more, can think about it."

The road made a swing between its high, heathery, barrow-freighted slopes, and abruptly the view before us was new. Hesting laughed afresh. "At least the peat bog is reasonably permanent," he said in Latin.

The sight enchanted me. Afar glimmered another lake, tree-encircled, reedy, clamorous with ducks, geese, swans, curlews, herons, storks. It had no definite shore; the foreground, in this low valley, faded from water to quagmire to fen. Flowers had exploded over the uneasy soil, white daisy, tawny marigold, heaven-blue cornflower, girl-pink primrose, fiery poppy. A few yeomen were digging the turf with long-handled wooden spades. They took it out in rectangular brown chunks which they stacked on higher ground to dry for some weeks before they brought it in for fuel and building material.

Hesting drew rein and gossiped awhile. I admired how casual-seeming a way he had of probing their feelings, especially about the war he foresaw. They answered him with respect but not servility, using his name and no honorifics.

I noticed that, in spite of water oozing from the sides to make the workers splash barefoot on the bottom, this trench was considerably deeper than one several yards off. In fact, the latter had been partly filled in. As we rode on, I asked Hesting the reason.

He scowled. "They'd not want to grub up a dead body," he said. "The bog won't have let it rot away."

"Oh." I recalled what I'd heard earlier. "A lawbreaker buried there?"

"Yes, in this case. He was a thief. I hanged him myself." He pointed to a huge old ash on the marge of the fen, which I learned later was man-planted generations ago. "My single time as executioner, and I hope the last."

"It's kinder than crucifixion," I said, for his look was grim.

Turning eager, in that mercurial play which went ever across his basic calm, he said: "Oh, you misunderstand, Philon. This is no disgrace. Rather, it's the way the man gets

his honor back. He's sanctified to Her, don't you see. His life
goes to make the earth live, and his kinfolk can hold up their
heads again. It's not necessarily a punishment, even. Once in
a long while—'' He grimaced. ''Never mind. I didn't like
seeing and feeling him struggle while I hauled him aloft.
Let's make a wish it won't be needful anymore.''

He leaned toward me. This time he clasped my wrist. His
hand was hard and warm. I wasn't sure if I felt his pulse
knocking in it or mine. ''Maybe it won't be, Philon,'' he
said, ''not because men will get any better, but because ways
will alter. I *am* glad you've come! You southerners—this
writing you have—it gives you such a long view. You mentioned a Bronze Age before anybody knew about iron, and
the rise and fall of . . . you called them republics?
. . . and—so many things I have to ask you about.''

My face burned like the sun. I stared at the mane of my
horse and mumbled. ''I'll tell you what I can, . . . Hesting,
. . . but my patron knows far more.''

He chuckled. ''Aye, I expect to get considerable out of
Memmius. However—don't pass this on, no use giving
offense—he strikes me as a narrow man. Sharp, but his
cutting edge strictly on business and politics. You may be
callow, but you think beyond yourself, and you're always
trying to learn. The night before we left, I watched you gaze
long at the stars.''

''Well, they're different here—''

''You want to know them. And I'd like to hear about your
stars, Philon.''

I will not seek to write down the discourses we had, hour
by hour as we rode or strode across those mighty hills, over
wind-scoured moors and down into wolf-haunted woods, or
at evening when low blue peat flames brought his face out of
shadow, and the hands he held forth to them. I dare not.

Let me say that we came to a oneness of giving, that both
our minds were widened by what we shared. I was learned in
books; he could read every leaf and spoor. I drew pictures of

the Parthenon or an athlete sculptured by Phidias, in charcoal on skin; he took me to a hiding place where we watched a family of otters at play, lovelier to see than I would have believed. I recited verses which he said grabbed him by the heart; he roared forth olden lays which shook me by the throat. I spoke of exotic animals and physical laws described by Aristotle; he made me familiar with the life around me and in smiling patience taught me how to make a skiff of the northern sort obey my will. I told him about theories of the ideal state, deeds and misdeeds of historical statesmen; he introduced me to the running of a here-and-now day-to-day kingdom.

Memmius came along on some of our trips after he got well. He was particularly interested when Hesting went on a diplomatic mission to the Cimbrians, failed to make alliance against the Danes but succeeded in winning their pledge not to side against the High Jutes—which he admitted to us was as much as he could hope for. "Our host's a fox of a bargainer," Memmius said to me. "If he'd been born a Roman, well, we might have a different Caesar. To be sure, we've not seen how he can fight."

That chance was soon forthcoming. One cricketful eventide the beacon fires he had had made ready over the land blazed. I saw the nearest to Owldoon kindle afar, a bloody spark like the planet of Ares descended onto earth. Wildness erupted around me. Men ran forth yelling, the torch was put to our own heaped wood, iron and teeth gleamed in the dark, weapons dinned on shields. Inside two or three hours, warriors were arriving from outlier settlements. We set forth before dawn.

Ioran and her daughters bade Hesting and her sons goodbye with Spartan sternness. Yet I saw hands linger together, and my own ached to be among them.

At least I would be under his banner. Memmius and I had brought Roman gear for ourselves, in case of emergency. We could have stayed home, but that would have destroyed our repute and thus our usefulness. Anyhow, my patron wanted to observe events. "Observe only," he reminded me. "Don't get into combat if you can possibly avoid it. Barbarians have so feeble an idea of military discipline that we probably can hang clear without it seeming on purpose."

But these are my friends! cried in me.

A strenuous day's travel—most of the men being afoot—brought us near the coast. There the smoke of a burning village told us just where the Danes had landed. Hesting sent out groups of mounted scouts, leading one himself. I asked to go along, drew a scowl from Memmius and a cheery nod from the king. "Good lad," he murmured. I felt momentarily dizzy, then exalted beyond mortality.

Galloping across a ridge, we saw a few islands upon a bronze-calm sunset sea. These were not the wellspring of the lean black oar driven ships, big enough to be named galleys, which lay beached in their scores or prowled the water on guard. King Knui, who led them, was the strongest lord on Zealand, across the strait from Scandia. Between it and the Chersonese, almost butting into the latter farther south, lay principally the other major island, Fyn.

They were more tall and fair than Jutes, the warriors who cooked, rolled out sleeping bags, took turns raping what women they had caught, near the ashes and corpses of the village. Mail and helmets were more abundant among them, too, though most had to be content with leather cap and doublet—if that—like most of our yeomen. They swarmed across miles. I estimated their number at three or four thousand.

Anguish twisted Hesting's mouth. He smote fist in palm. "I warned those folks to move," he groaned. "I begged them. They wouldn't heed, they wouldn't heed—"

That is the price of being free, I suppose. A Roman proconsul has authority to command evacuation. I have never decided whether it is worth it.

The Danes saw us. A beast-howl racketed from their throats. They ran toward us, arrows buzzed, but we riders left them behind and lost them in gathering dusk.

That night we camped on a high, defensible hill which Hesting had established as our rendezvous. From time to time, men would arrive in groups from remoter parts. The king did not sleep. He sat at a fire before a boulder engraved with sacred figures—the Sun Wheel, the Death Ship, the Goddess and Her consort coupling to renew the world—like a carven image himself. The light flickered over his countenance; so did the smile which greeted each newcomer band.

Between times, he was willing to talk. "How did you know the invasion would be here?" Memmius inquired. "Wouldn't your rival subjugate Fyn first?"

"No, that's too hard a nut until he's gathered much greater might," Hesting replied. "He has sworn oaths with some of the Fynish kings. They'll not help him—I've made arrangements of my own thereabouts—but they'll not fall on him either. He must break us, the High Jutes, before he can do anything else on the mainland. This is the best spot for a beachhead, especially if the Cimbrians swarm gleefully over our backs . . . as I've, hm, led him to think they will."

Memmius wearied and dozed off. I myself listened throughout the night, utterly caught in his stories of spying, bribing, promising, weaving a net to catch the pike which menaced his people—tales harsh or suspenseful or even comical, each fascinating. This was no book by a long-dead Herodotus, Thucydides, Xenophon, Julius Caesar; this was the living stuff with which these men had dealt in their days. How they would have understood and respected Hesting!

Thus did I come to some knowledge of actual, as opposed to theoretical, statecraft. Soon I learned about actual war and generalship.

Hesting's plan had a simple skeleton. He knew the Danes would strike for Owldoon, but in leisurely wise, pillaging, butchering, capturing slaves along the way. When his whole force had assembled, it was a bit larger than the invaders', albeit inferior in equipment. He divided it in two. The first half engaged the enemy. In a running battle, they let themselves be driven up a valley which slanted inland from the sea between thickly overgrown slopes. Meanwhile he led the other half in a circuitous night march. They surprised the fleet, overran its guards, seized the beached ships, launched them, and cleared or put to flight those which stood out at sea.

Knui got word, naturally. In horror he brought his pack around. Cut off from home, they would be an irresistible temptation to the Cimbrians (who had *not* joined them), the Heruls, even more distant tribes, to hunt them down for their arms and loot. He tried to disengage, and failed. The Jutes followed, harassing his rear, sniping with bows and slings from the brush.

When he reached the strands, he found Hesting had re-beached the ships in formation and added stakes and thorn-tangles, to make a fortress which he must storm.

His men tried, roaring, battle-drunken, scarcely heeding when their pursuers attacked from behind. They sought only to get at our livers, where we stood behind the dear hulls. We cast them back, sallied forth, and crushed them in the jaws of our twin hosts.

It is easy to write of these things. It was not easy to be in them. I do not believe any other living barbarian could have done what Hesting did. Perhaps Vercingetorix himself could not have. Untrained, the northerners fling their bodies at a foe and think that that is war.

Hesting had spent patient years with the headmen of High Jutland—and more with their sons, and still more with humble folk who would be the backbone of what strength he could ever muster. He had explained, over and over and over, the concept of discipline and concerted action which had made Rome the mistress of half the world. He had orated, he had argued, he had browbeaten, he had gotten them to drill, and in the end he achieved enough organization that it was possible to execute an elementary strategy.

On this day his toil bore fruit. I wonder what seed he may have planted to sprout in later centuries.

Only in retrospect do I know what happened. The doing itself was tumult, terror, pain, exhaustion, and marvel.

Obedient to Memmius' orders, I had held back when we fell on the ships. That was not difficult, for the fight was short and most of us never got near a Dane. Nonetheless shame grew thick in my gullet, I could not meet anyone's eyes, I slunk about helping in the most menial parts of arranging our defenses.

When the tall golden-braided men boiled whooping from inland, I left Memmius' side. He clutched my arm. I struck his hand loose. "Let me go or I'll kill you," I heard myself say. He lurched back, appalled, to stand in the reserves at the center of our ring. I sped toward the floating banner of Hesting. It bore a stag.

Amidst shouts and chaos, he saw me and waved me to him. For an instant he squeezed my shoulder. I thought I could feel him through the loricae. Earlier, fear had dried my mouth and given sight and sound an eerie, dreamlike quality—a dream from which I could not will myself to waken. Now glory took me.

They came, they came, iron ablaze beneath the sun, to surf against the ships. Arrows, spears, slingstones hailed into them, they fell in windrows, the sand squelched red. Yet they came. I saw a warrior whose guts trailed out of his belly crawl over a rail. When he fell inside the open vessel, a gigantic comrade leaped to him, picked him up, cast him—still grinning, still gasping his death-chant—against the face of a Jute. The Jute staggered back. The Dane crossed the hull, trampled him underfoot, and was among us, hewing.

Cool as a Roman, Hesting met that colossus. He fended off ax blows with a shield and cut a leg open. When the Dane went to one knee, Hesting smote his neck asunder.

I glimpsed that much before the attack reached me. They *had* broken through at this point. They were not many who did. We killed them and sent their followers reeling back. But for a while it was wild around us.

There I slew my first man . . . most likely my only man, peaceable clerk that I am. He was my age, I think, and had cast off his garments in frenzy as northerners are wont to do.

His assault shocked in my shield, helmet, bones. He was awkward, though, his sword already bent and blunted to a mere club. I got under his guard, thrust home, and twisted. The motion felt heavy.

He tried to run up the blade at me. I retreated while twisting, probing his entrails till he fell in a spout of crimson. At the time it simply happened. I was not even conscious of being Philon, a unique point in this vast thing. Strange how often afterward I see my swordthrusts, how white his skin was, how handsome his face beneath its Medusa contortion.

Otherwise I mainly see Hesting fight. When the Danes broke and scattered, the divine fury came on him too. But—I might have known—for him it took the form of mirth. Laughing through ever yell and thunder, he hunted the murderers of his people; and I, close behind, knew that he was indeed the vessel of a Power, himself a god whom I longed to adore.

The last Danes threw down their weapons. We bound them to hold for ransom. They'd not make safe slaves, Hesting said, calm again in a quietness whose immensity was hardly touched by the noises from hurt men, the hush-hush-hush of waves upon strand. Thereafter we gathered our dead and did what we could for our wounded. Badly injured foes we left to the village women we'd freed.

Then Hesting looked about in the yellow sundown light, between green hills, metal-bright waters, darkening blue heaven, over his folk who sprawled at rest too weary for triumph. Into the peace he asked: "Where is Geyrolf?"

That was his second son. Walhauk, his first, came to him and said, "Geyrolf fell. I think it took three of them to bring him down."

Hesting stood moveless awhile, though I saw knuckles whiten around his sword haft. At last he said tonelessly, "Bring me to him."

His friends had already laid out the youth, swabbed off most of the blood, bound the fallen chin. They had left it to Hesting to close the eyes. He knelt on the sand to do so. "Sleep well," I heard him whisper. He kissed his boy, rose, and went about his overseeing of the live men. I wondered if he wept. We were all so sweaty that slow tears would have passed unnoticed. I ran to him, seized his hand, and blurted, "Oh, Hesting, I'm sorry—"

He could not keep pain from his voice. "It was a good ending," he said, and broke from me. I imagined myself laid out, my slain enemies around, wind in my hair, and he kissing me farewell.

Overhead, the gulls and ravens gathered.

Why are the greatest hurts, until the very last, set in the greatest beauties? I can still hardly endure to remember one light night.

The invasion had come shortly before midsummer. Soon the exigencies of getting home, seeing to the injured, dickering out peace terms with Knui's successor, starting the next phase of work on the land—picking up life again—blunted the grief of those who buried their loves. They always live close to death, the northfolk. I wonder if they may not feel loss more keenly than Midworlders do; but they keep it mastered.

And we had won our war, stamped out a threat, taken a booty of ships and arms, a ransom of more, which opened the way to our becoming unassailable. Considering the ferocity of the battles, our casualties were not excessive. Even those families which suffered them had cause to rejoice.

The midsummer festival lifted hearts in still more hope and gladness than was usual. It happened to fall in a spell of singularly fine weather—a good omen, as well as pleasurable in itself—yet this was no drought year and crops flourished. Nerthus smiled upon the world.

Though they have their solemnities, the summer solstice and the autumnal equinox are less portentous, more merry among the Jutes than the other two high holy days. Those concern themselves with the coming year. In the milder seasons, one knows fairly well what the Powers intend; one reaps the rewards of toil ; it is meet and right to show appreciation of Their hospitality on this earth by feasting, dancing, singing, lovemaking, partaking of everything They give.

True, the moment was awesome when we kindled the balefire. From that hilltop where we did it we saw others come to life, wider than eye could reach, stars across the land. Robed and garlanded, Hesting bore among us the bowl of mingled milk and blood from Her cows, the bread from grain grown at Her shrine, that we might be nourished. As I knelt to receive it from him, I knew he was Fro (and Apollo of the Sun) and through him She entered me and I Her. Can the Orphic mysteries give more?

Nonetheless worship ended in revelry which continued for a week. They call this time Wink, because most parents turn an indulgent glance away from their half-grown children. Should something happen beyond a flirtation and kisses, it is not considered the deadly offense it would be anywhen else. If necessary, betrothals are hastily rearranged, marriage dates advanced.

For this is the peak of the light nights, that we do not know around the Midworld Sea. The sun is down for a mere few hours, and true darkness never comes.

I had spent a day at the lake among people my own age or younger, for swimming, ball games, foot races, wrestling, loafing on moss and turf, yarning, joking, a stolen touch of nude bodies and cool lips in the water. It did much to ease my mind, which had kept imagining what sorrow must dwell behind the face Hesting wore . . . and Ioran too, though she did not really occur to me at the time. In truth, the day excited me, until I was relieved to see the slave girl Asrun at liberty when Memmius had already closed his shut-bed.

We needed no more than a look. She followed me from the town, onto the common. In systematic search for privacy— she didn't mind auditors—I had discovered a spot where bushes screened soft grass. She was eager and our passage went hastily. I got a bare minute to squeeze my eyes shut and put before me Wulf. He was a cousin-child of Hesting's whom I believed must resemble the king at age thirteen.

Afterward at peace, I meant to spend the whole night in love but felt no hurry. Raising myself on an elbow, the springiness of every moist blade underneath me, I drank of wonder.

In mild air full of earth, blossoms, green growth, the land reached to the lake, which glimmered like a misted mirror. Leaves were silver-hued beneath a heaven more silver than purple, where only a few tender stars dwelt. Dew glistened, fireflies swooped and darted, blink-blink-blink. On the far side of the water, a hill tall enough to be called a mountain upheaved itself, ghost-wan, unreal, seeming to float. Frogs chanted chorus to a nightingale's Pan-pipe. An own passed splendid and soundless overhead.

Surely, I thought, Hesting let his own soul go free into all this. He did not speak of it, that was not the way of his people, but surely he too could become one with it, he and I and the light night of summer.

Asrun nuzzled me. I turned about, annoyed, for she was just a vehicle. Still, this was no hour to provoke a quarrel.

"I like you, Philon," she sighed. "I like you real good. Bettern'n old Memmius."

"Thanks," I muttered.

Pale and clear in the moonless glow, she shook back her hair and giggled: "Not that he makes any difference to me. You know? Maybe twice a month, and hardly started when it's over." She stroked a hand across me. "You've not been such a stud horse either, sweet. You can when you want—oh, how!—but you don't want very often. Why?"

"I've many things on my mind."

"Awww, now. You ought to unload 'm." She nibbled my earlobe, rubbed my belly, and tittered anew.

That sound was abruptly irritating. I wanted my own thoughts, my own dreams, until at last I grew ready—"Let me be!" I snapped.

She bridled. She was not spiritless; Hesting and Ioran treated their slaves decently. "What's the matter? Aren't you up to more, lover boy?"

I swung on her, lifted a hand to cuff, let it drop but spat in a shivering rage: "You'll do what you're told, which is keep quiet till I lay you again. Or must I tell my host he's lent me a useless mare?"

She choked down a shriek. The terror upon her struck into me. I rolled about, scrambled to my knees, caught her arms, and exclaimed, "What's wrong? I didn't mean— What happened, Asrun?"

She cowered from me. "Y-y-you . . . won't, Philon," she got forth. "You won't, you won't. Please, please, please. I'll, oh, no, *plea-ea-ease*—"

I have seen underlings in Asia actually grovel. They know how. She didn't, which made it hideous.

I slapped her to cut off the hysterics, held her close to lessen the sobbing, and asked for her dread. She stabbed me:

"If he doesn't think—I'm good—I know I'm not a good housemaid, and I'm barren, and if, if, if men don't want me for fun— He'll drown me! He will, next spring, he'll drown me!"

"Nonsense. Why in the world—"

"Nerthus! She takes three each spring . . . girl, woman, carline . . . th-th-they see Her, they handle Her, and then he, he holds their heads under . . . Holy Lake's full of their bones— Oh-h-h-h, Philon, darling, don't tell him!"

I remember little more until the moment when I stumbled past his house. I must have raved around for some while, because my bare feet bled from thorns and stones, my weeping had gone dry and hurt my ribs, dawn stood white in the east where we had been victorious.

He came out. To this day I do not know how that occurred; it was always too hard to ask. Maybe he chanced to be awake, for one sleeps very lightly on those nights. Maybe a watchful servant roused him to something unusual, and was told to stay behind. Maybe the Goddess had Her will, whatever it is. I do, ludicrously, know that this stretch of trail was lined with blackberry bushes, and that a silence had arisen between the nightingale and the lark.

Suddenly, there he was, in a wadmal tunic whose roughness scratched my bare skin when he cast an arm around my shoulders. "Philon," he murmured, "what is your trouble?"

I wrenched free of the embrace. "Let me go, you murderer!" I may have screamed. A dog got excited and started to bark. From afar came an answering wolf howl.

"I don't understand," Hesting said. The first rays of the still hidden sun made a halo in his hair.

I fell to hands and knees, beat my fist on the ground, and cried, "A girl, a woman, a granny. Every year!"

"Oh." He was long silent. The light strengthened. I do not know if others came from the houses or the meadows and saw us. It was never spoken of; they have a sense for what is sacred.

At last he nodded. "Philon," he said, word by word, "this must be, that the land may live. Do you imagine I like it?" He lifted crook-fingered hands to the sky. I saw that his mouth was stretched quite out of shape. "It's hard to drown them— and yet, Philon, that's a release, an ending, a thing I can leave behind till next spring. Harder is putting them through their duties first, while I try to calm them, make them happy, make them drunk. . . . Hardest is to choose them, to choose them. Can you see that?"

Agamemnon and Iphigenia . . . Achilles who butchered the Trojan captives for dead Patroclus. . . . Maybe the gods, if they exist, do not demand horror of us; but we always do of each other.

I rose and laid my head on his breast. He held me close, ruffled my hair, and said shakenly, "I've been thinking of you as a son, Philon. A son in the stead of him we've lost."

Why was I shocked?

Well, he had been so relaxed, curious, jolly, the whole first while that we knew him. Had he shown any reluctance when he drove off to Holy Lake, those three bound to his wagon like cows, I might have guessed the truth earlier. After all, the Gauls and Britols practiced human sacrifice till Rome conquered them and suppressed their Druids. I have heard of it among German tribes.

Slowly I came to know that I had not wanted to know. From the outset, my mind covered the fact up. Memmius took for granted I had made a deduction obvious to him, and didn't think the matter worth discussion. He is a Roman, who enjoys the arena. I went just once, and fled vomiting. Whenever I pass a crucified felon at a roadside, I turn my eyes and cover my ears. I cringe a little when I see slave gangs stooped in the fields of a latifundium, their foreman passing among them with his whip.

However, I savor the fruits of their toil, and admit that criminals must be disposed of, and take pride in having killed an enemy. Thus I struggled toward a vantage point from which I might see the world as Hesting did. Before long I believed I had succeeded.

A kindly man at heart, he hated this duty, therefore dismissed thought of it until the ineluctable annual moment. Nevertheless, to him it *was* a duty, along with many others. The Goddess must be served, yet Her mysteries might not be profaned, lest death come over the land. It would not even be proper for him to show distress over his obedience.

Philon, I scolded myself, you've been stupid. You blindly assumed that he, the father of his rugged people, the incarnation of their male god, shares your squeamishness.

I wondered if he could be won from his superstition. He had seen that different ways are possible. . . . No, it would be no favor to change his belief, when his folk would never let him change his act.

Was it a superstition, indeed? The Goddess has uncountable aspects. Aphrodite, She is not only that grave beauty whose image stands at Milos; She is the foam-born Virgin of Dyprus, She is the Mother of Eros, She is Our Lady of the Weddings, She is the foolish slut Whom Homer mocks.

Artemis, She is the moon-crowned maiden huntress, and She
is the Ephesian, many-teated and fecund as a sow. She is
Cybele the inspirer of madness, Hecate the terrible, Hera,
Ceres, Athene, Persephone Queen of the Dead. . . . When
She is Nerthus, can it be right that She takes lives? So gaunt a
land may need them.

Can it be wrong what they do, these people who still adore
Her while a weary Greece and a corrupted Rome relegate Her
to consorthood, turn more and more to Oriental he-gods or to
no gods at all?

I had felt Her nearness, my first evening upon these shores.

Thus did I assure myself it was not wrong to love Hesting
and be his—son. Meanwhile summer waned, days shrank
before nights, hasty clouds and spilling rains warned of
oncoming winter.

My reconciliation to the facts may well have been speeded
and strengthened by an absence of almost three months.
Memmius, having gotten considerable knowledge and made
considerable contacts among the High Jutes, wanted to do the
same in other tribes, albeit less thoroughly. When the fair at
Owldoon broke up, mid-July, he joined a party from the
southern end of the peninsula who would hawk their wares at
similar, lesser gatherings elsewhere. Perforce I went along.

Our companions were Heruls, Angles, a couple of
Teutons, a Saxon, and a Longobard, whose partnership was
years old. Despite their uncouth ways, this mixedness, this
partial uprooting from home soil, made them somehow
familiar to us. Memmius was more cheerful in their midst,
and won more friendliness, than he had among Hesting's
uncosmopolitan folk. I liked them well enough, and in a way
enjoyed being on the road again, new sights, each day
unforseeable. But a weight lay always on my heart. I recognized it when we watched the autumnal equinox being celebrated in a tiny fisher settlement and I felt nearly ill at not
being elsewhere. I was homesick for Owldoon.

Our course took us north through Cimbri and Vandals, then down the bleak west coast nearly to Chaucian territory. There Memmius and I said farewell, hired a few local men to accompany us, and rode back up the middle of the country. This was at the end of September. We had seen much of interest, accomplished no little of value or profit. None of it is worth my writing down.

I will see him soon, it sang in me: soon, soon, soon.

Thus I was dashed when we entered the town and Ioran informed me he was away on one of his circuits. She expected him presently, however. I composed myself and settled down to record our results in orderly fashion. Memmius dictated most of this, then let me interpolate what I wished as I transcribed from wax tablet to paper. So passed a few days.

Asrun approached me; but though we'd had no women on our journey, I said the house lacked privacy and outdoors was now too cold. "Not really," she sniggered. "Go!" I commanded, and she crept off in fright. I'd not spoken badly of her, but neither had I been able to bring myself to praise her talents to the king as she had begged.

"I'm afraid we have another dreary winter ahead of us," Memmius sighed. "Worse for you than me. I'll at least be conducting interviews, looking for somebody who's got sufficient wit and will that I can make a factor of him. You— Well, of course you can inquire too. Maybe you'll hit on a promising man. However, I do suspect we want one of mature years, perhaps too old or handicapped to risk his neck in these silly little wars. I can't expect you to become intimate with that class of person." He smiled and patted my shoulder. "Amuse yourself as best you can till we sail. On the whole, you've earned it, Philon."

We chanced to be alone, in a turf-and-wattle shack Hesting had lent us for the storage of our goods. These were gone, in trade and gifts, replaced by native products. We were taking inventory, subsequent to this latest venture of ours. Light seeped through thick clouds and wicker door, forcing us to illuminate the dusk within by four lamps which had also made the space fairly warm. His hand continued down my side till it rested on a flank. The aquiline head drew near to mine. "You have been a good boy," he breathed. "No flutterbrain slave. You're better-looking than Asrun is . . . by a long shot . . . did I ever tell you?"

I stepped back. Confusion whirled in me. "Is something wrong?" Memmius asked.

"I feel a little sick—the smell of that burning blubber—"

His eyes narrowed. I'd never voiced objection to odors before, as he occasionally did. At last he shrugged. "Well, let's knock off, then, Jupiter knows we've ample time between here and our ship."

When the trestle tables were set up in the house for the evening meal, I merely picked at my food; later I drank but a few sips of the winelike beverage brewed from berry juice and honey—though my appetite and thirst were normal. This made it plausible for me to sit apart, to stretch myself early on a bench. Not that Memmius would have invited me to his shut-bed. Such would have outraged custom, we knew. It might even require death in the peat bog. The Jutes are as narrow in that respect as other Germanic tribes. I have declared before that I do not idealize them, and try to see their failings as well as their virtues.

What I couldn't afford was to let Memmius realize that I had repulsed him.

Why had I? The question kept me long awake and found no answer. My dreams were troubled.

When in the morning I asked leave to take a walk, he agreed. "You look poorly," he said. "Fresh air may help. I hope so. The nearest proper physician is quite a ways off."

Can even Aesculapius heal the spirit which keeps wounding itself?

After a night's rain, morning had been born in beauty.

Many women were about in the town, taking this chance to air bedding, butcher and pluck fowl, and otherwise batten down against winter. Some men worked on their houses. Most had gone off before dawn with nets and club-headed arrows, to the fen after migratory birds. I met few on my northward tramp, none by the time I stopped for a bit of bread and cheese.

I tried to lose myself in the land. This had been a lingering fall, as if She were reluctant to take summer's ghost from us. Across the high heath I had reached, the ling still bloomed, purple billowing beneath a wind which smelled of it and of distances. Southward whence I had come, plowland rolled brown, black, tawny, till brilliance flared on lakeside woods. The air was loud and swift but unutterably clear. I could see every barrow along roads and fields, Owldoon like a ranking of little hedgehogs. Somehow today the mountain across the water did not look humble beside my memories of southland peaks; it sailed blue and gold into heaven. The hugeness of that sky was broken only by last flights of geese and storks, by a sun which swung pallid and low.

I should have made nature my medicine, as wise Vergil advises. But I kept thinking of the winter ahead. The Jutes hate it. True, they have sports like hunting, sledding, or ice-sliding in the normally short period when the weather turns cold enough; they have games at home, visits with friends, a week of festival after the sacrifices at solstice. But the sunlessness! More than one had admitted to me that hope wears as thin as the stocks of food, that quarrels among penned-up wretches are much too apt to bring manslaughter. How was I, Greece's child, to endure a thicker murk than in Colonia?

Why, there would be Hesting . . . and never a minute to be alone with him, in a crowded and ever more foul sty of a house. And when Spring brought back light, cleanliness, freedom, Memmius would take me away.

Long lean shadows reminded me that not much time

remained till dark. I shook myself, sprang erect, and started back at a brisk gait. Maybe that would flog the sadness out of my blood.

It seemed to, a little. After a mile or so, regardless of the chill streaming over my skin, I grew thirsty. I recalled a brook which ran past a barrow I recognized. It wasn't far off the trail. I turned, picking a careful way through stiff heather and prickly gorse.

Rounding the mound, I slammed to a halt. My temples drugged. Two hobbled ponies cropped what they could find. The single man showed that one beast was a remount. He had undressed to wash off the grime of travel. Against dappled luminance in the brush, sun-darkened face and arms, his body shone white as a girl's.

I stood amidst a roaring and a soaring.

He sensed me, whirled, snatched for his sword. How the muscles flowed! Across their hardness was strewn the same ruddy hair as hung loosened around his cheeks. I had never seen him naked before. The king must maintain a degree of aloofness.

He knew me at once and straightened. "Philon!" he cried gladly.

A far-off part of me decided that he must have dismissed his last set of warriors several miles back, to let them reach home before nightfall. In the peace he had wrought, he need not fear to end his journey alone. And it was like him to stop here first, that he might meet us clean.

"Hoy, what good sprite brings you?" he called through the wind. "How went your trip? Come!" He spread his arms wide.

I ran to them. He hugged me. How powerful he was! Under the wetness glowed warmth. Our hearts beat together.

"I've missed you so—" I began.

He stepped back, but the hands still rested on my shoulders. "You're weeping, lad," he said. "Why?"

"For joy and—sorrow—I know not," gulped from me while the tears whipped forth. "The, the Goddess has me, and I must leave you, Hesting—'' I sank, hugged my knees, lowered my face to them.

The brook rang over stones. A horse whickered. Wind sighed under heaven, soughed in the heather. I shuddered and fought for air.

The warmth descended on my neck, clasped me by the left upper arm, touched my right ribs and thigh. I raised my head. He had sat down beside me, laid that arm around. His free hand turned my face to his. ''Philon, be glad again.'' His smile was shy and, oh, very near my lips.

I kissed his.

There was an instant which was eternal, when my tongue and my hands sought, when my whole being tried to say what words cannot. And then, and then—

I lay sprawled. Blood ran from my mouth. The bruise of his fist would remain for days. I did not feel the pain. I looked up to him where he stood crouched, fingers bent into talons as they had been when he asked for my forgiveness. Behind him reared the barrow, helmeted by its dolmen.

His teeth gleamed. Amidst the chaos in my skull, I saw that Dane who had run my sword into his guts as he strove to get at me. ''What in death's name were you doing?'' he screamed.

I rolled over, dragged myself to my knees, reached out, and stammered, ''I love you, Hesting.''

He stood quiet for a space. His hair tossed in the wind. At last he turned, beat fist in palm, went to the stream, and likewise knelt. He rinsed his mouth several times, scrubbed his body, stared forth at earth and sky.

''Kill me if you want,'' I said into his silence.

Rising, he shook his head. ''No.'' The voice was flat. ''It was a . . . surprise. I'd heard about Greek ways, but never thought you— You were like a new Geyrolf to me.''

''*Was* I?'' I yelled, and stretched my neck for the mercy of his sword.

He gasped.

Presently I opened my eyes. He had toweled himself dry and was scrambling into his clothes. ''Speak to none about this," he slurred, never looking my way. "It's the bog if you do."

"I might welcome that, I said. A leaden steadiness had come upon me.

"Then I must be your hangman. I'd rather not. Even now."

Dressed, he fetched his horses and rode off at a hard trot.

I followed afoot, so slowly that it was night before I arrived. Walking, I worked to reconcile myself to this latest truth. I had been a fool again, had reached too far and thus lost what had been mine. Well, at least I could take it like a philosopher. At least I could spare him a scandal and the pain of making me, for whom he once had cared, sprawl choking on a rope. We could both endure the winter. I would lie about the cause of my injury, and contrive an excuse to move elsewhere. When spring resurrected the world, I would leave his sight forever.

Dogs clamored until they recognized me. Nobody seemed roused by that brief noise. I groped to the king's dwelling and stealthily into its gloom. Fires banked on the hearths threw enough light for me to find a clear floor space to try to rest on.

From the royal shut-bed drifted a whisper. He must have supposed that everyone else was asleep, that none save Ioran heard his hoarse, agonized curses.

By day the lakeshore trees stood skeletal athwart water and sky that were iron-gray. But day was turning to the shortest of glimmers in the middle of night.

Through gifts and glibness I wormed out an invitation to stay with a yeoman named Sigern who dwelt at the opposite end of town. Memmius arched his brows when I asked his permission to accept. "The oldest son and I are good friends," I said. "I'd have a better time, and maybe gather more information, than here."

"You would that," he agreed. "This house has become a tomb." He peered closer. "Have you any idea what's wrong?"

''No. . . . Winter's influence. . . .''

''Not this early. It's the king and queen. As moody and curt as they've become, they cast a pall over the whole company.'' His eyes ransacked me. ''You've not been any comedian yourself of late, Philon.''

''For that same reason.''

I did not quite tell a falsehood. Mainly, however, it was the trouble in Hesting which picked and picked at my own wound.

What was his, though? I couldn't imagine. Very well, I'd shocked him, much as knowledge of the vernal sacrifice had done me. Those slayings went on, and I could live with them. As for him, nothing he would call untoward had really happened between us, nor ever would. We scarcely spoke anymore. Each time his vision chanced to cross me, straightaway he looked elsewhere. That attracted no attention, because he had withdrawn his comradeship for the entire world.

So I had disappointed him. He must be able to shrug that off!

Something else, then. What? Often I saw Ioran his wife touch his hair or the back of his hand. Her mouth had grown pinched and she was liable to start at loud sounds or to shrill at her underlings. Meanwhile she could not always refrain from showing him in public that tenderness which hitherto she had saved—I suppose—for the shut-bed. And he, he seemed to tauten when she did, as if to keep from flinching.

His face was a mask these days, save when anger livened it and a word barked forth more likely than not to be unjustly harsh. He went about his duties, including his duty to be a fairly courteous host, like Talos the automaton. Otherwise he drank heavily and joylessly, or went for long solitary gallops.

''Hesting, what is your pain?'' I wanted to cry. ''Can I ease it? Hang me aloft if that will help.'' Of course I could speak nothing.

When I told him and Ioran that I wished to move, and thanked them for their hospitality, he closed fingers on knife haft. I had seen him grip his sword that hard, on the strand after the last battle. For an instant his gaze touched mine, then snapped to the dusk beyond. "As you will," he said. "Yes, it might be best."

Ioran's reserve broke briefly in puzzlement. I knew he had not told even her what happened at the barrow. Nor would he. She would be certain to get me slain, if not by denunciation and formal execution then by inciting some ruffian to pick a death-fight. I, who betrayed her man's faith!

The house of Sigern enfolded me. They were glad to lighten winter's burden by hearing my tales, recitals, translated songs, whatever I chose, whether or not they had listened to it before. In entertaining them and their neighbors I found a measure of comfort.

Zeus knows we had little else to do. Darkness, and raw chill which could bring inflamed lungs if we ventured too much outside, caged us. Food must be hoarded, to see us through till the first catches of spring, the first reapings of summer. Solstice and equinox would see feasting, but this heightened the need for parsimony at all other times. Cheese, butter, honey, preserved meat and fish, dried apples, stored nuts were scarcely more than seasoning for flatbread and gruel. The latter was made out of grains both cultivated and wild—bindweed, rye grass, burdock, whatever could be picked by the children while it grew.

Chores like caring for beasts or bringing in fuel became outright welcome. One slept as much as possible.

A day in late November or early December (I'd long lost track) happened to be comparatively warm. I went for a walk. Beneath an overcast which it seemed I could reach up and touch, the woods stood bare, shadowless, above steely waters. No snow had fallen thus far. Dead leaves lay sodden, plowlands stiff and black. Now and then a flock of crows mocked me. The sound was soon lost in dank stillness.

It startled me to come upon Asrun. She wore her usual drab, soiled gown, but in this bleached universe her hair was a shout. I stopped, reminded of Hesting, though his locks were bronze and it seemed to me that each time I glimpsed him there was more white in them. I doubled my fists, determined not to be overwhelmed.

"Philon!" she piped. "What a nice surprise!" Reaching me: "Where've you been? I mean, you've moved, but you could drop in on your old friends once in a while, couldn't you, naughty?"

"No doubt. What are you doing?"

"I got sent to empty the weir, if anything's in it." She drooped her basket and laid hands on my waist. "Nothing moves fast in winter. I could stay here a little and nobody'd notice."

I glanced around at trees, lake, desertion. She simpered. "Sure, it is kind of wet and cold here, Philon. If we're, you know, quick—"

"I'd better be getting on."

"Really? Awww." She rubbed her breasts against me. "I've missed you. You're always gentle, and you know what a girl wants and care that she gets it." When I didn't respond, she grew sly. "After the letdown, yes, the fright I've had, you might be nice to me."

Somehow that didn't suggest idle chatter. My stomach tightened. "What's this?" I exclaimed.

"I mustn't tell."

"What is it?"

"No. Honest. I swore and— You wouldn't want me flogged, would you? Or killed?"

I grabbed her. She watched me, made her shallow calculation, and breathed, "The king . . ." then immediately shut her lips.

A wind struck through me. "The king? What of him?" I shook her till her teeth rattled. "Tell me! Tell me, or, or by Fro, I'll be the one who kills you, you bitch!"

Frightened now, she whined, "You'll hear soon anyway," and, "Let go, you're hurting me, how can I talk when you hurt me?" and, "M-m-m, well, for a *friend*—" and

perceiving that I had no wish whatsoever of that kind, "You
too, ha? At least friends give gifts. Don't they?"

In my wallet I generally carried some Roman coins, which
northerns value as amulets. I offered her one. She demanded
three. "All right!" I yelled, and cast them at her dirty feet.
She collected them before she confronted me, fluttered her
lashes, toyed with a braid, and dragged it out:

"Well, you know, us girls . . . the queen's sent us each
by each to his bed. . . . He wouldn't have me. I don't know
why. He—" Fear crossed her again. "I thought he'd murder
me then and there. I, I, I ran away, and— The rest of the slave
girls he did try. From different houses, too. We were told not
to talk, and we don't, 'cept mongst each other—" She
relaxed back into self-importance.

"What do you talk of?" My hand rested on my knife.
Earthquakes went through my head.

I wonder if she guessed something. Why else should such
spite dwell in her grin? Perhaps it was just the slave's unending impotent hatred.

"They'll get them a new king soon, I bet. He can't be Fro
anymore. Not with anybody."

She dared laugh before she saw my face. Bleating, she
fled. I caught her, hurled her to the earth, nearly slashed her
open. Mastering myself in bare time, I stabbed the nearest
tree instead, again and again, while I wept.

None but men, heads of households from all High Jutland,
might attend the abdication. It took place on the mountain
across the lake, in darkness. That night was clear, numbingly
cold. A rare aurora shivered among the Boreal stars. My eyes
were only for a crimson gleam upon the unseen peak.

None spoke about it afterward, not that I would ever have
asked. I can but imagine him as he stands on a great boulder
before their eyes. A balefire roars below, flames whirling red
and yellow to claim from the northlights their right to show
him forth. He is clad in his best, silks, linens, furs, chased
leather, massive gold and amber. To his breast has been fixed

a sprig of mistletoe as if piercing the heart behind. In his upturned hands lies a drawn sword.

He says, iron steady: "Nerthus has taken Her blessing away from me."

He does not hear the horrified calls, the wild questions as to why. Maybe there are none. Maybe the folk accept that Her will is alike beyond cruelty and pity. He says—he will give those who love him this much of his self—"I had not looked for it. Not at my age. I hoped, as every man does, to die before She wearied of me. That could not be." Duty comes back, takes every softness from his voice. "Choose then your next king, and give Her that which She will have."

He casts the sword down into the fire. Sparks rain upward. And suddenly he smiles.

He smiled.

He walked among us and our griefs, through those last sleety days, in more than the mirth-underlain serenity we remembered. Often tears met him, a harsh "Landfather, abide!" He stilled the outbursts and proceeded to order affairs, give counsel, make everything ready for his son who would follow him. When there was a small child, he liked to hold it on his lap while he talked and jest it into laughter.

He went off by himself many times, though, hours and miles upon end. I think he wanted to be on and of his land, however stark a look it wore, before he must sink within it. And he no longer sat in the royal house. He and Ioran dwelt apart, in a cottage borrowed from a peasant: a lowly place, suitable for two who had scant need any more of earthly goods.

She could not help showing how hard was her fight to match his peace. No doubt he consoled her when they were alone.

"What is this barbarian lunacy?" Memmius stormed at me. "Can you comprehend it? He's gotten his virility back—"

"How do you know?"

"How do you think? I slipped out after sunset and listened. Those flimsy doors—"

"What made you do such a filthy thing?"

"What ails *you*? Listen, Philon, we've spent some nine unrecoverable months in this hole, and now the baby we hoped would come to term . . . won't. Walhauk isn't like his father, he's more interested in enlarging the kingdom than its trade, he's suspicious of Rome, you know that. When he succeeds, he won't encourage any permanent outpost. Everything we've done could be wasted!" Memmius drew breath. "Anyhow, about Hesting, his recovery is common knowledge. Owldoon knows him, sees it shine. You must have heard gossip."

I nodded unwillingly.

"Then why must he die?" Memmius demanded. "If he can carry on the rites at spring as before, why must he die when I need him?" He leaned forward. "You and he were pretty close once, Philon. I don't know what happened—I never did quite believe you tripped and landed on a rock—still, lately, I've seen him greet you quite pleasantly when you chance to meet. Can't you learn, and maybe talk him out of his idiot aim?"

If I could . . .

Like a cat at a mousehole, save that the fear and entrapment were mine, I watched. Hitherto I had not dared trail him on his lonely stridings. Now Midwinter Day was so near that nothing remained for me to lose.

I caught him at the edge of the heath. The first snow of the year, no, the last snow of the old year had fallen overnight, a fine whiteness and silence across dead plowlands. Barrows and leafless bushes reared above. Their shadows were blue, under a pale sky and dim, low sun. The air was heavy with chill.

"Hesting," I called, and stumbled to overtake him.

He stopped, leaned on his spear, crinkled upward his lips and the crowsfeet around his eyes. "Hail, Philon," he said in Latin.

I stopped before him. My lungs burned from running. "Speak your own speech," I pleaded.

"If you wish." The breath smoked from him and vanished.

"Hesting, you— Is it that—I mean, what I did, if that brought a curse . . . or if Nerthus wants a death for any reason, I'd gladly, gladly—"

Had his tone carried scorn rather than politeness I could have borne it easier. "It is well thought of you. However, I am the one who is wanted. She would not be appeased, might well be angered, by a different offering." Altogether levelly, he uttered it: "What if She did not call the sun home?"

"But the curse was lifted!"

"That makes me double sure of Her will. She did not smite me—not the little while wherewith She punishes most men who offend, but week after week—She did not smite Her Fro for nothing. Nor is it for nothing that as soon as I vowed myself to death"—all springtime broke forth in his tone—"She made me whole again!"

I could not ask what he meant; my tongue locked. Nor can I to this day follow his thought, nor reach that final haven he shared with Orestes and Oedipus. The Goddess has never touched me since; my world is a drumskin above a void which has no ending.

He finished in a kindliness as impersonal as if already it spoke from the grave: "Don't blame yourself. Now, if you will forgive me, I have only this one night left with my wife."

He turned and walked off across the snow.

At dawn he went alone to the shrine of Nerthus. They tell me he took along just a bowl of hallowed gruel to eat. I wonder what his musings were on the shore of Holy Lake.

The day after was Midwinter. It had warmed, snow melted in soft little gurgles, the sun swung red behind overcast. Somewhere I heard a rook caw.

I must stay in town, of course. None but the heads of

households, and Walhauk his son, might meet him when he returned down the forbidden road.

They accompanied him to the peat bog. I never asked what the ceremonies were. I could not help overhearing talk of them—whatever was known to everybody, whispered in darkness. He undressed, stood naked until they gave him a leather cap to cover his head from the light and a leather belt to hide the scar of his birth. Of leather, too, was the noose his son laid around his neck. Not being an evildoer condemned to slow strangling, he himself ascended the ash tree. He secured the other end of the cord to a lofty branch, smiled upon them, and stepped free.

They buried him there, with no grave-goods save the rope and his honor. Owldoon would not sacrifice a bullock this year. It had given Her a king.

Nonetheless the winter turned hard, winds whistled down from the Pole Star, cold rang in the earth. The time grew long before our ship was able to come and bear me back to people I can understand.